MOON LAKE

MOON LAKE

AN EAST TEXAS GOTHIC

JOE R. LANSDALE

MULHOLLAND BOOKS

Little, Brown and Company

New York Boston London

Copyright © 2021 by Joe R. Lansdale

Mulholland Books / Little, Brown and Company
Hachette Book Group
1290 Avenue of the Americas, New York, NY 10104
mulhollandbooks.com

First Edition: June 2021

Mulholland Books is an imprint of Little, Brown and Company, a division of Hachette Book Group, Inc. The Mulholland Books name and logo are trademarks of Hachette Book Group, Inc.

The publisher is not responsible for websites (or their content) that are not owned by the publisher.

The Hachette Speakers Bureau provides a wide range of authors for speaking events. To find out more, go to hachettespeakersbureau.com or call (866) 376-6591.

ISBN 978-0-316-54064-3
Library of Congress Control Number: 2021936124

Printing 1, 2021

LSC-W

Printed in the United States of America

For Pamela Lansdale Dunklin and Scott Dunklin

The moon is up. The water is high. Dark souls walk the earth and cry.

—Jerzy Fitzgerald

MOON LAKE

PART ONE

THE NIGHT, THE BRIDGE, THE PALE MOONLIGHT

1968

(1)

My name is Daniel Russell. I dream of dark water.

My first memory of Moon Lake was as a youngster, on a dark night in October of 1968 with a nearly full moon seeming to float on the surface of the water. I remember its glow and the way the shadows of the trees on the sides of the lake reached out for it like chocolate fingers groping for a silver platter.

Me and my dad were parked on a long, narrow bridge that went over the lake. The bridge was made of rusty metal and cables and rotting wood, not to mention a few lost dreams, for the town beneath the water had been flooded and the great lake was supposed to be the new town's savior. People were expected to come from miles around to picnic on its shores and fish its depths.

They didn't. At least, not enough of them.

I was fourteen years old when I learned this, or learned some of it. Looking out at the moon on the water, it was obvious how the lake got its name.

We were in our broken-down Buick that had come from a time when cars were big and the American dream lay well within reach for just about anyone white and male and straight who wanted to reach for it. All others, take a number and wait.

We had skipped out on bill collectors two days after we had an interruption in electrical service due to a tardy light bill, as my father called it. Two days in the dark and without heat, with the house soon to be repossessed, a blackened head of cabbage and a quarter jug of curdled milk in the useless refrigerator, Dad got rambling fever, and away we went, tires whistling over concrete.

As we sat parked on the bridge, Dad told me why my mother had left a few months back. Believe me, I had wondered. Dad said it was because she thought me and Dad and the world were holding her down. I guess without us, it was less heavy out there. I suppose when you're shedding weight, every lost ounce counts.

I had rarely mentioned my mother after she left. I wished to remember a time when she had held me or spoken softly to me or loved me, but if such a memory was in my brain, I couldn't find it. She was prone to long hours of depression, late-night drunks, and had a somewhat unearthly beauty. Dark hair and eyes, creamy skin, jittery movements like a squirrel on amphetamines. She had a silver star in one of her front teeth. It was a cosmetic procedure she'd asked the dentist to perform. She had a hippie look and a Wall Street mind.

Not long after my mom's departure, Dad took her remaining clothes, odds and ends of hers, and hauled them to the dump. He kept a pair of her black panties, and that made me a little uncomfortable. He kept them in a drawer by his bed. He told me once, "They smell just like her."

Some things a child doesn't need to know.

The day we packed up and left, those panties came with us. I saw Dad put them in his suitcase. We left most of our stuff and traveled light, a suitcase apiece, scrounged from behind Christmas decorations. The luggage was placed in the trunk and in the back seat, along with some refugee clothing. Shirts mostly.

We spent a few nights in motels so cheap that in one of them, roaches moved under the wallpaper in our room with a crackling sound. In another we could hear the next-door neighbor coughing and showering and straining to shit.

We were parked on the bridge that cool night in 1968 because we had no home and no more money for a motel room. Dad said he had read about a job in some newspaper somewhere. He was vague. He was by original choice a librarian but had left that job to make more money, as my mother felt she needed to live in style. She wasn't crazy about a husband who had what she said was a woman's job, shuffling books and filing dusty cards and memorizing the Dewey decimal system. She liked to party. Dad liked to complain.

Dad had some math skills and was smart in many ways, had a lot of educational paper that said so. He became an accountant, and I think that things between him and Mother must have been all right for a couple of years, though he hated the work. He missed the smell of old books and chasing down people with overdue items on their library cards.

I know this somewhat from memory, somewhat from my dad, and it's just possible I made some of it up.

As we sat there on the bridge and the wind whistled around the car, my father patted his fingers on the steering wheel. The big silver ring he wore on his left hand made a snapping noise against it, and the moonlight caught it and made it wink.

Dad said, "Beneath that Moon Lake water is a town called Long Lincoln. It was named after a tall man named Lincoln. How about that?"

I didn't say anything, because I couldn't tell if it was really a question. Moonlight was shining through the windshield and it made Dad look like he was coated in shimmering gold paint. The bones in his face appeared sharper than usual, like you could use one of his cheekbones to open a letter. His lips trembled. There were beads of sweat on his forehead, and I remember thinking, Why is he sweating? It's a cool night.

Leaves were picked off the trees by the sharp fall wind and they flapped through the air, bright in the moonlight, red and yellow, orange and brown. Many came to rest on our windshield and on the bridge, as if they were birds settling to roost. Where they coasted onto the windshield, the moonlight formed a camouflage pattern over Dad's face.

"Long Lincoln is where I was born. It was where I met your mother. We were in high school. We thought love was enough. We thought a lot of silly things. A few times I came back here, after it was a lake, parked here, looked down, and on days when the sun was bright, I could see buildings, could even read the words POST OFFICE on a building where I had mailed letters to Santa and applied to colleges, sent sweet notes to your grandparents when they were alive. When they died, there was only me and you and your mother. Three against emptiness. Now it's two. You and me. Jesus, it's a sad old world."

I wanted to ask why we were parked on a bridge and why he was telling me these things, most of which he had told me before, and often. But there was something about the way he was talking, something that made me stay silent for longer than I might normally have. Being on the actual bridge he had described to me while living in our home made it stranger and more real to me.

"I loved your mother," he said. "I want you to know that. Without her, we're lost. My hands feel damp with the blood of dead hopes."

He talked like that sometimes. My mother said he read a lot of books. When he worked at the library, they were readily available.

I couldn't hold it in any longer. "Daddy, you're scaring me."

Dad turned away from me, faced forward, and him doing that caused me to do the same. I could see our headlights lying on the bridge, extending outward, leaves still whirling about in the beams, coming to land on the frail bridge.

That bridge was narrow and long, the railing on the side was made of thin, rusting strips of metal, and when we drove onto it, it shook and moaned like a sad old woman about to die.

"Sometimes you have to do what's best for all involved," Dad said. "No one should suffer famine and worry, not have love and support at home. Of course, they would first need to have a home."

He laughed a little when he said that. It sounded like cracking ice. He was acting so strangely it felt as if the interior of the car were colder than the weather demanded.

"Once upon a time, the town down there had people in it. They had jobs and they had homes, and then it was decided by someone that the town should be moved and renamed and that the old town would become a lake. There was a great dam then, so broad at the top you could walk across it. It had a high spillway, and it was pretty up there, and there was water that came from the spillway and ran through the center of town as a creek, rolled by a post office, gas stations, a school, a general store, and so much more. There were trees on either side of the creek and they made much of the town shady, and on the outskirts of the town on both sides there were houses. I lived in one of those houses. I was raised there. Did I already say that?"

"Yes, sir."

If he heard my reply, I couldn't tell.

"Money was paid, and the town was evacuated. A new town was built in a different location. But there were some down there that didn't leave. Can you believe that? They waited there thinking that if they stayed, the water wouldn't be released. But it was. Gone in a flash, and the remains, along with the bones of those who didn't leave, are lying down there at the bottom of the wet. I was born there. I grew up there. I met your mother there."

A theme was developing.

"Danny, I feel like there isn't any true light or warmth in the universe anymore. You should never have to feel that way. Do you understand?"

I didn't.

" 'The moon is up. The water is high. Dark souls walk the earth and cry.' An old poem. I know what it means now."

Dad shifted the car into drive and inched us forward slightly with a gentle tap on the gas. I was glad we were finally moving on.

"I want you to know how much I love you," he said.

Before I could say "I love you too," he punched his foot down hard on the gas, and the car leaped and the bridge shook. He jerked the wheel to the right, and the great big Buick, five payments owed, smashed through the rotting railing and sailed out into space like a rocket ship.

Wet leaves swirled about us, and then the car dipped, and there was the Buick's shadow, smack-dab in the center of the gleaming reflection of the moon. We went down in what seemed like slow motion, the car lights shining onto the lake, the moon's reflection a golden bull's-eye.

When the car struck the water, I took a deep breath. There was a slapping sound as it hit. The headlights glowed briefly, even underwater, but only for a moment, then they snapped off. The windshield caved in, folded like a blanket, and banged up against me. Cold water and the impact of the windshield washed me loose of my seat and towed me away.

(2)

Had it been now, I would have had a seat belt on, but then, even if a car had them, we didn't wear them, and thinking back, I wonder if in this case a belt might have done me in, if I might have been fumbling with the release, sucking in water all the way to the silty bottom.

But there was no belt in that giant Buick, and the impact and that dislodged windshield and the water drove me over the back seat. The clothes we had thrown there swirled around me and something caught over my head, and then I felt a pain in my spine. Realized I had been driven through the rear windshield.

The safety glass molded around me and then went away. I clawed the cloth off my face and looked down. It was dark where I was but light enough I could see the rear of the car and the dying taillights for a moment, and then I couldn't. The dark took the Buick and Dad.

Above, I could see moonlight through water, and it beaconed to me the way dying people say they see a warm, bright light that invites them into it.

I'd been swimming all summer, but no one had ever praised

me for my aquatic skills. I struggled like a dying frog with no real breath inside of me.

Then I saw a mermaid. She came swimming down toward me, and she was dark of shape and swift of motion.

I felt weak. I had the sensation of filling up with something and floating downward, and then the mermaid grabbed me, and up we went, her pulling me by my jacket. It had burdened me during my rudimentary efforts at swimming, gathering around me like a suffocating cocoon.

The light grew bright and the mermaid broke the surface of the lake, still dragging me by my jacket. The mermaid was black. I registered that. I coughed and spat, but the water wouldn't leave me. I felt as if I was being absorbed by moonlight. Then the light was gone and the universe became a murky place and there was only the beating sound of the mermaid's swimming arms and legs. Or so I thought before I realized it was the sound of my hammering heart.

(3)

When I awoke, a black face hung over me like the dark side of the moon. The dark moon was the face of a girl about my age.

It was the mermaid and she was outlined in the moonbeams. She was sleek of build. Her dark skin was wet and shiny. Moon-glistened beads of water dripped off her nose and cheeks, lips and chin, and wilting Afro hairdo. She looked at me as if examining a formerly unknown species of fish. She had at first seemed nude, but now I realized she wore a dark shirt and dark shorts. No fishtail.

I rolled my head to the side to let some water flow out of me, and I remember when doing that I saw across the lake a little light moving through the trees like a large firefly, and then I didn't see it anymore.

Then another black face leaned over me, this one larger and rounder and older and not so beautiful. The man who owned that face was fully clothed and wore a fedora.

The older, dry man lifted my head, said, "Breathe easy. You been to the bottom of the lake."

I hadn't actually, but I had certainly come close to it.

Feeling nauseated, I turned my head and coughed up enough filthy water to start a fish farm.

"It's all right," said the man. "You're going to be all right."

The girl was still staring at me, her eyes wide, her lips parted, her chest heaving slightly. Sight of her didn't take away the pain I felt that night, but it was a mild balm to a soulful wound. I felt some puppy love howling around inside of me.

"You saved me," I said.

"Yep." She smiled. Oh, heavens, that smile.

"My daddy?" I said. "In the car."

The man shook his head. "Sorry, son. You're all that came out. He's gone down with the car, and he didn't come up. It's deep out there."

"You have to get him," I said.

"I'm sorry. Lake owns him now."

I started to cry and I don't remember when I quit crying. I don't remember them helping me up and out of my wet coat and into their pickup, loading up their fishing gear, for they had been night fishing on the bank of the lake, tucked up between trees and dark shadows—a lucky break for me—but I remember the drive to town.

It was long and lonely. The world came back in starts and spurts. Cold, wet memories, slices of this, slices of that, the car in the water, going down, down, down.

I sat in a puddle of my own making, shivering. The girl beside me was making a puddle of her own. She wore a jacket now over her wet clothes. We shivered together. The truck was full of warmth, though, as the heater was turned up high. Gradually I began to lose the chill.

The town wasn't too big, but it had bright streetlights, and the main highway split it right down the middle. On either side of it there were businesses and old houses and great trees with limbs that dangled over the edges of the road. Many of the houses were two stories, and a few were three stories tall.

I saw a Dairy Queen all lit up, and I was suddenly hungry and felt ashamed of the feeling. I was alive and craving a hamburger, and my father was at the bottom of the lake, maybe still behind the wheel of our car. In my happier thoughts, he was driving along the lake bed, and all he had to do was find a place where he could drive up from the deeps, onto the bank, and into town, where he would find me. It seemed perfectly reasonable.

The police station was a blur. A big white man with a big round belly wearing a dark blue cop suit with a badge pinned on it was there. He was also wearing a white cowboy hat with a brim wide enough to use as a patio awning, and when he turned in his chair, I saw he had a colorful patch on his sleeve that had all the flags that had flown over Texas, including the Dixie flag.

On the wall were a lot of photographs of him with other law enforcement officers in uniform. One photo had him with three older looking people, a woman and two men. Beside him, solemn and pale as they were, they looked like wax figures of executioners.

There was another man in the room. Also large of size but better proportioned. He was dressed in slacks and a crisp white shirt and he had a thick head of red hair. He was placing a tray with a cloth over it on the sheriff's desk. There was a placard on the desk that said SHERIFF JAMES DUDLEY.

The redheaded man removed the cloth from over the tray as if it were a magician's trick, and there was a plate with fried chicken and mashed potatoes and white gravy on it.

"Thanks, Duncan," the sheriff said, and smiled at him. The redhead nodded, smiled back, and left the room, trailing a cloud of Old Spice.

The sheriff studied me. I was still damp and dripping. Questions were asked of me and of those who saved me. Notes were taken by the sheriff on a pad with a pencil.

I did the best I could to say what I knew, but my mind wandered. I could see a room off of the office with the words COLORED WAITING ROOM above it. The words had been painted over with white paint but were still visible under the thin coating. Just a few years back my rescuers would have had to come through the back door and sit in that waiting room, where they would be attended to. Eventually.

"What the hell am I going to do with him this time of night, Jeb?" the sheriff said. "Get some foster folks or some such, I guess. I can get a wrecker out to the lake in the morning, couple of boys who can really swim, see if they can find the car."

"You'll need swimmers who can use diving rigs. It's deep there," the black man said. I would find out later his full name was Jeb Candles and his daughter, Veronica, was known as Ronnie.

"That'll cost the county a good chunk," Sheriff Dudley said. "More to the point, this boy needs a place to stay, some food, and dry clothes. I'm not sure what to do about that."

In 1968 the idea of protecting children was different. There wasn't a whole lot of thought put into the struggle of orphans. Not in that small East Texas town, anyway.

"He can stay with us for now, Sheriff. May I borrow your phone?"

The phone was borrowed, and the next thing I knew, I was brought dry clothes from somewhere and given a large beach towel. My donations had come from black folks Mr. Candles knew. They arrived quickly and quietly and left the same way they arrived, like beach-towel ninjas.

I went into the bathroom and dressed, looked in the mirror at somebody I didn't know: snow-faced, dark hair drying in a matted wad, eyes seeming as if they were without true color, my skin popped with goose bumps.

I could hear the sheriff talking in the other room. I heard him say, "If you're up late, I'll be by later and we can discuss a few things. I got to do some thinking on this first."

"We'll wait up," Mr. Candles said.

When I came out, I was wrapped in the beach towel by Mr. Candles and loaded back into the pickup. We drove away, leaving the sheriff happily alone with his notebook and fried-chicken dinner. It had been all I could do not to grab a chicken leg and shove it into my mouth. I was starving.

(4)

Later, I would be asked many more questions and could answer only a few. It was hard enough right then for me to remember my name or where we had lived.

I did eventually tell the sheriff my mother had abandoned us and that I had no idea where she was. I had an aunt on my mother's side somewhere in Europe, but I didn't know where, and I didn't know her that well. Her husband, my uncle, a rich oilman who I had never met, had died and left her well fixed. My aunt and I had met, and that was about all I could say.

The Candles house wasn't too far from the lake in a section of town where there were no streetlights, and the houses on the block were lit by porch lights that were swarmed by insects.

Inside their house there were shelves of *Reader's Digest* books as well as others; a big fat black Bible was open on a wooden stand. There were knickknacks of all kinds on the shelves in front of the books; ceramic elephants were favored. The air smelled slightly and pleasantly of baked bread. There was a delicate-looking black woman there. She had a sweet face. She said her name was Millie and to call her that. She moved about swiftly, like a bird on the ground.

The house was bright with light and warm from a fire in a stove that had been constructed from a black barrel and a long, wide pipe that ran from stove to ceiling. A door had been cut in the barrel. Hinges had been made for the cutaway and welded to the barrel. The little door was open, and I could see inside. A bright fire was chewing up sticks of split wood.

When I touched something, it seemed not to have substance. When I spoke, the words didn't seem to be mine, so I preferred not to use them. I felt like a phantom dissolving into the warmth of the house.

"Come, child," said the woman. "Closer to the fire. Let's get you warm."

I moved to a chair by the stove. The beach towel was taken away, and a blanket was put over my shoulders. I was brought a hot cup of cocoa with marshmallows melting in it. The cocoa steamed under my chin and warmed my face. When I sipped it, it filled my insides the way the fire filled that stove, only without the burn.

It was late when the sheriff came by. He seemed smaller to me now than he had before, but perhaps it was because he stood with his hat in his hand, out of his element, beneath an orangish hallway light.

Mr. and Mrs. Candles were standing with him. They spoke in low tones. I caught a word here and there, but mostly it was all a mumble. All I knew was they were talking about me and my situation.

Ronnie was with me in the living room. She said, "You scared being in the lake like that?"

"What do you think?"

"Stupid question."

"Thing is, I was scared until I saw you swimming down to me. I thought you were some kind of mermaid."

"I'm a damn good swimmer. You're not that good. You thrash a lot."

"You do that kind of thing when you're drowning."

"Guess so."

"I'm glad you were there."

"Me too."

I could tell there were other things she wanted to ask me. She had to be curious as to what led my father to drive us through a bridge and into Moon Lake. But she didn't ask.

Had she asked, I couldn't have given her an answer. There were moments when I thought my father felt he could drive off the bridge and back into the past and take up life there. It was an idea right along with the one I had about him driving along the bottom of the lake. None of my thoughts and feelings that night were exactly stellar.

Later, I was alone on the couch in the dark beneath warm blankets, and from time to time, I would wake up whimpering, and each time, Millie was there. She stroked my head, said, "Now, now, sweetie. Now, now. You're safe here. Sheriff says you can stay with us for a while."

"My daddy tried to drown me," I said.

"Ah, now, baby. It was just an accident. He lost control."

I nodded, but I knew better.

Millie stroked my head until I slept. I never knew when she went away. Daylight came. I woke up late, exhausted from trauma, nibbled at some crackers and tomato soup. Both Ronnie and Mr. Candles were gone, her to school, him to work. Millie didn't press me about anything. I ate and went back to sleep on the couch.

When I awoke again, it was dead dark and there was only the glow of the porch light sliding through a split in the curtains of the window next to the couch. As if sensing it was time that I would awake, Millie was there. She ran her fingers through my hair again. My mother had never done that, not that I recalled. I remembered my mother staring at me from across the room as if she were surprised that she had a child.

"Listen," said Millie. "I know it's not something you'll love to hear, baby boy, but it has to be said. Dudley came by again, while you were sleeping. He said they dragged the lake for your father's car, and nothing. They can see clearly right to the bottom in some spots, but it's a little murky there close to the edge because of mud. Car could have slid down there."

She patted my arm.

"Did your father . . . hurt you?"

"He tried to drown me. Does that count?"

I thought for a moment she might laugh, but she contained herself. I think she was trying to decide if a laugh was appropriate or not. She settled on clearing her throat.

"He wasn't in his right mind, baby."

"I loved him," I said.

"Of course you did. Thing is, Danny, you are here and you are safe, and if they find the car or if they don't, the world turns and you have to be ready to turn with it."

"Yes, ma'am," I said.

"You hungry?"

"No, ma'am. Just feel really tired."

"That's okay, honey. You go back to sleep, and if you wake up before we do, there's bread and meat and cheese in the kitchen. You can make yourself a sandwich."

"Thank you."

"Now, you need something else in the night, don't hesitate to call out, knock on our bedroom door. I can sit here by you until you go to sleep, if you like. Would you like that?"

"Yes, ma'am."

"Parents certainly taught you manners, baby. Now, you sleep, dear. Sleep."

She sat with her hand on my arm, and after a while she hummed softly, sang under her breath from time to time, some old song where only a word now and then came with the humming. The words had something to do with Jesus and an old rugged cross.

Fear and exhaustion, the warm room, the soft touch of that sweet lady's hand, helped me fall into a deep sleep, and I dreamed of Daddy driving that big-ass Buick along the bottom of the lake, seeking a way up and out and onto the drier world.

(5)

I ended up staying with the Candleses for longer than a day or two; it was as if Dudley had forgotten me. One month rolled comfortably into the next. Winter came, wet and cold and icy with some early-morning blows of rare East Texas snow, but the Candleses' house was warm and cozy, and I felt safe there, and even a little happy.

I felt my father would never be found. They had swept hooks on cables through the lake and come up with nothing and called it a day. New Long Lincoln, the town that had replaced the old, didn't strike me as a community that wanted to worry much about a murderous father whose son had been rescued from a purposeful attempt to drown him. I began to feel much the same way. Let sleeping demons lie.

Late at night, listening to the cold winds blow and the panes in the windows rattle throughout the house, I sometimes sensed my father at the foot of my bed, for I had been set up with a small one in a storage room for food goods.

There were shelves on either side of my bed and behind me. They were stocked with jars that had been packed with pickles, beets, and jalapeños soaked in vinegar. Above the back-wall shelf was one high window touched gently by the swaying limb of a chinaberry tree. The limb made little shadows in the sunlight, and when the moon was bright, the lunar shadows trickled in.

Some nights Dad would be down there at the foot of my little bed. I put my head under the covers, but I could sense him there. I could feel his touch on my ankle, foot, or leg. The air seemed to smell of water and fish and mildew. I would keep my eyes closed tight under the pillow, and finally the touch of his hand would fade, and the bed would move slightly as if he stood up, and then I could sense him no more.

The stench in the air would be replaced by the faint aroma of cedar, the wood the shelves were made of. There was only the natural cold of winter then, for the fire in the barrel stove had been put out, and the portable electric heaters had been turned off, and there wasn't any central air.

In time, I learned to live more comfortably with the visits from my father. I couldn't decide if those visits were false or real, if my father's wet ghost actually came to see me there in my little warm bed. I couldn't figure if he wanted me down there in the lake with him or if he was there to assure me that he was all right.

Time plowed on. Ronnie was in school, of course, went there during the week, and me and her went fishing with her dad on weekends, nowhere near the bridge over Moon Lake. I didn't ask them not to go there; they just didn't. We fished off the bank or sometimes from a little aluminum boat.

Ronnie liked to box. She loved watching it on TV. Liked gloving up. Her mother didn't care for it, thought it was unladylike and feared Ronnie would break her nose or chip a tooth, but I could tell her father, who had boxed, was delighted. I was delighted too.

We practiced together. We learned punches and hammered the heavy bag that Mr. Candles kept in a walled-off section of his garage. There was also a speed bag, and we worked that.

From time to time, wearing light gloves and mouthpieces that Mr. Candles boiled in a bucket of water and a dash of alcohol, we were allowed to box inside a circle Mr. Candles drew with white chalk on the floor of the garage. It was about half the size of an actual boxing ring. We didn't go for the knockout. During our little bouts, we suffered only bloody noses and now and again a split lip, a black eye, or a light blue bruise.

The whole process made me feel stronger, more confident. It felt good to become tired from physical activity. On those nights, I slept deep and my father's ghost stayed in its new home at the bottom of Moon Lake.

The Candleses bought me some clothes, a few odds and ends. According to the law, I was supposed to be in school, but instead of having me go, the county let Millie, who had been a teacher at the black school before integration, teach me. When the black school folded, so had her job. She told me that for a time, she had been a lunch-line lady at the new school.

She said, "It hurt my pride, after being a teacher. It was honest work, and I was glad to have it, but it was as if I was being punished, demoted, after acquiring an education and teaching kids to spell and write and do math. Next thing I knew, I was serving up tuna surprise and corned beef hash, Wonder Bread and straw-berry Jell-O. I didn't like it. Worse, the food was so bad, the cook they hired might as well have been mixing cement."

She didn't work in the lunch line long. She quit and worked from home baking this and that, selling her wares to both black and white customers. Her loaves of bread were brown as autumn, firm and soft as your one true love, and soaked up butter like a brand-new sponge. Her cookies were sweet but not too sweet, and her pies and cakes were like gifts from heaven. Their smell as they baked could almost cause me to levitate.

Fact was, if there was a heaven, something I sincerely doubted, then Millie would have run the bakery there, personally delivering to God and Jesus and the Holy Ghost, bringing cookies to the angels on Sunday. She might even toss a devil's food cake down to Satan on a friendly day. Bottom line was, they let her keep me in the educational loop, and I had the added benefit of baked goods too.

Millie was sweet, but there was toughness under that sweet veneer. She taught me my lessons—reading, writing, history and geography, the basics of algebra, which I never really understood. My lessons were graded by Millie, then sent to the school and checked over by white teachers who, in the Jim Crow South, were considered more competent. They rarely changed a grade or a suggestion, but it made them feel good to judge the papers she had graded and give them white sanction.

In the history department, there were some mark-outs where I had written about the Civil War from a less sympathetic point of view than most Southerners, had given opinions not in line with the Daughters and Sons of the Confederacy. No doubt those opinions had been the influence of Millie, who gave me numerous books about the war, not just the ones they taught in Texas history class.

On school mornings when it was cold and the mist rose off the wet grass, I watched Ronnie leave to catch the bus.

I normally watched from the window, rubbing moisture off the pane with my sleeve so I could see her. But one morning, we were standing on the porch, waiting for the bus, breathing white foam into the air, and suddenly she leaned over and kissed me on the cheek with lips soft as cotton and warm as a wool blanket. I couldn't have been more surprised if I had discovered I had acquired the ability to lay painted eggs and pee lemonade.

"I like you, Danny Russell," she said.

Moments later the bus arrived. The door wheezed open. A black girl in a white dress with a white bow in her gathered-up hair swung down from a front seat onto the bus steps and yelled out, "What you doing with that white boy?"

"He's a guest," Ronnie said, stepping off the porch.

"Get on back up in here," the bus driver said to the girl in white. The driver, who did the same sort of job as Mr. Candles, was a heavy black man with a fedora hat wearing khakis and work boots.

"That white boy staying with y'all?" said the girl, ignoring the driver.

"Get on back up in the bus, Earleen, before I punch you in the nose," Ronnie said.

Earleen took this as a serious warning and retreated. Ronnie went up the bus steps, turned slightly, looked at me, and smiled. It was like a sharp, sweet dart to the heart.

Then the door closed. I saw her through the steamy windows, moving like a shadow along the aisle of the bus. Then she was seated, and I could see her seated shape through the glass as the bus reeked away, spitting exhaust loud enough to make me jump.

(6)

Dead center of December I heard word the law had found my aunt. I don't know how they did it, but they did. She was still abroad, spending my dead uncle's money and doing it in style. She was on her way to France and had plans that she meant to keep, orphaned nephew or not. She wouldn't be home for another three months.

She reminded me of my mother in that respect. Her own interests superseded those of anyone else, no matter the circumstances. It was like she was saying, "So, his father drowned and Danny barely survived, and his mother, my sister, has run off like a frightened deer? That's some tough stuff there, but I got plans to see the Eiffel Tower and then go on down to the South of France and sample the croissants, which I hear are simply divine. And you know, maybe his mother will show up before I get home. It could happen."

I wasn't bothered by this. I was glad to stay longer with the Candles family. I knew them better than my aunt, as my memory of our one meeting was a thin recollection.

Christmastime, the Candleses gave me a jacket they called a hunting coat along with the first three John Carter of Mars books, some socks, underwear, and a pocketknife with all manner of devices on it. It was like a Swiss Army knife, but not quite as expensive. I thought it might have been bought used from a pawnshop, but I was glad to have it. The three books bent me happily out of shape for the next few days.

During the Christmas holidays, school closed and the weather was a disaster. We all stayed at home, and at night Millie read us poetry. She was partial to Robert Frost but also read Robert Service, the bard of the Yukon, a poet Mr. Candles liked. Me too. Mine and Mr. Candles's favorite was "The Shooting of Dan McGrew." Ronnie liked the poetry of Langston Hughes.

After a few days of us boxing in the garage, reading poetry at night, watching a bit of television, Mr. Candles looked out the window one late afternoon, said, "There's been a crack in the weather. Let's go fishing."

Me and Ronnie, bored from being inside, practically jumped to put on our fishing clothes and grab our gear from the garage. I wore my new coat because it was the warmest thing I had.

Mr. Candles had an aluminum boat that was on a trailer in the garage. We fastened the trailer to the hitch of his pickup and away we went, stopping off briefly at a bait shop to buy some worms.

When we got to the lake, I was glad I had the coat I had been given, along with some gloves and a wool hat with earmuffs Mr. Candles loaned me. Ronnie was snuggled up good too; in a wool pullover she had struggled to pull over her hair.

It was damn frosty even though the sun was shining and no wind was blowing. The sky was clear. The trees around the lake were bright with icicles that dangled like glass decorations on fancy chandeliers.

We launched the boat off the trailer rack and into the water. In the sunlight, the water was silvery and blinding to the eyes. It looked warm because of the sun, but when some of it splashed on me as I was leaping into the boat, it was icy.

The fishing boat had a small motor and there were paddles in the bottom. Mr. Candles ignored the paddles and motored us out on the lake. We were down well beyond the bridge, but I could see it in the distance, looking like a strand of tangled string from where we were.

I pointed at the bridge, said, "Would it be all right to go over there?"

Ronnie and Mr. Candles looked at me like I'd just asked if we might taste the worms we had brought for bait.

"I don't know, son. I thought we were even farther down. I meant for us to be."

"It isn't making me feel better or worse not going back there. Can we?"

"I suppose so," Mr. Candles said.

"You're sure?" Ronnie said.

"I'm sure."

Mr. Candles wrinkled his face, worked the boat around, geared up the motor, and set us off for the bridge. I watched as it grew in size and looked less like a long and tangled length of string and more like what it was, a bridge of cables, crumbling boards, and rusty rails and bolts, a wide section split open where, just a few months past, our Buick had broken through.

As we motored under the bridge, we could see the shadow on the water that the cables and slats and rails made. The water was calm except where the boat disturbed it, and that seemed to be calming quickly as Mr. Candles shut the engine off. I tried to look through the water and see the town below, but the water remained silvery from the sunlight and the glare hurt my eyes.

Mr. Candles, knowing what I had in mind, said, "You can't always see what's down there. Legend is you can. And sometimes you can. Or parts of it. The higher roofs. But mostly you can't. Some shadows mainly. When the water's a bit low, there's a place over there"—he pointed—"where the old high school use to be, and when it's low enough, you can step out of your boat and appear to be walking on water, but it's the roof of the high school. I did it once."

"I've done it," Ronnie said.

"Is it low enough now?"

"No," Mr. Candles said. "Has to be a dry time of year. Usually dead summer it gets a little low, and once it does, you can do it. If it's real low, and it sometimes happens, the roofs of the high school and other buildings stick up out of the water.

"Under the bridge here was Main Street. Main Street usually has good fishing. Ronnie caught an eighty-five-pound mud cat. It damn near straightened out the hook. They say they don't grow that big. Biggest ones I'd seen up until then was thirty-five pounds, but I'd heard of fifty-pounders. Still, this one was ancient and bigger than any I'd ever heard tell of. I wouldn't have believed it, but that's what it weighed when they put it on the scales at the feed store. Got it home, we weighed it twice on the garage scale, had friends over to see and photograph it. Even with that, most wouldn't believe us. It was an old man of the river. No telling how long it had lived before it washed into the lake and made its home there. We kept it hosed down and in a tub of water for a while, its tail flipping up over the edge of the tub. Then we took it back to the lake and let it go."

"I enjoyed watching it swim away," Ronnie said. "Could see it partly on the surface for a moment, see how long it was, and then it dipped and was gone. It was like magic. It visited our home, got weighed, and was sent back into the water. It was like a doctor's visit without a prescription."

A shadow moved across the water. For a moment, I thought a

great bird had passed before the face of the sun, but when I glanced up, there was an abnormally big man up there, young, white, and ragged-looking. From where we sat, the sun seemed to be resting on his shoulders.

He looked down at us for a long time as if considering hawking up a wad of snot and spitting it onto us, but all he did was look. He had a flashlight in his hand even though night was hours away.

I waved. After a long delay, he waved back, and then he moved on.

"Winston Remark," Mr. Candles said when the man was gone. We could hear the bridge squeaking, see it swaying, and I could see through gaps in the slats Winston's feet stepping from one board to the next. His shadow moved on the water along with that of the bridge.

"That poor young man," Mr. Candles said. "He comes out here and wanders and looks at the water. Even at night, wandering around with that flashlight. No one knows what he's looking for, but I got a guess. His past. He's a bit head-addled. I've seen him quite a few times. His tongue and his mind kind of ramble about. Might be mute. Just kind of makes noise."

"Where does he live?" I said.

"Good question, but I haven't an answer. Me and him and even you, Danny, have something in common."

Mr. Candles was interrupted by Ronnie saying, "Oh, I got one." She pulled a sun perch in, unhooked it. Mr. Candles dipped a bucket we had brought into the cold water and she put the fish in it.

Then I caught one, and Ronnie another, and then Mr. Candles, and then me. They began to come as fast as we could put worms on our hooks and catch them and put them in the water bucket. Pretty soon the bucket thrashed with fish.

As the day continued, the fish hit hard and for a long time, and then they didn't hit at all. By that point, the bucket was nearly full, and Mr. Candles took out the smaller fish and eased them over the side.

"Can only eat so many, and for me, fish three days in a row is one day too many. We can keep some in the freezer for a while, though."

"I could eat them every day," Ronnie said.

"I bet you could at that," Mr. Candles said. "Ronnie has always liked fish, liked water, swimming. She's like a seal."

"Her being a swimmer was my good luck," I said.

"It was indeed," Mr. Candles said.

I suppose we could have moved on when the sun went down and it grew quite cold, but we didn't. We night fished, even though now we weren't catching anything. There was a scimitar moon. It was bright even though it was thin, and you could see its shape on the water. Water so still, I felt I could step out of the boat and walk across it.

"You were saying about Winston," I said. "That we had things in common."

Quite a bit of time had passed since Mr. Candles had mentioned it and been interrupted by our run of fish, but I hadn't lost interest.

"Oh, I forgot," Mr. Candles said. "I said me and Winston had something in common, and in a slightly different way, so do you, Danny.

"Down where the lake thins, and the spillway, fed by the river, leaks water through the new dam, that was the colored section of town. We were under the shadow of the old dam during the time the town was segregated. White people lived on the other side of this bridge. Town was in the middle and there were houses on both sides of it, the colored section and the white. Those who lived on the border between white and colored, they were what you might call the elevated colored people. That was your mother's family, Ronnie. Your mother, she's what saved me, how I got what real education I ever got. Rest of it I learned from Shakespeare and the Bible."

"We say black now, or Afro-American," Ronnie said.

"Oh. Well, it changes all the time, the names we get called. Long as it's a good name and not meant to be a bad one, I'm okay with it. Black, then. Afro-American sounds like some kind of desert."

Mr. Candles paused as if studying the moonlight on the water, the dark line of trees on both sides of the bank, then the white barrier of what they called the new dam, way off at the far end of the lake.

"The old dam was built to keep most of the water out. The new dam is designed to keep the lake from flooding broader. That way it doesn't spread too far, overflow everything. The spillway lets in more than the old one did, though, because there's no town to protect from the branch off the Angelina River. Back then, there was just enough water to fill a pleasant little creek that ran through the center of town."

I remembered Dad talking about that, the creek.

"In the summer, in our section of town, close to the water, we got mosquitoes and blackflies in abundance. There were colored businesses on either side of the creek, though not many. We had a picture show and a couple of small stores, a car lot and so on.

"Town was built during Prohibition, and there were secret places to drink in both our part of town and the white side. I knew black men who had hauled liquor into the white and black sections, made extra money. Hauled it out of town to customers all over East Texas and likely beyond. Anyplace that was dry of alcohol and wanted to get wet, the wet was provided. There were vast tunnels under the town—suppose there still are. They were built by rich men and used for shipping liquor about so as to make them richer. They were the ancestors of the city council folks who run everything now. Come right down to it, they made all the money.

"Most everyone else worked at the sawmill, which was up the hill beyond those trees, close to the rails, next to the junkyard. Not far from that was a colored cemetery—black cemetery.

"You had a place to work, junk your car, and be buried, all within a rock's throw of one another. Later, when Prohibition was repealed, the sawmill gained more workers and I guess the old tunnels were forgotten, maybe filled up with water.

"Where we lived in town, it was down in a kind of earthen decline, like a bowl, deeper than the rest of town, and the noise from the trains would travel through gaps in the woods and make our house rumble. We could hear the big sawmill blade too, chewing trees up, turning them into lumber, railroad ties and such. The air smelled like turpentine.

"Junkyard wasn't quite as high on the rise as the mill. It was full of old cars. White man who owned it was said to be the meanest man that ever learned to walk. Said he treated his son bad and let others treat the kid worse. Boy mostly roamed the woods with a flashlight."

"Winston," I said.

"That's right. What we have in common is we both lived in the old town or around it. He mostly grew up in his father's wrecking yard up there beyond the trees, near the top of the hill, back when it was still a working business. No idea about his mother, but whoever she was, she wasn't in the picture."

Mr. Candles dipped silently into his memory for a moment.

"That black cemetery. My mother and father and brothers are buried up there. Other relatives. People I know. I don't visit, I'm sorry to say.

"One day, walking home from work at the mill, my father's

heart burst. Exploded like a bomb. Mama said he worked himself to death. I was the man of the family suddenly. Had my mother and four younger brothers to take care of, so what there was for me was the sawmill. It was full-time, god-awful work. Hot and nasty, backbreaking and dangerous. It wasn't just the air that smelled like turpentine—you did too. That odor got in your hair and clothes. It took a lot of lye soap to get rid of the smell, and then next day, you were up there again.

"Saw a white man get his sleeve caught up in the big saw one day. Jerked him into the blade and chewed him up. Like Humpty-Dumpty, he couldn't be put back together again. The saw room was red with his blood. Days after, we kept coming across pieces of him. I found his ear. Terrible stuff. Sorry, kids."

"Keep talking, Daddy."

"Sawmill began work early and went on late. I'd start walking home about dark, sometimes just after. We didn't have a car. Closest thing we had to that was watching one drive by.

"There were nights I'd go home and couldn't sleep, because I felt I was wasting my life away. Wasn't in school anymore, didn't have any real future. Being a colored fellow, I wasn't never even going to make leadman at the mill.

"When I couldn't sleep, even tired as I was, I'd get up and wander outside. I'd walk the streets. There weren't any streetlights in our section. Somehow the all-white city council felt colored folks did just fine in darkness, like we were a bunch of bats. Also thought we did just fine with holes in the road, faulty sewer and water lines, electric wires that sometimes fed us electricity and sometimes didn't. But you can be damn sure we paid for the services if we got them or didn't. Complain too loud, you didn't get anything at all. I remember not being able to pay all the bills, and the lights getting cut off, and us doing our evenings by candles and lantern. Wasn't so bad, but it wasn't so good neither.

"Won't kid you, I was angry. Angry at my life. I was young and had dreams and knew that I'd have to forget them or dress them down from a tux and bow tie to short pants and sandals."

Ronnie laughed at that. "One thing I don't see you doing is wearing short pants and sandals."

"We're talking what your mom would call a metaphor."

"So, you walked," Ronnie said.

"Lights on the white side of town would pull me like some kind of bug that wanted to flitter around a porch light, and when I got close to that side, I could hear music, see cars rumbling along, people walking about with all the confidence pale skin had given them.

"Later, I started dating your mother. She lived right on the border between colored and white town. Her house was painted bread-slice white, and there was a golden light on a high pole not twenty feet from her yard. At night that light would fall across her house and yard, splicing it in light and shadow.

"In time, I knew her and her family and came there to hear her father read poetry, her mother play boogie-woogie on the piano, watch your mama sing and dance in the living room, and I sang and danced with her. Her grandparents lived with them, and they knew more gospel songs than were in the hymnals, and some of them were so inspiring they made you jump up and dance.

"But what I'm telling you now was a little before that. Back then, I'd walk at night to that dividing line, and some nights I would walk up to it and step over. I thought maybe I'd feel different in the lighter part of town, and in a way, I did. I got so I started coming out late at night with a couple cartons of eggs in a tote bag that was tucked up under my arm, bold as you please. I'd come into white town with those eggs, and in the dead middle of the night, I'd plaster parked cars and toss them at houses."

"Daddy!" Ronnie said.

"I was angry, darling. Angry for being black, and I was angry at them for being white. I was angry about every damn thing, and a lot of it with good reason, some of it with little to no reason at all. Not saying what I did was right, and I wouldn't want you to do such a thing, but that's what I did, and that's the truth of it. And Danny, no offense, son, but back then I hated those white people in their white houses on their brightly lit streets. Hated them bad, God forgive me. I felt cheated. Robbed. Not like I was dealt a card and lost due to the luck of the draw, but like I wasn't ever given any cards.

"One late night I was on my way with my eggs, knowing full well I was going to get caught eventually, and I passed this house in the colored section. It wasn't far from the white line but wasn't as close as Millie's house. But you could damn sure see the streetlights glowing from the white section.

"I'm strolling by this house, and the garage door was open next to the house, and it was filled with light. I could hear a steady thumping as I came nearer, and then I could see this muscular, dark-skinned man with close-cut gray hair in there. Had leather gloves on, was hitting this big bag hanging from a rattling chain. Way he hit, how hard he hit, fascinated me. I stopped and stared at him, watched him float around that bag, light as an angel's ghost, slamming it with his fists.

"He looked up and saw me standing there in my patched clothes and ragged shoes with cardboard soles I'd cut out and placed inside, my bag of eggs under my arm, and it was like he was seeing right through me.

"He said, 'What you doing there, boy?'

"'Standing here.'

"'I can see that. Come on over here.'

"I didn't know this man, not really, but I recognized him. Seen him around, here and there, and he had a powerful presence. I go to the garage, and he says, 'I see you pass by sometimes. Got an idea that bag under your arm isn't full of hymnals. I sit on my porch in the dark and drink a beer and see you come by, and I think you're up to no good. Doing whatever you're doing in white town, that's going to lead to something bad. I'm suggesting to you, kindly, that you don't do it. I don't want to read about you in the morning papers. Give me your name, so at least if your name comes up, I know who I'm reading about.'

"I told him my name, and he said, 'Come on up in here.'

"He took off his gloves, using his teeth to untie the strings on one, sticking the glove under his arm and pulling his hand out of it, then untying the other glove with his free hand. He handed me the gloves.

"I sat my package of eggs aside and took the gloves. 'Let me help you put those on,' he said.

"The gloves were sweaty, but I liked the way they felt. He said for me to hit the bag a little. I don't know why, but I did. I hit it a few times, and he said, 'Naw. That ain't right.' And he started showing me how to punch.

"His name was James Turner. He was retired from the railroad, one of those jobs where you actually got a pension. He liked to sleep days and stay up nights. Had once been a professional boxer, and good, too, or so he said, and I believed it. But he killed another black man for insulting and knocking down his mother, and he went to prison. Killed that man with a hard right cross.

"First night I trained a couple hours with him, and we fried up about half them eggs, ate them until we near popped. His house was full of photos of children grown up and a wife long dead. I came to realize that Mr. Turner was an older man than he seemed.

"I dragged out of there early morning, went on back home long enough to drink a cup of coffee with my sweet mama and say hello to my younger brothers, then went on to work. I felt fine, though. I had found something that meant something to me. Never threw another egg, and I tossed the meanness out of me on that bag. I spent a lot of time with Mr. Turner, and he taught me more than boxing. Despite prison time, he was a good man. I wasn't so angry anymore, and I began to feel sorry for white folks. They were what they were taught.

"Then there came talk of the lake, about how we had to move, and many did. But some of us, white folks too, we thought if someone stayed in Long Lincoln, they couldn't release the water. Wouldn't release it.

"A peculiar thing was that the whites and the colored found themselves meeting together at the town hall, which was in the white part of town, of course. Started out sitting in different sections, and then we weren't. We had a common concern, and we were all underdogs right then. But we also talked about fishing and families, this and that, and we had pretty much the same going on in our lives. We weren't so different.

"Met your mother at one of those meetings. Fell for her so hard, it was like I broke a leg. Don't know if she felt the same about me right away, but in time I won her over. One night, as part of our courting, she invited me to a singing over in Garrison, at a church there. She had a car. That was a big thing, being colored—black—and having a car. I walked to her house, dressed in as good as I could find, and we went over there.

"Now, Ronnie, I haven't told you this part, just hinted at it, and your mama, she won't talk about it. That's why we go quiet when you bring up about your grandparents, our old life. Because night it happened, we were singing in a church in Garrison. It was a little black church that was hot as sin and loud with our voices. We were thrilled to be there. We felt special.

"While we were there, the bigwigs didn't come in and drag the stay-at-homes in Long Lincoln out by the heels. There were no more warnings. Not a word in the last two weeks, and because of that and all the petitions we'd filed, we thought maybe we'd won something. But you don't beat the moneyman.

"While we sang, back home the dam was blown, and the water roared along, carrying concrete and all manner of stuff. Water wiped the sad little buildings and houses of colored town off the earth as easy as you could take your hand and wipe checkers off a board. Just took it all the hell away, swept away my loving mother, brothers, washed over Millie's parents, and stole Mr. Turner like a mean thief in the night. Drowned most everyone, all those people who had held out, that had refused to move.

"By the time we got back from Garrison, our souls full of heavenly blessings, the moon lay on the black water where Long Lincoln had been. Water was high on the road, and had we been driving faster, we'd have gone right into it. Those heavenly blessings faded."

Mr. Candles got a catch in his voice, a bit of hesitation, before he said, "So you see, Danny. We have something in common with this lake. It took our families. They found the bodies of some of the people that drowned on the edges of the lake, like my mother, and she was buried in that cemetery on the hill up there"—he pointed toward the woods—"next to my father, who, like my grandparents, had been lying and waiting for her in his grave for years. Not a one of my brothers were ever found. I guess they are now part of the earth and food for the trees or covered up deep by mud and silt. Mr. Turner was never found, and no one went into the deep water to look for them back then. The fat cats said it was an accident. They said they thought everyone was gone on the night they let loose the water, but they knew, sure as birds sing and fish swim, that they were not. So many of the stubborn drowned and so many of them were poor that though some could afford suits or funeral dresses, a lot of them had to be buried in blue shrouds supplied by the colored funeral home that had already set up shop in New Long Lincoln. They were made of cheap cloth and looked like choir robes. But what money those people had, black and white, was lost in that flood, and some whole families were gone and had to depend on charity to be put in the ground. It was a terrible night. Winston and his father were still up on the hill, but the people who lived in the town had fed their business, and now the town was gone. Winston was pretty much let loose. What do you, me, and Winston all have in common in one way or another? Moon Lake. Winston because when the town was gone, his father's business was gone, and his father went away. Winston was left on his own like a wild dog."

"Don't you hate it?" Ronnie said.

"The lake? Water is water. Why should I hate water? Family members of those who drowned in the town, like me and your mama, we had lawsuits back then, but in time we didn't hear no more about it. Our lawyer, a good Negro lawyer, followed by a good white one both died in a short time, and the whole thing fell silent.

"The city council saw to that. The new Long Lincoln had been built, and most people from the old town were already living there, and now those who had survived the flood moved there too. It was done."

Almost on cue, as Mr. Candles wrapped up his story, dark clouds rolled in and wiped out the moon. The lake and everything around it became dreadful dark. Then I saw a light bobbing on the far bank near the base of the bridge. Ronnie and Mr. Candles saw it too.

"That'll be Winston again," Mr. Candles said.

I watched the light. It went into the deeper woods and finally it moved away. I realized the light I had seen that night on the lakeshore, recovering from my plunge, had been him.

"We better head in," Mr. Candles said.

We pulled in our lines, and as Mr. Candles was cranking the motor, tugging on the pull cord, a flash of lightning smashed across the sky, and in the light, I could see the lake and it was suddenly rolling.

Thunder grumbled, and then the bottom of the sky fell out and rain came down in a gush, drenching us and splashing in the bottom of the boat. The water under the boat swelled and heaved us about.

(7)

It took us more time to make the shore than expected. The water pushed at us like a thug wanting our lunch money.

When we were finally on land, we loaded the boat on the rack in the pouring rain with the wind trying to lift it up and carry it away, and then we climbed into the truck. My feet felt like blocks of ice.

Mr. Candles turned on the engine, and the air from the heater was cold at first. We sat there while it warmed, listening to the rain smash, the lightning sizzle, and the thunder rumble. The wind was so fierce the truck wobbled.

Finally, we were moving, the wipers beating at the rain like a fool waving in a parade.

When we got back to the house, we unloaded the boat and rushed inside, laughing as we went. We toweled off and took off our cold, wet shoes, cleaned up where we had dripped on the floor, then had some corn bread that Mrs. Candles warmed in the oven. We buttered slices of the crusty, brown corn bread, crumbled it into glasses of milk, and dipped it out of the milk with spoons. When the corn bread was chewed up and tucked into our gullets, we drank the remains of the milk. We told Millie about the fishing and the rain and how Mr. Candles had struggled the boat ashore. The way we told it, it sounded like a great adventure.

"It wasn't any big thing," he said.

"You know better than to be on the lake with it raining," Millie said.

"Wasn't raining when we went out there."

When we were finished eating, Mr. Candles told us to get ready for bed, he'd clean the fish. I wanted to help him. I had never cleaned fish before, and I wanted to know how, but he insisted our night was over.

I went into my little room and pulled on the pajamas the Candleses had given me, then went down the hall and into the bathroom. I brushed my teeth and did my bathroom duty and washed my hands.

When I came out, Ronnie, dressed in blue footie pajamas, her beautiful, wild hair tied up in a ribbon that couldn't quite contain it, was coming out of her room and down the hall. She passed the doorway to the kitchen as I was turning from the bathroom toward my sleeping place. She rushed up and grabbed my shoulders and turned me, easy as a top, and kissed me.

It was a warm kiss and I liked it more than the one on the cheek she had given me before. I felt it all the way down to my toes and it made the milk and corn bread in my stomach spin around.

Wasn't a long kiss, but it was strong kiss, and when her lips left mine, I said, "What was that for?"

"Because," she said, and she turned and padded quickly down the hall, looking back at me once with a cute smile, then she went into her room and closed the door.

Hallelujah.

In my bed, I lay awake and thought about that kiss. Warmth and memory of it glided me into sleep. And it was nice for a while, until I felt the bed move, and I knew my father was back, and he reached out to touch my foot.

When I awoke from that shake, there was just the dark and the slight chill of the midnight room. It took me some time to get back to sleep.

*   *   *

Since it was Christmas holidays, for a few days following our fishing trip, Ronnie didn't have school, and Mr. Candles didn't have work. We stayed home in the warm house. I liked having Ronnie near. She smiled at me a lot during that time, in memory of our kiss, I guess, though she was the one that had done the kissing. I could have kicked myself for not kissing her back.

(8)

Beginning only a few days after the fishing trip, the joy that had overwhelmed me tumbled down a dark tunnel to nowhere. It came over me suddenly, like a dose of the flu.

The stars didn't twinkle and the moon didn't shine. Raindrops were heavy as lead, and my poor heart was like a wet rock in the shade. Maybe it was because it was just after Christmastime and all the good moments were gone. Ronnie had gone back to school and Mr. Candles had gone back to work. At least I had Millie nearby, her good mind, her good heart, and her good cooking.

Another thing that made me blue was it was almost my birthday. I hadn't mentioned it to anyone, but when the new year cracked, I would be fifteen. I think the idea of a celebration so soon after the wonderful Christmas holidays didn't seem fitting. That was a broader celebration, but my birthday, my existence due to my mother and my father, didn't seem worth mentioning. The idea of it depressed me.

On a shiny, cool morning, a couple weeks of rain having finally passed, the sun peeking out from between a blanket of gray clouds, I was sitting in the glider with Mrs. Candles, both of us wrapped in our heavy coats, full of breakfast and hot chocolate. She was reading to me from a book, teaching me about the mysteries of ancient Rome, preparing me for a history quiz she was going to give me at the end of the week. While we were doing that, Sheriff Dudley pulled up.

He wasn't in his company car but instead in a black bomb of an automobile that looked as if it had been fished from the same lake where my father in his big-ass Buick resided. He was wearing his hat and khakis, no badge or gun. He was cleaned and starched and seemed proud to be there.

There was a man in the car with him on the passenger side, and I recognized him as the one who had brought Sheriff Dudley the fried-chicken-and-mashed-potato dinner on that cold, wet night when I first came to New Long Lincoln via the lake. I remembered his name was Duncan. The man had his window rolled down, and I could see he wore a dark hat and shirt, and his face was turned toward us. He wore a thin smile like he had farted and thought it was funny.

Sheriff Dudley got out of his car, removed his hat as he came up the steps to stand near the glider. He nodded at Mrs. Candles, called her Miss Millie. She nodded back.

"Dudley, how are you?" she said.

"Fine, mostly, and in places I'm not fine, nothing can be done about it. I'm going to get right to it. Son, your aunt is home in Tyler, Texas, and she said you could come live with her, get registered in a Tyler school."

"My mother?" I said.

Dudley shook his head. "Can't find anything that has to do with her in any kind of place. Your aunt said she has no idea where she is and that your mother didn't have any real friends she might be with."

I assumed that was correct. My mother was beautiful and mysterious—that silver star in her front tooth, her charming hippie outfits—but if you knew her for long, you realized how peculiar she was as well. It's like she had clawed open a hole in the universe, gone into it, and clawed it back together again.

"Daniel, you be ready tomorrow morning, and I'll come get you, drive you over to your aunt's. I'm happy for you. Happy she's home."

Sheriff Dudley made with a few pleasantries and started for his car. I said to Mrs. Candles, "I don't know I want to go live with my aunt."

"And I don't want you to, Danny," Millie said. "I want you here."

"Then I can stay?"

Millie's right cheek quivered. "You don't have a choice. They let you stay with us longer than I expected. You see, Danny, baby, they don't see things the way they are. They see them how they believe them to be."

"How's that?"

"Colored with colored, and white with white. They'll tell you that's how it is with the birds and such. That they keep to their own. But people aren't birds, Danny. They think they're rescuing you, and they have the power of the law on their side. Do you understand?"

In theory, I did, but in my heart I was confused.

*   *   *

Next day, Ronnie stayed home from school and Mr. Candles took off the morning hours and, of course, Millie was there. They stood on the porch with me, waiting for Sheriff Dudley. It was cold, but the sun was bright and the birds were singing. For me, though, it might as well have been stormy weather.

The Candleses had given me a travel bag to carry the few things I owned, and I had eaten a big breakfast.

As the sheriff arrived, this time in his official car, Ronnie leaned in and hugged me and put her lips to my ear and said, "I will miss you, Danny."

Her voice was choked, and in that moment, mine was so choked I couldn't say anything.

I hugged her back and thought of that kiss in the hallway. I let my pretty mermaid go and hugged Millie. She said, "I love you, baby. You do well."

When she let me loose, she gave me a brown paper bag she had been holding.

"For the road," she said. "Cookies. You can share with Sheriff Dudley."

Me and Mr. Candles shook hands and he asked if I had my books in my suitcase, my pocketknife in my pocket. I did. When we parted hands, I rushed him and hugged him.

Sheriff Dudley came and directed me down the steps, him with my travel bag in hand, me with the sack of cookies. I felt something had torn loose from me, and whatever it was, it hurt. I got in the car and looked at the Candleses standing on the porch, certain I had seen them for the last time. Ronnie and Mrs. Candles were crying, and Mr. Candles looked like he wanted to.

Smiling, Mr. Candles lifted both hands into boxing position, called out to me, "Keep your hands up, Danny."

"I will," I said, and waved at them.

*   *   *

It was about a two-hour drive. Sheriff Dudley played the radio; mostly mournful country tunes came out of it, and most of the songs fit how I felt. I think that was the day I became a country music fan. A George Jones song about how he stopped loving her today hit me hard.

I opened the sack Millie had given me. A warmth came out

of it along with a fine smell. The sack was full of large chocolate chip cookies. I offered one to Sheriff Dudley. He took it without hesitation.

Around crunching, he said, "Millie bakes the best cookies. The best anything."

I nodded, had a cookie myself, even though I wasn't even close to hungry.

Sheriff Dudley glanced at me out of the corner of his eye. "It won't be so bad, son. You get to be with your own."

"I liked the Candleses just fine."

"Up to me, you could stay with them. They're as fine a family as there is, but it's just not customary."

"Does that matter?"

"Some things just are," he said. "You might can work around some of them, but black and white living together, like you're a son of theirs, what it does is it makes things hard on you, and to be honest, it could make things harder on them. Not saying I agree with that, I'm saying things are what they are."

"It doesn't make much sense."

"Hate to say it, but sometimes you do things that don't make much sense, or you feel you have to do things you don't like, and sometimes it can weigh on you. Heavy. That's the side of life they don't tell you about. Dreams get crippled from time to time, and the people dreams cripple the most are those without the right kind of backbone. You keep your backbone."

"Is that hard?"

"You wouldn't believe."

"Have you kept yours?"

"Can't say that I have."

Couple hours later or thereabouts, we arrived at the little blue house sitting on the winter-brown lawn with the wide white porch and the big green and blue metal rocking chairs on it.

Sheriff Dudley cut the engine and we sat in the car and looked at the place.

"It's nice," Sheriff Dudley said. "Talked to your aunt over the phone, she said she bought it soon as she came back from traveling. Said she used what money she had left to buy it."

We got out of the car, me with my sack of cookies, the sheriff with my bag.

We had just stepped up on the porch when the door opened, then the squeaking screen door in front of it, and my aunt stepped out.

My teeth almost fell out of my mouth.

(9)

My aunt looked remarkably like my mother. The gene pool had been kind to both, but if my mother always looked and seemed sad to me, Aunt June looked as if she were waiting for the slightest reason to fly off the handle and beat you to death with a shoe heel.

She lacked the silver star in her front tooth. She was a little heavier, and there was nothing hippie about her clothes. She had on a black-and-white dress that had all the style of a borrowed quilt. Her hair had a long patch of gray in it that I thought was most likely designed by the beauty parlor. She wasn't wearing makeup, and I was to learn she seldom did. I tried to remember if my aunt was the younger or the older sister. I realized I really didn't have anything to remember on that matter. It had never come up when my mother spoke about her, which wasn't often.

Way she looked at me, I might as well have been a small-pox blister.

"I take it you're Daniel," she said, and her voice sounded as if the inside of her throat had been slightly sandpapered that morning. "It's been a while."

"Yes, ma'am," I said. "Once, I think."

She looked over my shoulder at Dudley. "And you're Sheriff Dudley, of course."

"Yes, ma'am. We spoke on the phone."

"Come in, Sheriff."

"That's all right. I'll check back on him for time to time. To let him know if we recover his father's body."

"Don't bother," she said.

"Do you have any idea where his mother is?" Sheriff Dudley asked.

"No."

"So, you and your sister weren't close?"

"Sometimes yes, sometimes no. Mostly no. We didn't do each other's hair, trade dresses, and swap boy stories, if that's what you mean."

"I see," Sheriff Dudley said, handing my aunt my travel bag.

Aunt June stood with one hip cocked, waiting to see if Dudley had more. He didn't.

"Okay. Thanks, Sheriff. Daniel. Come in the house."

I told Sheriff Dudley goodbye and marched through the open doorway with my sack of cookies held before me like a shield. Before I knew it, the door was closed and I could hear Sheriff Dudley's car starting up and motoring away.

My aunt looked at me like I was an unidentified animal discovered in the Amazon. She had my travel bag in her hand. She lifted it up and down, said, "Not much here."

"Didn't have much."

She set the bag by the door, kept eyeballing me.

"I'm trying to see your mother in you," she said. "Trying to see me, for that matter. Did you know your mother and I were twins?"

I shook my head. I realized I knew more about the Candleses than I knew about my own family.

"I'm the older one by nine minutes," she said.

The only response I could come up with was "Oh."

It was warm in the house, and it was nice, but considering how I'd imagined my aunt's taste, given the fact that her husband had been a highly successful oilman, I had expected more. Perhaps the Taj Mahal and a troop of elephants. The house was simple and well kept, and except for the overwhelming smell of cigarette smoke clinging to the curtains and the padded furniture, it seemed cozy enough.

Aunt June, still studying me, seemed to know what I was thinking.

"That cigarette stink," she said. "Comes from the previous owner. That's their furniture too. I'm having all that stuff thrown out next week, walls painted, new furniture. You'll get a new bed out of it."

I nodded.

"What's in the sack?"

"Cookies," I said.

"I like cookies," she said. "That colored family give you those?"

"Mrs. Candles," I said.

"Colored women can cook. How was it staying with those kinds of folks?"

"It was fine."

"Wasn't too nasty, was it?"

"Wasn't nasty at all."

"Good to hear. I know there are some clean ones."

I hadn't been through the door five minutes, and already I was starting to hate her.

"Want a snack?"

I nodded as if I really knew what I wanted. Truth was, I was still stuffed to the gills from breakfast and the cookie I'd eaten.

She guided me to her kitchen. There were wooden roosters on

the wall in several places. There was a framed cloth with GOD BLESS THIS HOUSE on it that hung over the doorway. There was a clock on the wall and it beat out the minutes with a sound like someone driving railroad spikes.

"That goddamn clock makes me crazy," she said. "I been here, what now, three weeks, and I keep thinking I'll get used to it. I won't. I'll be glad when all this bullshit goes and I got new stuff. People owned this house, all of their taste that wasn't in their mouth was up their ass."

She took the clock off the wall, beat it soundly on the counter until it quit ticking, then threw it in the trash can under the kitchen sink. "I'd rather guess the time. Sit at the table."

She was as subtle as a drill sergeant but without the charm. I sat.

She got out a glass jug of milk, set it on the counter. She reached back inside the refrigerator. There was a sandwich already made and on a plate. The plate was nestled between some blackened bananas and something in a clear bowl with a lid on it. The contents of the bowl looked suspicious. She placed the sandwich in front of me, then poured me a glass of milk and placed it by the plate. She put the milk back, and from a pot on the stove she poured herself a cup of coffee. She took a bottle of whiskey from a cabinet shelf, leaked a little of that into her coffee, said, "Eye-opener. Eat up. I got to get more groceries with you here."

The sandwich turned out to be pimento cheese. The bread tasted a little damp. I only ate a few bites. I was so stuffed by that time, I feared I might burp and shit myself.

"I need to go shopping. You should go with me. Listen here, Daniel. I don't know a goddamn thing about taking care of a teenage boy."

"Not sure I know much about being one," I said.

That made her laugh.

"Me and your mother, we didn't exactly have great examples for how to parent anyone. We didn't get much in the way of examples for how to do much of anything. I married well and your mother tried to. Unfortunately, she married your dad. She expected more than she got."

"He was all right."

"Was he?"

"He was all right," I said like a mantra.

"Let's look at some facts. Your mother is missing. Your father drove you out to his old hometown, your mother's old hometown, my old hometown, then drove his car through a bridge with you in it, and you had to be rescued from drowning by colored people and had to stay with them for a few months. How all right was your father again?"

"I don't think he knew what he was doing."

"Someone had to know, and I pick him. He tried to kill you, Daniel. He put you in a position where you were on your own and you had to stay with coloreds."

"I didn't mind staying with the Candleses," I said. "Ronnie says they prefer to be called black."

"Ronnie? That the little girl Dudley told me about? You don't have a little crush on a pickaninny, do you, Danny?"

I could feel myself blush, but not because of Ronnie—because of what my aunt had called her. I didn't know what it meant, exactly, but I knew it wasn't good.

She looked me over as if seeing into my thoughts.

"Remember this, kid. I wasn't supposed to raise your ass. That wasn't my job. That was my sister's and her no-account husband's job."

I really couldn't argue with that.

My aunt sipped her coffee. She kept looking at me as if by looking long enough and hard enough, I might vanish in a puff of smoke.

Perhaps then I might cling to the curtains like cigarette odor and she could throw them and me out with the spring cleaning.

Her eyes widened. A sudden thought had hit her like it was shot into her head by a bolt of lightning.

"You're not going to want a goddamn dog, are you?"

(10)

For the record, Aunt June never mentioned my birthday had recently passed. I don't think she knew the date until sometime later.

The little blue house became my home, but I never thought of it that way. Not really. It was just where I stayed. Aunt June had all the warmth of a refrigerated ice tray in winter. She treated me well enough, the way you might treat a dead relative's pet that you didn't really want to look after.

The house was a house where everything had a place and everything better damn well be in its place. I was expected to keep my bedroom as clean and neat as a military barrack. I went to school. Watched TV. Read books. In school, I didn't adjust right away. I was thought weird and was as popular as a prostate exam.

It wasn't that my aunt wasn't kind in her own way. She wasn't one to hold your hand or put her arms around you or kiss you on the cheek. She made me go to school and to church, which I always found depressing, especially since she didn't go and had absolutely no interest in anything theological. I think she thought it would somehow make me part of the community.

I remember one boy from my school said church was a great place to pick up girls. He might have been right. I never found out. I quit going as soon as I could drive a car and was no longer dropped off like laundry and collected an hour or so later.

For a couple of years, I wrote Ronnie, and she wrote back. Sometimes I wrote Millie, and she wrote back. Eventually the letters dwindled, then stopped. I guess even good memories must make way for new ones. I was almost happy we quit writing. That way I could quit thinking about what I had lost.

My aunt and I, if we were in the house alone and were both suffering from boredom, would talk a little. It was usually what I think of as functional talk. Do you have this or that? How are things at school? Anything you want to add to the grocery list?

I tried to direct our conversations to other places, but it was almost like you couldn't get there from here. I wanted to know more about my father and mother, the things that as a child I might not have noticed.

My aunt surprised me one day, saying, "You know, I dated your father first. But it was your mother that caught his eye. Sad day for her. Lucky day for me. It was like I dodged a cannon full of grapeshot when he lost interest in me. Your father wasn't worth the collected cells that made him, that handsome bastard. There was always something dark and suspicious about him, like a snake in your underwear drawer. Your mother and I weren't close, especially for twins, but I remember telling her she should take a powder, as they used to say. Head for the hills, leave that marriage like a cow plop in the pasture."

"Do you think she's dead?"

She looked at me as if she might reveal a dark secret, her face quite beautiful, but she didn't say anything. She suddenly found things to do in the kitchen.

Aunt June was like that. In a moment when you thought you

might have connected, you realized, like throwing a dart, the release felt good but often the toss missed the target by more than a few inches.

One thing that changed during my time with my aunt was my father's ghost. He didn't visit me anymore. Perhaps he found my life too boring to haunt.

There were a few calls from Sheriff Dudley over the years, and this surprised me. When he walked off Aunt June's porch that day, I assumed I would never hear from him again. But he called. Not once a week or once a month, but at least once or twice a year. He called to check on me. I always told him I was doing fine, and then he spent the rest of his time on the phone talking to my aunt while I stood or sat somewhere nearby, hoping there would be news of my father's car and body.

When his call was finished, I would look at my aunt, and she would say each time something like this: "They don't know anything more than what they didn't know before. Dragged the lake again. Found some tires and a dead horse, but they didn't find him. Way I figure, that fat sheriff couldn't find his ass with both hands and a well-marked instruction manual."

As I moved into my junior year I began to feel more like a true teenager. My aunt bought me a used car, the one that kept me out of church, a '64 tan Impala, and boy, did it run. I had to work part-time sacking groceries to pay for the insurance, tires, gas, and so on, but I liked that. It meant I spent less time with my aunt, moving through silence like a ship through fog. I kept my studies up enough to pass. I dated. I had sex in my car with two different girls quite a few times—never at the same time, I should say. Neither of those pretty sex partners turned out to be my one true love, or me theirs.

The second one, Jennifer Kitchen, a blond beauty with a figure loaned to her by Aphrodite, was quite an obsession for a time, but football players proved irresistible to her, so her favors were taken from me and given to them.

At home I sulked about for a few weeks. It wasn't a loss of love, as I said, but it was a loss of something. Sex, most likely. I had never discussed it with my aunt, but she surprised me by recognizing my disease.

"Got your heart broke, huh?"

"What?"

"Some girl?"

"No."

"Bullshit. You got the look. They come and they go, Danny, and mostly they go. It's no big thing. You would have got her pregnant anyway, and then there would be a child, and what a burden. You'd be stuck with some girl who is going to change as much as you are. Hell, buy some condoms and use common sense. Enjoy yourself for a few years. Better yet, die a bachelor. It saves on groceries."

I didn't know what to say to her. It was embarrassing. But that's how it was with my aunt. Absolute silence or something insightful or mean phoned in from left field. I once asked her why she had ceased to travel after so long in Europe, and her answer was as blunt as a tossed rock.

"I have you to take care of, don't I?"

PART TWO
THE ROAR OF THE FLIES
1978

There was nothing in the dark that wasn't there when the lights were on.

—Rod Serling

(11)

When the wrecker pulled my father's car out of Moon Lake ten years after it went in, I was at my house working on an article for a daily newspaper.

I was writing about some poor lady who had died in her home and been partially eaten by her two dogs. They found her in a house full of dog crap and stacks of old newspapers. Both dogs were small and cute and had on little red dog sweaters with MOMMY'S BABY stitched into the material with red and white thread, and according to the cop who climbed through the window and found her and them, the doggies had blood on their teeth.

When the cop discovered her body, it was so covered in flies, he said he thought it was a buzzing black electric blanket on the fritz, but when he moved forward and startled them, they rose in a tight wad of beating wings, and in the narrow hallway where she was found, it sounded like the roar of a lion. Being religious, the cop thought it was her soul leaving her body via bloated houseflies. Interesting.

I was about to wrap the piece up when I got the call. I was trying to find a way to put the emphasis on her animal-rights work and leave out the part about how her starving pets had snacked on her and the putrid detail about the roar of the flies.

As for the dogs, I sympathized. Had I been trapped in a house and not had thumbs or fingers to call for help or pizza delivery, I would have eaten her too, but the public didn't want to read about that, not in a small-town newspaper.

The call was from old Sheriff Dudley, who was still on the job, although he was now with the New Long Lincoln police force and was Chief Dudley. He told me they had found the remains of my father, broken and scattered across the front and back seats by water and time, and, in the trunk of the car, suitcases and bodily remains—meaning bones and withered flesh—wrapped in a blanket that had turned into a kind of mud-covered cloth mush. Their guess was the remains belonged to my mother.

It was a startling moment, to say the least.

At first when I was invited to come there and hear what they had to say, make some kind of funeral arrangements, I was both confused and reluctant.

It wasn't that my part-time job for the newspaper was making me real money that I feared to lose, as I had recently sold a second novel proposal for enough money to keep me in good shape for about six months; it was that, by that point, after feeling pain and loss for so many years, I had to a great degree disconnected. It was a part of my past that had wandered off into the weeds, and if it hadn't died there, it was badly wounded and lying mostly still.

I wrote a poem about my past once. It remains unpublished.

Thing that was foremost in all this was that I was going to have to cancel my therapy session to go to New Long Lincoln. My session wasn't with an actual therapist but with a YMCA boxing coach.

I was getting pretty good, and as I had learned from Mr. Candles, boxing centered me. It was my therapy. I had also learned to protect myself with skepticism and, at times, a smart mouth.

I finished up the piece on the partially dog-eaten woman, wrote a half a page of the novel I had started, then tried a few poems, and as usual, all of them sucked. But writing, like boxing, lets the pressure off my mind, no matter what I'm writing about. I wondered if the ancients drilled holes in skulls to let those kinds of pressures out, thinking they might fly away, although instead, the patients ended up with infections and a new fondness for hats of some sort. Still, the urge to drill would be strong.

I drove to work with my article in a manila folder, and when I was inside the newspaper building, the air had gone foul and it was sticky warm.

Saul Albright, who owned the business, was the only one there. He was red-faced and white-haired, thin as a starving model and sharp as a samurai sword. He always seemed at attention, even when sitting down, but today he appeared to have shrunk in height. He was standing outside his office door, leaning against the doorjamb. His clothes hung on him as if they were draped over the back of a chair. He looked tired and dank.

"Daniel," he said.

He melted into his office, and I followed. He tucked in behind his desk as he always did, his long legs stretched out, his hands in his lap. I placed the folder with my article in it on the edge of his desk. He eyed it sadly, like a hungry man on a diet who was looking at a dessert he knew he shouldn't eat.

"I got a call this morning. From the police department in New Long Lincoln," I said, then summarized it. "I'll need to be gone a few days."

"Oh, that's horrible, Danny."

"I suppose it is."

"You'll have to go, of course."

The realization that my father must have murdered my mother meant that the night we drove over to Moon Lake and parked on the bridge before playing submarine, her body was in the trunk the whole time. I had helped load that car trunk, and I couldn't figure out how my father had put my mother's dead body there without me knowing, though one of the suitcases was large enough to contain her.

"Damn," I said. "It's hot in here. Where is everybody?"

"I've turned off the central air. The electricity and water are next. Not the best of times to hit you with this. I've already told the others, but I'm worn out, old enough to remember when I could remember. These days I'm putting my pants in the refrigerator at night."

I didn't believe that, but it was Saul's way of sneaking up on something he really wanted to tell me. It was his method.

"I'm closing the paper, Daniel. I was going to call you but decided I wanted to see you in person. You, like the Scarecrow, I will miss the most."

"Why are you closing?"

"Nobody reads it and they don't wrap fish in it anymore. I thought about selling it. But who to? Tyler newspaper and the TV news have taken all of our little-town thunder. I'm not making any money. I'm in arrears on damn near everything. I been borrowing from Peter to pay Paul, and Peter died. Today is the last day.

"Got up this morning, looked at what I owed, figured I could get it all paid, but the idea of struggling through another month, wearing cold pants from the fridge, it wasn't all that appealing anymore. I got your check here. Shit, Danny. Money you make here is about enough to buy a birthday cake and a party hat. You don't need this, being a novelist and all."

"I felt like I needed it."

"Maybe as a hobby, but not much else." He opened the desk drawer and pulled the check out and gave it to me.

"Look, if you can't afford this——" I said.

"Don't be silly. I can't afford the goddamn paper, but this I can afford. Drop in and see me from time to time. Not here, of course. Come by the house and wear refrigerated pants with me. I'll keep an extra pair ready. I'm sorry about your father and mother. I don't know exactly what to say."

"Not much to say. Turns out my father murdered my mother and was trying to kill me too. I think that's enough said."

"You don't know the whole story, Danny boy."

"Mom didn't crawl into the car trunk and die on her own."

"I suppose not. But you're a reporter, even if it is for a half-assed paper that dies today. You know enough to realize what seems real at first might not be. Assumptions instead of facts can make an ass out of everyone."

"Some things are so obvious, it's not about where there's smoke, there's fire—it's where there's fire, there's fire."

Saul stood up and stuck his hand across the desk. I shook it.

"You go to New Long Lincoln and decide to stay there, you might want a job. I know the lady runs the newspaper. Christine Humbert. She runs a bigger outfit than this one. They might even be able to pay you enough to drive to work in the morning. I could put in a word for you."

"Didn't say I was staying there."

"True. But I've known you long enough to know when you're truly curious about something, and in this case your curiosity is linked to a personal reason. Look, I'm locking up and going home, and tomorrow I'm going fishing. I've never been, so I thought I might. Course, I need to get some gear first, so I might not go after all. It seems like a big damn bother to catch a fish and clean it, more I think about it."

"Guess you won't be printing the obituary I wrote."

"Afraid not. Sorry to say, in the case of the poor old lady, she will lie in her grave with her horn un-tooted. At least, not by us."

"Sad."

"Beyond my powers now, Danny." Saul was already coming around his desk, heading for the exit. "Come on."

When we were outside and he was turning the key in the door, I said, "I'm going to miss this place."

"It had its moments, didn't it? Decide you don't want to go to work at another newspaper, take advantage of this time off. You're a remarkable young man. You got on here without a degree in journalism because you had already written and sold a novel. It's damn mature for your age. An old soul. I thought about writing a novel once. I'm still thinking about it. I know I'll never write it. But you, you've got one out there and a second sold. Forget this piecemeal journalism. Finish your book."

"Thanks for everything, Saul."

I went home to pack.

(12)

I slept at home that night, though I'm not sure wandering the house and dozing on the couch from time to time between glasses of water and snacks of peanut butter—coated graham crackers really counts as sleep.

Next morning it was hot as a cheap motel room in hell. I carried my suitcase and typewriter out to the car and tucked them in the trunk, and by the time that was done, I was soaked in sweat. I had a stack of cassette tapes on the seat that I hoped would entertain me on my drive to New Long Lincoln, but the truth was I didn't feel a whole lot like listening to music.

I looked back at my aunt's blue house that I had inherited when she died and knew in that moment that I was going to sell it. She had been dead for a couple of years now, heart attack in the grocery store while standing on her tiptoes trying to reach a can of lima beans off a shelf. An observer, also in search of legumes, saw it happen. He said the can of beans fell when she touched it and hit her square on the head but that she was already crumpling. That stretch to reach those beans had been more than her heart could stand, and it had exploded like a tossed water balloon. I buried her two days later, no church funeral, just a simple graveside service with me and the mortuary owner, his two gravediggers, and a solemn squirrel in a nearby tree in attendance. I couldn't quite decide if I missed her. I mean my aunt, not the squirrel. The squirrel I hardly knew.

There was nothing left inside that house that I wanted. The furniture could go, as could all the pots and pans in the kitchen. I didn't really have any reason to come back to this community. I didn't have anywhere I wanted to be after my trip to New Long Lincoln, but that was as deeply as I thought about things right then. It reminded me of the day I came into that house for the first time and Aunt June spoke of tossing everything out and starting over, and did. I was doing the same, but I was going to include the house with it.

New Long Lincoln was a two-hour trip. But first, I went by the bank and cashed my newspaper check and withdrew all my money. It wasn't a fortune, but it seemed like a lot to me.

After I got on the road, I stopped once for gas and to relieve myself at a filling station and buy a Sweet Mama chocolate fried pie, along with black coffee in a Styrofoam cup. I ate the pie and drank the coffee while driving. The pie was good; the coffee was awful. Perhaps the coffee machine had been filled with transmission fluid by mistake.

I drove too fast, but luck was with me—no flashing cop lights appeared in my rearview mirror. I arrived in town, and as I glided past the population sign, I saw that New Long Lincoln in ten years had gone from twenty thousand souls to thirty-five thousand.

Downtown, central to the square, was a huge statue of Jefferson Davis holding a book (probably a Bible) in one hand and grasping his coat lapel with the other. The statue had a look on its face that signified defiance, I guess, but it looked more like a man plagued with frequent constipation. On a tall metal pole, flying above Davis, rippling in the wind, was a Dixie flag.

That statue, like a lot of those glorifying the Confederacy, had most likely been built during the civil rights era as a slap in the face to black people, the government, and Lyndon Johnson. For a lot of folks in this part of the country, the Civil War might as well have ended yesterday. For some in that group, it hadn't ended at all.

I stopped at a Dairy Queen for directions. A pimply-faced girl behind the counter was my guide. I left there with instructions and an icy drink. It was midday by then, and the sun's rays had scorched the air. It was so thick you could chew it. It tasted like copper.

Upon arrival at the police station, I recognized it, though it had been expanded considerably. I had a bit of a flashback to that wet night that suddenly didn't seem that long ago, and I could feel the cold lake water on me, and then the cold air, and here it was dead of summer. So hot a camel would need a tent, but still I felt it.

The inside of the station had changed. It was heavily air-conditioned, for one. The air was full of blue cigarette smoke. There was a young black woman with close-clipped hair and a perky face wearing a blue dress and a black coat sitting at a desk before an open sliding clear plastic panel. She had a sign in front of her space that said SHONDA RAY. She smiled at me.

I was still a bit startled to see a black person working in an up-front job in an East Texas town governed by Jim Crow. Time and the old days were chipping away, and I was glad of it.

"You're wearing a coat?" I said.

"Air-conditioning gets to me after a while. I go outside, it's like I'm bread from a toaster, buttered with sweat."

I smiled and told her I was there to see Chief Dudley.

"Let me buzz him. Your name?"

I gave it. She picked up the phone and spoke into it. I looked around, saw there were a few men, all white, in cop uniforms sitting at desks, one wandering in from the back, a lanky guy who looked over at me and nodded. I assumed there were other cops out there on the beat. The department, like the town, had grown.

"You can go through," Shonda said, hanging up the phone. "He's three doors down and on the right."

She buzzed the side door open, and I trudged down a long hallway like a kid heading for detention. Before I arrived at his office, Chief Dudley stepped out of it and looked down the hall at me. He seemed the same except with thinner, gray hair. He had lost a lot of his belly, making him look more like an artillery shell than a bowling ball.

He grinned, waved a hand for me to follow, and stepped into his office. I entered after him.

"Close the door, son."

I did. On the wall, I saw that photo I remembered seeing that night in his old office. The one with the waxy-looking folks in it standing with Dudley, who looked pink-cheeked and much younger than I remembered.

Chief Dudley saw me looking, said, "City council folks. Think they look old there, now they look like death in a wheelbarrow. Thing is, though, old dogs can bite same as young dogs."

"If they have teeth."

"They got teeth, all right. Too many of them."

Chief Dudley lumbered behind his desk like a rhino looking for a soft spot to lie down, carefully planted himself in his squeaky chair, and looked at me.

"Have a seat."

I sat in the chair in front of his desk, slung a leg over my knee.

"You done growed up tall, son. Last time I seen you, you wasn't nothing more than a fart in the wind. Now you look like something for the girls."

"The girls seem uncertain about that."

"Ah, hell, you just ain't found the right one. Listen here, I hate to bring you in like this, but I really need you to sign off on a few things. Things being the bones of your father and, I figure, the remains of your mother. Makes sense it's her, right?"

"But you can't be sure?"

"Got our coroner looking the body over, may have to get some outside help that knows about things like that. Dental records are probably long gone at this stage. People didn't keep things like that back in the day, not if a patient quit showing up, and if they did keep records, it's hard to know who her dentist might have been."

He looked at me like I might reveal her dental practitioner. I knew nothing so said nothing.

"I promised you we'd keep looking for your mother, but to be honest, we didn't. Gave up a few years back, and the agencies we were in touch with that were supposed to be looking gave up too, if they'd ever started. Finding her and the car and your dad, well, that wasn't brilliant police work. It was an accident."

"What kind of accident?"

"Drought. Lake pretty much dried up, and let me tell you, it's a thing to see, deep as it was, and that old town being there, most of it in surprisingly good shape. Hell, looks like you could bring a team of janitors in, plant some grass, put in a few shrubs, and reopen the place in a couple of weeks. Thing that was most unusual was that there were several cars out there, pushed off in the water, when there was water. Your father's car was on the other side of the bridge, not where it went off. And here's the odd thing. There's a garage, still upright and solid, and the car was parked in it."

"What?"

"Washed in there by time, I reckon."

"Pretty remarkable."

"Lot of power in water. Stormy weather, and that car could have sailed along the bottom and ended up there. Wrecker man,

Buck, hooked a long-ass chain up to it and pulled it out. It was in rough shape, but it was all there. Remains of your father were spread from front seat to back. Your mother's bones, or what we assume to be your mother's bones, were more of one piece, had dried flesh on them in spots, and had mostly been in a suitcase that had come apart. The bones were wrapped in what was left of an old blanket. She and that blanket were curled around the spare tire in the trunk. Couple of places, you could see a pattern on the blanket. Blanket might have been blue or black or dark green, maybe. Had little designs on it, but I couldn't make them out."

"Blue. And the designs were seahorses. I remember that blanket. It came from our house. It was mine. My mother gave it to me. Until this moment, I had forgotten all about it. I kept it folded at the end of my bed, used it on cold nights. Where's the car?"

"In a garage where we work on cop cars. Got it being looked over by folks that are supposed to know what they're doing. Crime scene specialists. Meaning they took a course and have a manual. We're not exactly big-city folks, so we do what we can."

"Since you're chief now, not sheriff, where did the sheriff's department go?"

"Departments used to share different ends of this office, but not anymore. Sheriff's department's got its own layout now, on the edge of town. Me, I got cops working under me fresh out of diapers. Sheriff's department has fellow named Hiram Drudd in my old job as sheriff. Son of one of my old deputies. He's dumb as a bag of fresh horseshit, but I try to put up with him. Have to. But he's no help. We're thinking of bringing in the FBI, those government know-it-alls. And I figure we will, though I don't like it none."

"They could help close the case, though."

"It's our case."

"Solving it would seem more important."

"Son, there isn't much to solve. The rush is off of it, if it was ever really on. Your father had an argument with your mother, probably didn't mean it, but most likely hit her and she died. He rolled her up in that blanket, put her in the car trunk, and decided to abandon home and hearth and drive you and him into the lake. Nuts do that sometimes. Kill their entire family because they can't imagine them getting along without them. They're thinking about themselves mostly. They like control in life and death."

"Can I see the car, the remains, Chief?"

"Before the FBI comes in and throws a Fed bag over everything, I'm going to let you. Might catch hell for it, but shit, I'm an old man and should have retired years ago. I'm more honorary than anything. My roommate, he thinks I should retire and sit on the porch and drink beer or coffee, time of day deciding which. Can't say that appeals to me all that much. But he's the kind of fellow that don't have a lot of ambition, you know. Retired from his job soon as he could. Has a pension and is easing toward Social Security couple years ahead of me. If he has a slice of watermelon and a bowl of strawberry ice cream, his life is complete. Still, I like him. Good friend. Known each other for years. Come on, let's go over. We'll start with the car and then the bones."

(13)

The place where they were keeping the car was behind the cop shop. Dudley led me out the back way and walked me over. It was a gigantic aluminum building that I felt certain had not been there ten years before.

We stopped at the door to the garage, the side door, not the big slide-up door that was pulled down around front. There was a police cruiser parked nearby. The sun rested on the back of my neck like a weight.

Dudley put his hand on the doorknob, then said to me, "They make you put some covers on your shoes, and you'll have to wear plastic gloves and a shower cap. Gloves ain't enough anymore."

"Okay," I said.

"First, for the record, let me know for sure it's the car. Still remember it?"

"Like yesterday."

"All right, then."

Inside it was air-conditioned and there was a nervous little freckle-faced fellow seated at a desk near the doorway. He was doing paperwork with greasy fingers blackened by oil and automotive fluids. The pages he was writing on had smears to match his fingers.

Dudley nodded at him, said, "Give us some gear."

The nervous fellow got up, put on plastic gloves, opened a plastic crate, took out the stuff we needed, and brought it over.

I could see the car, which was parked over a grease pit. I could see hands reaching up from below, a wrench in one of those hands. The mechanic was doing something to the bottom of the car, but I wasn't sure what. Damn sure wasn't fixing anything; he was looking for something. Clues?

The wheel rims were rusted and full of mud, and there were a few strands of rubber tire hanging off them. I could see the top of a shower cap–covered head on the opposite side of the car.

"Is that it?" Dudley asked me, nodding at the car.

"Yes, sir, that's it."

The original color was gone and it had taken on the hue of the lake bed, brown and gritty-looking. The side windows were caked with mud, and there were little things I couldn't identify stuck in that mud. I had envisioned the car to be wet, but of course it was dry now, worked over by a drought and the burning sun as well as time under air-conditioning.

Looking at the car, I could almost hear the cracking of the bridge where the Buick had gone through the railings, could still feel the breathtaking plunge as it headed down into the moon-slicked waters.

We each put on gloves, cap, footies, and a plastic tunic over all of it. It crackled when I moved. I felt like I was wearing a condom.

When we got closer, I could see the gap where the rear windshield had been. I had been blown through it by the force of the water, while my father, being larger, had been pressured to the front seat. Inside the car there was a lot of mud and some twisted items I finally realized were the mud-coated remains of clothes.

I looked at the trunk where my mother's bones had been found. I knew she had been removed, but I visualized her inside, her once beautiful, now ruined body wrapped in a blanket next to a spare tire. My old man in the front seat, maybe clutching that pair of her panties he told me about.

Looking through the gap where the back window had been, I could see the front window was missing too, and as we passed the rear of the car, I saw the glass on the driver's side was still in place, but it was crusted with mud and had visible stars and cracks where something, perhaps my father, had slammed into it. Seeing all of this, remembering that night, it hit me like a freight train.

When we got around on the other side, the person who was there lifted her shower-capped head and looked at us.

She might have been ten years older and covered in plastic, but those shiny deep brown eyes were the eyes of my mermaid.

Ronnie.

(14)

This is Officer Ronnie Candles," Dudley said. "It's been a while, but you know her, of course."

"I can see the young Daniel in your face," she said.

"Truth is, you had to know I was going to be here to recognize me."

"Saw your face on the back cover of your book. Had on a tweed jacket with elbow patches. How writerly of you. But you look the way I remember you, only a lot taller."

"You read my novel?"

"Bought it but haven't read it yet. *The Stone at the Bottom of the Sea.*"

"That's it."

Chief Dudley said, "I remember you both standing in my office, dripping water. You interrupted my supper."

"I remember too," Ronnie said. "There was a colored waiting room still there, or the sign was, anyway, under thin white paint."

"Well," Chief Dudley said, "ain't there anymore. Why don't you take Danny to get some food, then take him over to the morgue?"

"I prefer going to the morgue first, if that's all right?"

"Fine by me, son."

Me and Ronnie walked to the desk, took off our gear, and put it in a disposable bin. We went out into the sunshine. It felt good at first, and then the heat turned weighty.

Now that Ronnie had removed the coverings, I could see she was compact with broad shoulders, catlike when she moved.

She reached back and unbound her hair, which had been gathered and contained by a huge hair clip. It sprang up and was soft and black and shiny in the light. She had found a style and was sticking to it.

Damn, she was lovely.

"Do you remember me, really?" I said.

"I remember how scared and wet and cold you were. I remember how scared and wet and cold I was. I remember you staying with us awhile. Yeah. I remember you."

"Your parents?"

"Older, but fine."

"Still got the books they gave me, the multi-tool pocketknife too. Got it with me right now."

"That's nice. Daddy still works the bag a little. Mama, she's buzzing around like she was twenty years younger. I feel a bit sad when I see the gray in their hair because it reminds me, as Daddy says, that they are moving closer to the barn. But they're okay."

I thought: Do you remember the kiss in the hallway? Part of me very much wanted to know, but I certainly wasn't about to ask.

We got in the cruiser and Ronnie started up the engine. The air-conditioning felt good. It was a short drive to the morgue, a moderate-size aluminum rectangle that looked a bit like a hangar for a small aircraft.

Another small building, also made of aluminum, was pushed up near it and there was a porch that led from the larger building to the smaller one. The porch had an overhang on it, and the sides of it were not wood or brick but hard plastic that served like long windows; a rectangular fish tank is what it reminded me of. Someone walking from one building to the next could easily be seen.

We stepped out into that dreadful heat, made our way to the smaller of the buildings, and went inside. There was a desk in there with a word processor and printer on it. A young woman was seated behind the word processor. She looked like she had not yet graduated from high school. Pretty in a pouty way, with a big tumble of red hair and eyes green as memories of Ireland.

There was a man, probably ten years older than me, putting a manila folder into a file cabinet. He had the physique of an athlete, was tall, and his hair was black as engine grease.

The air in there was almost cold and there was a dark curtain mostly drawn over a little window to the right of the desk, and where the curtain split was a slash of light that cut across the wooden floor like the edge of a solar razor. There were chairs in a row near a long, narrow table with a glass coffeepot on a hot plate. There was coffee in the pot. It looked dark and deadly.

The man turned and looked at us. There was an old-fashioned manly air about him. He was thin-lipped and squint-eyed; a lock of his dark hair hung down on his forehead. It was like someone had jacked up Elvis and driven John Wayne up his ass. He had on a loose Hawaiian shirt and khaki pants and white slip-on tennis shoes.

When he moved, the girl behind the desk studied him with a smile on her face, and I swear, I thought the air smelled of musk, but it could just as easily have been coming from me. The mere sight of Ronnie had fired up a lot of chemicals.

"Hello, Jay," Ronnie said. "How are you?"

"Good. You must be Daniel, the son?"

"I am."

"Chief called. Said you were coming over." He stuck out his hand. "Jay Scott."

We shook.

"Glad to meet you, Jay." I was lying through my teeth, because as he shook my hand, he was glancing past me, studying Ronnie as if he were observing Aphrodite rising nude and gorgeous from the foamy sea. A bolt of unreasonable jealousy passed through me and then was gone.

The redhead behind the desk cleared her throat.

"Oh, this is Shirley Rivers," Jay said. "Excuse my manners. Too much time at work. The dead don't need formal introductions."

Shirley lifted her hand and moved her fingers a little, said, "Hi. I'm not one of the dead."

If her voice had been any smaller and cuter, it would have needed a high chair.

"Intern from University of Texas," Jay said. "Nursing, right?"

"Anthropology. But that's okay, you weren't even close," Shirley said.

"Sorry."

"No, you're not," Shirley said.

"Yeah, you're probably right," Jay said. "Follow me, please. Not you, Shirley. You have paperwork."

"Yes, boss," she said, and saluted.

We went through a door at the back of the room. Jay led us along the clear plastic walled-in walk to the larger building. Inside it was icy and we were standing in a narrow pathway between a row of what looked like giant file drawers. Our breath puffed out in cottony clouds.

Jay walked directly to a long drawer and pulled it open. There was a cardboard box inside and there was a white cloth over the top of the box. It was hard to imagine that someone that had lived could now be stored in a cardboard box in a file drawer.

"You know, I have a saying," Jay said. "'Dying makes the dead better people, and if the living pay attention, it does them good too.' I think we find death puts things into perspective. Chief Dudley told me about your past. The bridge and all."

"I've made my peace with who he was and what he did," I said.

Of course that was a big fat lie.

"These are the remains of your father, Daniel." Jay removed the cloth from the box.

I looked in.

There were yellowed bones, a skull with a crack in the front of it, probably where it had banged against the steering wheel. I didn't feel anything right then. Without flesh, it could be anybody.

In there with him were pieces of his clothes in plastic bags, and in one of the bags was a single item, a silver ring. I knew it to be my father's ring. I remembered how it glinted on his finger as his hand rested on the steering wheel that night long ago. That ring brought the reality of his death home to me more than his bones.

"Hello, Dad," I said.

"We might need some information from you. A way we can check his dental records against these teeth, to be sure."

"I don't have any idea who his dentist was," I said. "Too many years ago. I may never have known. I don't even know what dentist I went to. Same with Mom. Chief Dudley asked me the same thing for her."

Jay nodded. "Maybe we can figure it out. Probably will."

"That's his ring, though. I'm certain of that."

Jay closed the drawer, moved to another, and when he pulled it open, the air inside felt solid, as if it were climbing out of that drawer.

There was a blanket in there, my childhood seahorse blanket stained with mud, and it was wrapped around a bundle of something. Of course, I knew what that was. There were also three clear plastic bags containing little blue-bud earrings, a silver wedding band, black dress shoes of the sort a woman might wear to church, and some fragments of mud-stained hair.

Jay, as if unwrapping a burrito, opened the blanket. I tried to see my mother in those bones, but of course I couldn't. Besides the bones, there was some leathery flesh holding some of the bones together.

I leaned over and looked at the smiling skull and noticed something important.

I took a deep breath. So deep and loud, both Ronnie and Jay turned toward me.

The words practically tumbled out of my mouth.

"That's not my mother."

(15)

In that same moment, I realized something else as well. That wasn't my seahorse blanket. At first, I had seen what I wanted to see. Chief Dudley had described the blanket as having a pattern, and I had filled in the rest for myself because it all seemed to fit, and I guess when I thought of my mother and home, I thought of that blanket, though the blanket had been far warmer to me than she had.

Looking at it now, though, I realized the designs on this blanket were different. They might have been drooping white flowers, though I couldn't be certain. But I was positive that the designs weren't seahorses. At one time, it could have been any color. Now it was mud brown and delicate with decay.

"I know it's a shock," Jay said.

"No. It isn't my mother."

"You can tell from the bones?" Jay said.

"The skull. My mother had a cosmetic addition to her teeth. My father always hated it. She had a little silver star in the center of one of her front teeth. She was hippie-stylish in an expensive kind of way. You know, hoop earrings, miniskirts, all that. One of those stylish things she had was that silver star. It wasn't a surface thing either. It was in the tooth. I guarantee you, this isn't her. Also, when I heard about the blanket, I was certain that was my childhood blanket, but that's not it."

"It's been a long time since you've seen it," Ronnie said.

"That's not it. I used to look at the seahorses on my blanket and pretend I was Aquaman, swimming between starfish while I roamed the seven seas. I loved that blanket, and this is not it. Those aren't seahorses. Another thing, that jewelry, those shoes—that wasn't her style."

"It could be another blanket from home," Jay said.

"Maybe. I don't remember it, though."

"She could have gone to a dentist, changed her style, and the blanket might be one you don't remember. It's been a long time."

I felt relief, but it was an uneasy kind of relief, as if a shark had eaten only my foot, not my leg. A body had been in the trunk of my father's car, so he still might have been a murderer, just not my mother's murderer. And in the long run, if he could murder anyone, he could also have killed my mother. It was hard to find a place in my brain to rest a decision.

If he didn't kill her, she would be in her late forties. Could she have stayed hidden that long?

The morgue drawers were pushed in, and we left out of there, went back to the main office, stood in front of the desk, and talked, Shirley listening. She went to the coffeepot in the corner and poured coffee for all of us. I guess that was part of her job, being an old-fashioned Girl Friday, knowing when someone needed something, and maybe that was just her personality.

We decided to sit in the chairs near the coffeepot and drink our coffee.

"That was a surprise," Ronnie said.

"You're sure about the star?" Jay said.

"It's not her," I said.

Ronnie touched my arm. "I don't know if I should say sorry or congratulations on it not being your mom."

"I don't know the answer to that either."

"Got a thing now, new thing, called DNA testing," Jay said. "It's not what it's going to be, but it's pretty amazing. Maybe we could have the doctor draw some blood from you to match against the bones if they still contain DNA. I don't know much about it, but it might be more help in a few years than it is now. We could have it on record."

"It's not her."

"It's okay. You're not obligated."

"It's not her."

I filled out some papers that said I didn't have reason to doubt that one set of bones was my father's, but as for the bones in the car trunk, I was certain they weren't my mother's, and I wrote down why I felt that way. I didn't refuse the DNA testing, but I didn't agree to it either. I knew the bones in the box that were supposed to be my father were his, due to his ring, and I knew the other box contained the bones of someone who was not my mother. Could she have fixed the tooth? Okay. She had been gone a while, so that was possible. But she always seemed proud of it, possibly because Dad hated it.

Ronnie drove me back to the police station and my car. We sat out front of the station for a moment, listening to the car's air conditioner hum.

"I don't think Jay believed me."

"His job is to be skeptical. Mine too, Danny. Ask the questions, and question the answers. In our line of work, we have to do that."

"I know."

"What will you do?"

"Think I'm going to stick around. Thought at first I'd come to check off some boxes. Father dead—check. Mother dead—check. Father a murderer—check. Then I'd go home. To a home I plan to sell. Now all I know is I'm going to stay for a time."

"I like that idea."

"Do you?"

"Sure. I mean, you'd like to see my parents if you're staying, or even if you decide to leave, right? You didn't plan to come here and not say hey to us."

"That was next on my list."

"I'll give you my phone number. We'll set something up that will suit all of us. Maybe a meal at their house."

"Live in the same place?"

"They do. It's a little more crowded than it used to be. They have taken in a lot of items over the years, and they're beginning to accumulate."

"Still a boxing ring in the garage?"

"It's smaller than before. Like I said, they have more junk."

"Do you still live there?"

"With Mom and Dad? Oh, heavens no. I'm all grown up, Danny."

She took a pad and pen from her shirt pocket, leaned the pad against the dash, wrote down her number, and gave it to me.

"Thanks," I said.

"You'll call, right?"

"Absolutely."

(16)

I found what used to be called a rooming house on Main Street. It had a large enclosed garage to the left side of it where it met the cross street, and on the right side there was a two-story house that needed a paint job with a sign out front that said For Sale.

I guess I should say *room* house instead of *rooming* house, as it let only one room. The one room was simple and on the second floor of an old but well-cared-for two-story house that looked sturdy enough to have a jet land on the roof.

The landlady, Mrs. Chandler, was thin and wizened with cottony pinkish hair that appeared to have been colored by a mixture of strawberry Jell-O and beet juice. There was something about her bone structure, though, that gave me the impression that she might well have been something before paved roads were invented. She led me up the creaking stairs to examine the room.

The room was basic, no TV. It had a bed and a desk with a wooden chair. There was another chair just like it next to the window, and the window had some blinds pulled halfway up and angled.

The lighting was good. There was a painting on the beige wall over the bed that looked as if it had been stolen from a motel. It was a homely thing of a bright day by the pond with a bird dog lifting his paw, pointing his nose toward some tall grass next to it. A duck was flying up. The duck left no shadow on the water. The artist seemed to have died during painting.

There was central heat and air. It hummed like a bee in a jar.

There was a door that Mrs. Chandler said led to a closet, and there was another she said went to the bathroom.

She opened the bathroom door. It was small and tidy with just enough room for a shower stall, a commode, and a sink. There was one of those metal mirrors over the sink that makes your image look warped. There were a couple of towels, one large and one small, as well as a washrag. They didn't match in color and were a little worn, but they looked clean and had been folded neatly over the towel rod. Everything in there was so close, you could almost shower while you took a bowel movement and combed your hair in the bad mirror. Lilliputians would have been happy there. I wasn't sure about me.

She closed the bathroom door.

"So, you're a writer," she said.

I nodded. I had already told her that. She had asked me earlier what it was I did, as if she thought I might be staying there so I could case the bank across the street. I guess she was making sure my story was consistent a minute or so later.

"Write anything I might have read?"

"I've had only one novel published," I said. "I'm writing my second."

"Bestseller?"

"No."

"Why I haven't seen it. Just read bestsellers. I thought maybe you didn't write under your own name."

She gave me the key to the room and the front door. I put it in my pocket next to my pocketknife. She wrote down the number for the phone downstairs in the short hallway, told me no long-distance calls, and said she didn't serve meals. She wanted me to know she wasn't a bed-and-breakfast. She said she didn't do laundry. She gave me a list of things she didn't do, as if I had expected her to come in each morning and hold my dick while I peed. Even if she had offered that service, it would have been tight with both of us in that little bathroom. Maybe if I put one foot up on the tub, we could make it work.

She said I could use the stairs and the hallway on the way out but to stay out of the living room and the kitchen. The rest of the house was her domain.

I had sort of expected to use the stairs and hallway. I wasn't thinking of bailing out of the window to go for meals and hadn't planned on climbing up the drainpipe to get back in.

She went out then, closing the door gently behind her as if to set an example of how it was done in her home. I listened to her trudge down the stairs, heard them creak beneath her weight.

When she was gone, I took my typewriter out of its case and placed it on the desk. I pulled out my paper, spare ribbons, Wite-Out, and carbon paper, stacked everything in neat piles on the desk beside my typewriter. I added a couple of manila folders and a little plastic case full of paper clips, then dropped a notepad and a pen next to them. I meant business. I closed the suitcase and set it on the floor.

I raised the blinds all the way up, sat in the chair by the window. The room was clean, but the window was flyspecked. I looked out of it. A street was in view.

A green lizard crawled from the edge of the house onto the window. It stopped in the middle of the pane and clung there. Its throat swelled in and out and was bright pink. I tapped on the glass, but the lizard didn't budge. Perhaps he had just seen a Godzilla movie and was emboldened.

I placed my suitcase on the bed and opened it. There wasn't

much there, but I hung up my handful of shirts on hangers in the closet. There was a short dresser under the clothes rod. The dresser had three drawers. I placed my underwear, socks, and T-shirts in the top drawer. I had one pair of jeans in the suitcase. I slipped them in the second drawer. I only had the one pair of shoes, the tennis shoes I was wearing. I took my shaving kit and placed it on the sink under the mirror.

I had a book in the suitcase, and I got that out, put the suitcase aside, and lay down on the bed and read awhile, my feet draping over the end so I wouldn't get my dirty shoes on the sheets.

My mind wouldn't wrap around what I was reading. I couldn't hold a thought for long. I was too overwhelmed with the Buick and the bones. And Ronnie.

I closed the book, slipped off my shoes, curled up on the bed, and immediately napped.

When I woke up, I put on my shoes, got the number Ronnie had given me, went downstairs, and used the hall phone to call her. I wanted to give her the phone number where I was staying, see if there were supper plans. She didn't answer. Of course not; it had been only a couple hours since I last saw her. She was still at work.

I drove along the streets of the town, trying to get my bearings. I found a little café, Rita's Place, by accident, had a grilled cheese sandwich and coffee. When I finished eating, I drove around again, still trying to learn the layout of the town, grocery stores and such.

I went to the bank across the street from the Chandler house and opened an account.

When that was done, I drove outside of town looking to locate the Candleses' house. Ronnie told me they still lived in the same place, but the same place turned out to be hard to find. I'd thought it was solid in my memory, but it wasn't.

I went to a grocery store and bought a few simple things—bananas, apples, a few Baby Ruth candy bars, and a carton of milk. I filled up the car with gas. I found a newsstand and bought the local paper and some magazines. I picked out a paperback and bought that too. It looked better than the one I was reading. It had an alien on the cover.

I took my prizes back to my room and placed them on the windowsill. I peeled one of the bananas and ate it. I stared at one of the Baby Ruth bars but didn't eat it. I stared at the paperback but didn't read it. I went to the desk and sat behind my typewriter and rolled a piece of paper into it.

There was a lot of white space on that sheet of paper. I stared at it for a while. I finally started typing, and when I looked up and checked my watch, I had been at it for three hours. It was still summer-bright outside, even though it was late afternoon.

I went downstairs and called Ronnie again. This time she answered. I loved hearing her voice. I gave her my location.

She said, "I was wondering where you ended up. I know that place. Know that lady a little. Not that we hang out or anything. My parents can't do dinner tonight. Some kind of event at the church they're going to. Thing is, though, I thought maybe we could grab something simple and drive out to Moon Lake, if that's not going to be too much for you. I thought you might like to see it, but if not, if it's too much, I understand."

I thought about that idea briefly.

"I think I need to see it."

"I'll come by in thirty," she said.

(17)

I took a quick shower and changed into fresh clothes, which depleted my extra jeans. I slipped my watch back on and looked at the time. If she really meant thirty minutes, I had ten left.

I almost skipped down the groaning stairs and through the hallway. I glanced into the open living room to the right. I could see into the kitchen beyond, as the door was open. Mrs. Chandler was at the stove stirring something in a pot with a long-handled spoon. Toil and trouble, I thought.

She turned and looked at me. I waved at her. She unconsciously lifted the spoon out of the pot and wagged it at me. There was something red on the spoon. Probably the blood of one of the former renters who had dared to step into the living room.

I went outside and stood in the heat and wished I had stayed inside longer, but just when I thought I might have to step back into the hallway to relieve my suffering, I saw the cruiser gliding up.

I got in. "So they let you use this as your personal car?"

"Small town, small favors. I have a car of my own, but I get to use this one if I want as long as there's a faint degree of law business going on. Us going out to look at the scene at the lake, I think that counts. It will when I report it. I see the Judson house is still for sale."

She nodded at the house with the For Sale sign as she eased away from the curb.

"Old man Judson killed himself in one of the closets. Blew his brains out and ruined a rack of clothes, I hear. His family lives in Connecticut. They've had it on the market for years. No one around here is interested. They don't want to buy a suicide's house, even if they are giving it away for beans and a prayer."

We drove through a drive-through and ordered hot dogs and fries and sodas, then we drove out to Moon Lake.

It was an eerie experience going out there. I had only seen it when it was wet as wet could be. As we grew closer, I felt a pang of discomfort in my stomach. By the time we parked at the lip of what had once been the lake, the feeling had passed. The water was gone, and from where we sat, I could see the tops of buildings, a sagging cross on a crumbling church steeple, the bridge my father had driven us through.

We sat there with the motor running in the air-conditioned cruiser and ate our dinner. Ronnie made small talk, nothing of note, this and that, and then she said, "Are you married?"

"No."

"Me either."

We finished eating and stepped out of the air-conditioned cruiser and into the heat. This time of summer, it wouldn't grow dark until way late, but even with the darkness, the heat would remain armpit-sticky for quite some time.

When we walked to the edge of the lake, it was a massive bowl of cracked and dried red mud. The way the light hit the clay made a glare that was hard on the eyes.

There were some puddles here and there, some of them large, most of them small. I saw a fish jump in one of them and splash back down. A few more days of heat and that puddle would be gone, and so would that fish. The air was sour.

We walked closer to the bridge. It was worse for wear than I remembered. I could see the break in it where Dad had jetted the Buick. We decided it looked sturdy enough to walk on.

Carefully, we mounted the bridge. I walked toward the gap. Ronnie put a hand on my shoulder. "I think it's best to stay close to the center."

I nodded. We walked along a little farther and stopped. I took a deep, hot, woolly breath and looked out at the dry bed and the remains of Long Lincoln.

Some of the structures were crumbling in places, and the glass was gone out of all the windows and the doors were pushed open. There were mounds of drying mud and silt in the open doorways. I saw the ragged and crushed remains of houses out in the far beyond, wondered if one of them was the remains of Mr. Candles's mother's home or of the man who taught him boxing. I wondered where my father's and mother's homes had been before they left Long Lincoln. They would have been closer to the bridge, perhaps on the other side of it. In the white section of town.

I wondered about the grandparents I had never known. I had never really thought about them much. Didn't have any photos of them and knew nothing about their lives.

There were cars from the era of the town and more of recent vintage scattered about. There were washers and dryers, broken furniture and television sets, and old wrecked cabinet-size radios that might well have been in those houses when the water washed in during the dead of night and destroyed them. Radios that might have played Big Band music and radio shows about the Shadow and the Lone Ranger, given the news of the attack on Pearl Harbor, broadcast Franklin Delano Roosevelt's fireside chats, the first hot beats of rockabilly, and bulletins on the state of the Korean War.

There was a lot of debris out there that couldn't have come from the town. It wasn't new but it was too modern for when the water drowned that little world. Much of it was things that lazy bastards or crafty bastards had pushed off into the lake.

"River that feeds the lake dried up too?" I said.

"Dry as the desert right now," Ronnie said. "Thing is, though, we have a few big rains, it'll flow again and the lake will start to fill. It won't take long."

I knew about East Texas monsoons, of course. We didn't exactly have a season for it, but unlike the rest of Texas, we were usually heavy with rain and river risings. Floods were as common as buttholes.

"Has the river and the lake dried up this much before?"

"You remember Daddy told us about the time it got so shallow they could step out of a boat and walk on the roofs of buildings and how one time he could see the tops of the tall ones. Far as I know, that was as low as it had ever been. Until now."

"What's the name of that river?"

"It's mostly a creek that becomes a river when it rains a lot. Technically it's a branch of the Angelina. But it's a big branch, growing all the time. It'll join the Angelina before long, making the river deeper and wider there than in most places."

Ronnie turned in the opposite direction, pointed. "See that yellow building that says 'Bud's Garage' on it?"

The building was the color of old mustard and BUD'S GARAGE was spelled out in gray letters that had once been black.

"That opening there, the carport at the side of the shop. That was where your father's car was found."

I remembered my dreams of him driving around down there under the water, looking for a way out. Perhaps he needed some transmission work, and with information from a snapping turtle, he found the garage there to park his Buick and have a fish and a water moccasin repair his car. I thought that idea might make a good children's book.

We strolled back to the shore of the lake and walked along it until we found a place made of concrete that had been used to let small boats into the water. It was moss-coated closest to where the water would have been.

We skidded down that and walked onto the lake bed itself. By this time, the backs of our shirts, our armpits, our collars, were sopping with sweat.

We walked past a scattering of debris: a bicycle frame, a toaster, a percolator, and a random wheel rim without a tire.

Ronnie said, "When it comes to trash, people can be such pieces of shit, tossing it in the lake like it has no bottom and there'll be no tomorrow."

When we got to the garage, we strolled over a hump of slightly damp dirt that led inside. You could see the raw wheel marks from where the Buick had been yanked out.

Inside there were still some tools hanging on hooks. They had somehow avoided being washed away by the plunge and swirls of the water. There was something mud-crusted on the wall that I eventually identified as a tire tube. The air smelled rotten, and the brick garage with its slab of a concrete roof held the heat in like an oven.

It was more than we could stand for long. Outside the garage, we weaved our way through the heat and garbage, even a spool of barbed wire and a ruined *Star Wars* lunch box.

Ronnie put her hands on her hips, narrowed her eyes against the sun, looked around a moment, said, "Listen, I'm feeling curious. Wait here a moment, and I'll be right back."

"Curious about what?"

"Just curious."

She went across the lake bed, up the ramp, over the bank, and out of sight.

I looked across the wide lake bed at the trees that grew along the top of the bank and up the rise of the hill where there had been a sawmill, a junkyard, and the graveyard Mr. Candles had told me about those long years back.

Not too much time passed before I saw Ronnie going down the concrete ramp again. She was carrying a tire iron. As she got closer, I called out, "I hope I'm not in trouble."

She grinned at me. I enjoyed watching her. She looked good in her sweaty uniform with the big gun on her hip, the hand-cuffs hanging from her belt, the lace-up boots shiny-black in the sun.

Ronnie headed toward a black bomb of a car. As we walked to-gether, she talked. "Lake has been dry awhile. Chief thought about that, realized we had a unique chance to look for your father's car. We came out here and looked around where we thought it would be, but it wasn't there. Then the chief found it in the garage, had it pulled out."

"I'm surprised he bothered."

"Don't be hard on him. Over the years he may not have had it on his mind from the time he woke up until the time he went to bed, but he thought about it. And he hired me. No one else would have, a black woman to be a cop? That shows something about him, gives him some room in my mind."

"I guess he's treated me all right," I said. "He was always kind to me."

We had reached the black bomb by then.

"I've been thinking on the possibility your father didn't kill anyone."

"Yeah?"

"Idea I got doesn't make much sense, but it won't leave me alone." Ronnie studied the car. "A '48 Ford," she said, and she stuck the tire iron under the edge of the trunk and pried. The trunk groaned, then we both put our hands and weight on the iron and pushed down. The trunk snapped open.

I pushed the trunk lid up and held it. It was roomy inside the trunk, and there was a spare tire in there. The air had gone out of it, but the rubber seemed to have held up well, though if I had reached out and touched it, it might have collapsed like a cake too soon out of the oven.

Near the remains of the spare tire were scraps of cloth, and under a sludge of mud that had oozed its way into the trunk was what looked at first like a volleyball, but when we looked closer, we realized it was the slick top of a human skull.

(18)

Vibrating with excitement, we walked around to other cars, popping the trunks. Most of them were empty of bones, but some were not. We found four sets of human remains in as many cars, all of them with fragments of cloth, and all the cloth was similar, though much of it had worn away under the water or fell apart once we popped the trunks and the air got to them.

All those cloth fragments seemed strung to something in the back of my mind, but whatever it was on the other end of that string was stubborn, and I couldn't drag it into the light.

After we finished with the car trunks, we walked through a heat so heavy you could almost hear it toasting the atmosphere. We walked so that we were under the bridge. There was some shade there due to the slats.

"I thought there would be nothing," Ronnie said. "But I needed to look."

"Good instincts."

"I thought, What if your father didn't do it? Someone else did it. Bodies were probably disposed of by being put in cars and pushed off into the lake. Maybe for years."

"So it clears my father?"

"I'm saying it could be that way. But he could have killed the ones in the trunks, then killed someone and put her in the Buick, drove you and her off into the water. That someone could be your mother."

"I'm saying it isn't."

"Still, there was a body in the trunk."

"A lot of trunks have bodies."

"They have been pushed off into the water, is the way I see it," she said. "Your dad's Buick, he drove it into the lake, so the body had to be in there when he did."

"I would remember seeing him load a body in the trunk."

"Did you have a freezer?"

"Yeah."

"In the garage?"

"Yeah."

"Did you ever look in there?"

"It was locked. Dad locked it so I wouldn't do something stupid as a kid, like crawl inside. I see where you're going with this."

"All you would have to do is go back in the house to the bathroom, chase after something you forgot and wanted. Again, not saying it's that way, but it's a consideration."

"To kill those others, he'd have to steal their cars, if those are their cars, and he'd have had to find his way back to his car after he dumped them. Means he would have had to walk his way out. He couldn't drive two cars at once."

"That's true. Don't be mad at me, Danny. Only saying how it looks, not necessarily how it is. I need to call this in."

When we were back in the car, the air conditioner humming, I began to feel more human but no less confused.

Ronnie called it in on her cruiser mike. We sat and waited and didn't talk much. I wasn't mad at her. I just didn't know what to say. Could Dad really have been a serial killer all the time I was growing up? He wasn't someone who ventured out that much. When was he doing all this murder, and if the cars belonged to his victims, why were the cars so far apart in age? I organized my thoughts enough to tell this to Ronnie.

"Sometimes serial murderers start early. And he is from this town, Danny. Merely saying it's possible."

"Thinking like that could be an easy way out for the cops too."

Ronnie turned in her seat and looked at me. "I wouldn't do that, Danny."

"Hell, I know. I'm just in the moment."

She patted my hand. "Of course you are."

Three cop cars arrived. Chief Dudley got out of one of them. With hesitation, we got out of the cruiser and stepped into the wall of heat.

Other cops were climbing out of cars now, and there were cars from the sheriff's department as well. A massive orange wrecker came cruising up. The man who got out of that one was a black man. He was dressed in khakis that looked freshly starched and ironed. He appeared way too prim for my view of a wrecker driver.

Chief Dudley came over and started asking questions. I stood silent, let Ronnie answer them. I felt more capable of calculating a mathematical formula for time travel than figuring out why all those bodies were in those cars and what they had to do with my father.

"Goddamn," Chief Dudley said. "This has turned into one steamy pile of lumpy dog shit."

He gave me a glance like it might be all my fault. He sent a couple of the cops that had come over to stand with us down to the lake bed to look at what we had found, told them to break into the trunks of any cars they came across that we hadn't touched. That meant they would have to walk the entire lake bed, which was sizable, to see all that was there.

"Well, Danny," Chief Dudley said to me. "You may have gotten more than you expected. Jay called, said you say the bones aren't your mother's. Something about a tooth."

I explained what I suspected he already knew. My guess was he wanted to hear it directly from me.

"People can get their teeth fixed," he said.

"I know."

Across the lake in the shadows I noticed a light. It moved. I touched Ronnie and pointed at it. Chief Dudley looked too.

"Flashlight Boy," Chief Dudley said. "Always wandering the woods, flashlight on in the night or in the shadows, and then he's gone. Some people try to catch him for whatever reason. That's like trying to catch a will-o'-the-wisp in a fruit jar. Most of us just leave him alone. He's not hurting anything. Lived in the woods around the lake for years. No one knows exactly where."

"He was the boy on the bridge that night we went fishing with Dad," Ronnie said.

I nodded. The light went away, and the thought of it was lost as the wrecker driver came over.

He was tall and black and walked like he had a free lunch ticket for a nice buffet. He had a brilliant smile and crow's-feet around his eyes that made him look distinguished. I judged him to be older than me by several years, but he wore his age like a starlet wears a negligee. All in all, he made me feel slightly inadequate, especially when Ronnie looked at him the way she did.

He smiled at Ronnie, dimming the sun, and then he said to Chief Dudley, "What? Another?"

"Yeah," Dudley said, removing his hat and slapping it on his thigh at a big fly, then placing it back on his head, having missed the insect. "More than another. Several others."

"Now, that's weird."

"Tell us about it. Be careful with them cars when you pull them out. Handle them like you're paying for their college. Officers down there, they'll tell you which ones to pull out. Don't know how firm that lake bed is. Firmer than last time, I suppose."

"It's pretty firm," I said.

"On top, maybe," the wrecker driver said, "but underneath it isn't. Weight of a big wrecker like mine, I could sink up to the axle." He stuck out his hand. "I'm Buck Rogers, by the way. And yes, that's really my name, and no, I don't know Flash Gordon."

We shook hands, and I gave him my name, which was considerably less dynamic.

Buck studied the lake bed. "It'll take some finagling, long chain like last time and my expert driving and towing experience. But I always get my automobile."

Buck didn't smile when he said that. He meant it.

"Why you get the big bucks," Chief Dudley said. "But I remember one time you didn't pull one out."

"You would remember that. Dumb kids drove an old army jeep off into a slough in the backwoods. They got out, but the jeep sunk in a goo of quicksand made of oozing oil from an old derrick and a deep swath of mud. I stuck a twenty-foot rod down there and didn't hit that jeep. It could have slipped along, I guess, ended up farther out. But there was no way to pull that one out. Those kids were lucky they were close to shore and got out on firm land."

The disappointment of that job lay heavy on Buck's face for a moment, then he turned his attention to Ronnie, said, "You been good, Ronnie?"

"I've been good. You, Buck?"

"It's really good to see you. Miss our trips to Shreveport."

Ronnie smiled at him.

Buck's smile got wider, then he lifted a hand in adios and went away like the Lone Ranger after the completion of a dangerous mission.

"You bring friends to the scene of the crime?" Chief Dudley said to Ronnie, nodding at me.

"Figured you might not think of, you know, looking for clues like policemen do, so we did it for you."

"Thought that, did you?"

"Actually, we were having a picnic."

"A picnic?"

"Am I not speaking loud enough, Chief? Yeah, a picnic."

"Lady, I am your boss."

"I was on my own time, and I'm only mean to you when I'm off work."

"This is true."

It was obvious this was common banter for them.

"After we ate, we walked on the lake bed, and I saw all the cars, and I got to thinking what if, you know?"

"Wish you hadn't. Now we have our hands full. All manner of problems. And oh, shit, the paperwork you're going to have to do, Officer."

"You usually call me Ronnie."

"When I think about paperwork, I call you Officer, even if you are off duty. Look here, drop Danny off wherever he needs dropping, and you and me, we got to figure on some things, like why all these bones are here. Never mind that. No way to figure. I'm going home for supper. Duncan is cooking. That means one of four dishes, because that's all he can fix, but all four are good. Me, I can cook four different dishes, none of them particularly well, so I'm looking forward to supper. Figuring it'll be chicken and dumplings tonight.

"You go back to the office, start writing down what you found and how you found it. I'm putting you back on the clock. Without overtime. And when you write it out, print so I can read it, and be thorough. For that matter, don't write it down—type it up. You know, with a carbon, and make us a file for all that shit. Hell, they may even find more bodies in cars. Whatever all this means, I can tell you now, I don't like it."

"Would you like the reports on colored paper?" Ronnie asked.

"That would be nice." Chief Dudley paused. "I'm partial to blue."

We walked over to Ronnie's cruiser and got in.

"He does seem all right," I said.

"Buck?"

"Chief Dudley."

"Oh. Most of the time he is. Likes me because I don't underestimate him. I think he likes to be underestimated in a way. Gives him a leg up on the bad guys. Also gives me a kind of hope."

"How's that?"

"I've been underestimated by white people all my life because I'm female and black. Underestimated by black people as well, being a woman, being uppity, doing a white job, a cop job. I get shit on by both sides. Don't you think Chief looks like that cartoon dog?"

"Deputy Dawg?"

"That's it. But again, don't underestimate him."

"I'm starting to believe you. So, you and Buck Rogers—can't believe that's his name—know each other pretty well?"

"Couple years back, my car broke down. I had to walk, find a phone, call Daddy to give me a ride home. Next morning, I called the wrecker service to come and pick the car up. Buck was the wrecker service. He came by my house and gave me a ride out to the car so I could show him where it was. He pulled my car in. I rode up front with him in the wrecker. We got friendly."

"How friendly?"

She studied me carefully. "We had a few dates."

"Yeah? Anyplace special?"

"Are you asking for all the details?"

"Not at all."

"He took me to Mars in his rocket once . . . oh, shit. I was trying to be funny there, you know, the Buck Rogers name, but that could be taken the wrong way, I guess, to Mars on his rocket . . ."

"I get it."

"Nothing special came from our dates. Certainly no trip to Mars. Problem is, a lot of women like Buck. They collect on him like fleas on a dog. There's too much competition, and he encourages it. And sometimes I sense darkness there, or I think I do, and I don't know if I find it mysterious and appealing or a bit nerve-racking."

"Just curious," I said.

(19)

In the night, I awoke and lay there listening to my own breathing. It was loud, and I couldn't control it. I still had my eyes closed, but I felt that sensation I hadn't felt in a long time, the feeling that someone was in the room. Even with closed eyes I could sense him, and I knew damn well who it was.

The room was frigid and seemed damper than central air set at seventy-four degrees ought to be. There was a tremble to the air, and I was sure I could smell the odor of decay.

He came through the door to my room. I knew that door had not been opened because it was locked, but he came. I didn't see him enter, but I could hear his footsteps. I tried to get up but couldn't.

I felt the bed move.

There was a rustling sound, the sheets and blanket being moved at the bottom of the bed, and then I felt his hand on my ankle, like a bracelet of ice. I wanted to pull my foot away. I wanted to yell out, but I didn't. I couldn't. It felt like I had a cork in my throat.

"Danny," my father said. "Do you remember what Mr. Candles told you? About what was up there on the hill in the woods? Do you remember?"

His voice sounded as if it were coming through a wall of mud.

I tried to gather a response, but nothing came. I lay there with that cold hand on my ankle. I trembled as if experiencing an epileptic seizure and awoke to an empty room.

It was still dark outside. I sat up in bed. I was still breathing hard and my heart jumped like a jackhammer.

I checked the end of the bed. The covers were still in place, but for a moment, the streetlights sent pale gold through the open window near the bed and the light lay on the wooden floor, and I felt certain I could see a little puddle there where water from my father had dripped, but when I rolled out of bed and turned on the light, the floor was only shiny, like the wood had been over-polished in that spot.

I took a deep breath and gathered myself. I thought about writing, reading, anything to get my mind off things, but I didn't do any of that. I ate a banana, left the skin on the windowsill. I went to the bathroom, got dressed, and went outside, carefully locking the door behind me. My car was parked at the curb where the walk ended. I didn't remember parking it there.

Next thing I knew I was driving out in the country, and the trees and shadows in my headlights were as mysterious as some sort of dark enchantment.

I came to the lake. It wasn't dry now; it was quite wet. I wondered when it had rained, and how had it rained enough to fill the lake in such a short time. It wasn't raining now, so what was going on?

At the lake, the night was clear and the moon was full. I didn't think it was supposed to be a full-moon night, but it was, and its image floated on the lake.

Standing on the bridge, I saw a light move through the dark trees off to my right, flow quickly up a hill into the woods and beyond, and disappear.

It meant something, but I wasn't sure what.

I shone a flashlight that I discovered in my hand, shone it out at the dead black water. Swimming in the water were skeletons held together by bits of skin and muscle. Their heads bobbed up and then dipped down. Their skeletal arms and hands pulled at the water, and the water flowed through their fingers and into their empty eye sockets and open mouths. They were swimming toward the bridge, and then in no time they were under it. I followed them with the beam of my light.

Looking down between a split in the bridge slats, I could see them. All their skulls were tilted up to look at me, even though there were no eyes in those deep sockets, just darkness. But the darkness in their skulls seemed alive. They lifted bony arms up to me, and though I was high up, they could nearly reach me, and I couldn't understand how that was. Skeletal fingers were poking through the splits in the bridge slats, wiggling at me. I started to run, and as I ran my feet tangled in the covers and I rolled off the bed breathing hard again.

I worked myself out of the cocoon of sheets and blanket and slowly stood up. The streetlights that came through the window were on my face and on the floor and I was cold.

I went to the bathroom for real this time, washed my face and took a pee. I picked up the covers and remade the bed, and then I saw on the windowsill the skin of a banana, just like in my dream, and I felt a dark shadow move around me and then in me, and I sat on the bed and thought about things for a long time but arrived at no answers. Eventually, I crawled under the covers and slept.

*   *   *

They say dreams try to tell you something that you already know or need to sort out, that ghosts are when your brain sends messages to the eyes instead of the common way, when the eyes send messages to your brain.

Some believe that explains ghosts and so many things that we see, from Bigfoot to dancing gremlins in Bermuda shorts. The brain thinks it, believes it enough to tell the eyes to see it.

I once read that it happens when we drive late at night. When we're tired, and we keep pushing and are on the edge of sleep. The brain frequently tries to warn us. It wants us to stop and rest. It recognizes we are in the danger zone. It gives us false images, a dog or a person running across the road, for example. Something to alert us before it's too late.

Had the ghost of my father spoken to me last night, or had the ghost of my memories roused something from deep inside, something connected to those bodies in the trunks of those cars?

I showered and shaved, brushed my teeth and so on, went by the café I had found the day before, had coffee, then drove out to the lake and walked out on the bridge. There were birds singing, cawing, and screeching, and there was the sound of frogs bleating and crickets chirping. A wave of blue-black insects flew past me and into the trees on the far side.

Unlike in my dream, the lake had not filled back up with water. If anything, it looked drier today than the day before.

As I stood on the bridge and looked over the lake bed, spotted with debris, the wind swirled up a wicked-looking dust devil that lifted powdery clay and twirled it in my direction. It came at me for a few moments, then died down as suddenly as it had begun. The dust scattered and became too thin for me to see, then there wasn't any wind anymore.

I crossed the bridge and came to the end of it without having it fall apart. I remembered clearly the story Mr. Candles had told me and Ronnie long ago, about what was up on the hill.

It was a steep hill. There was a kind of trail there, and it was easy to tell it wasn't much used anymore because it was narrow where the trees and weeds had grown close to it.

The trail forked as I neared the top. One fork was wider than the other, and the smaller one branched off before the peak of the hill and meandered into the greater thickness of the leafy trees.

It was cooler under the trees, in the shade, but I still felt as if I were breathing the contents of a vacuum cleaner.

I paused for a moment to catch my breath. A red fox slipped out from between the trees at the top of the hill where it was bathed in harsh sunlight. The fox paused and looked down the trail at me. After lifting its head in what seemed like a "What's up?" manner, it darted swiftly and gracefully out of the sunlight and into where the foliage grew dense. It did this without making so much as a rustle.

I climbed up the slanting trail to where the fox had stood, took a deep breath, and looked around.

Off to my left I could see the remains of the sawmill. The mill was now nothing more than a collection of gray buildings of different sizes. The walls of the buildings were made of crude wooden slats with gaps in them you could throw a fat pig through.

I trudged to the biggest building. It had a tin roof, and the front double doors were like those you would expect on a barn. They were thrown wide open, and as I went inside, pigeons burst out past me in a gray-white explosion, causing me to flinch. A moment later I was inside and I could see a gigantic rusty saw with ragged metal teeth tipped red with rust.

Running out from it was a long tin chute resting on concrete blocks. That's where trees had been fed into the gnawing monster. There were the scattered remains of busted chains and rubber belts that helped work the saw. There was a block of concrete where I assumed a gas-driven engine had once been mounted.

I walked around inside for a bit, but there wasn't much to see outside of bat shit on the ground. When I looked up, I could see a colony of bats hanging upside down from the rafters. Did they poop like that? I wondered. Wouldn't it run down their bodies? Or did they do their business on their way out at night in search of insects, let loose with guano bombs to lighten their flights? For a moment, it seemed like an important mystery. I left the bats to their shadows and rafters.

Outside of the building, I strolled around, into, and out of the other buildings. On the hill, I could look down on a lower level where there was a massive patch of green, closely mowed grass that sprawled over several acres. It was a golf course. Behind the course was a huge structure that looked like an English manor. Around it there were outbuildings so luxurious, you could have called them elite housing.

I turned and looked the other way down the hill. There was a junkyard with a shiny tin fence around it. From my position, I could see inside the perimeter of the fence. There were rusting cars and a large, faded red, tin-roofed shed in the middle of the sizable lot.

I walked down to it. The gate between the pieces of tin fence was made of pipe buried in the ground on either side and the gate was made of metal rods and tight mesh wire. There was a strand of barbed wire at the top of the gate, and a big padlock held a looped chain in check. The chain locked the gate. The gate was old and corroded, but the lock was shiny as a gift from Santa. There was a sign on the gate that said No Trespassing.

I looked around and didn't see anyone. I climbed on the gate without snagging my pants or myself on the barbed wire at the top and dropped over it. I walked around among the cars, half expecting a large dog to come out from between the wrecks and take me down and eat my face.

When I got to the shack door, I tugged at it gently. It was

locked. I went to one of the windows. There weren't any curtains except natural ones made of dust and flyspecks that coated the glass. I wiped one of the windowpanes with my hand. That made it a little better, but most of the dust and specks were inside.

I looked through the glass and could see nothing but emptiness. Where sunlight came through a thin slit in the ceiling, I could see a chair and a small table. The floor was carpeted in rat turds and grime. The place gave me the creeps.

I went back to the gate and climbed over it. I wasn't sure what I had accomplished by doing all of that, but I felt I was pulling at a string with something substantial but not visible on the other end.

I walked down from the junkyard to a little road that led along the lake. It went in the direction of the bridge. I hadn't gone far when I gave it up, turned back to the sandy road leading up to the junkyard. I walked past it again, past the sawmill, and then I knew what I was really looking for.

When I got back to the hill, I ambled down the trail and found where it forked. I took the other fork this time and went into the deeper woods.

I hadn't gone far when I saw off to one side overturned gravestones. Some were broken. As I stepped off the trail and into the woods, the mosquitoes dove down in a hungry pack and went to work on my face and poked their bloodsuckers through my clothes. Slapping at them proved useless. Their numbers were legion.

Drawing closer, I saw there were open graves near the stones, rectangles that were about six feet deep with leaves and dirt in the bottom of them. Some contained the broken remains of wooden caskets and little fragments of colorless cloth. The graves had been plundered.

I heard movement out beyond the cemetery, in the trees, bigger than a fox, maybe a deer, and then there was silence. Something had been there, but it had stopped moving or had moved beyond hearing.

I wanted to look around more, but the mosquitoes were too much to bear and the heavy movement made me nervous. I got back on the trail pretty quick, scampering maybe as fast as that fox had. Those damn vampire bugs buzzed all around me, thick enough to sew together and wear as a suit.

Hurrying back to the bridge, I felt myself pulling on that string again, and this time the thing at the other end seemed to be coming into view.

(20)

At the police station, in the chief's office with him and Ronnie, I told them about my dream and what it had led me to do.

"Dreamed that, did you?" Chief Dudley said.

"No. I had a dream that led me to the cemetery and the junkyard, the old sawmill. Look, I know how it sounds, but it isn't like that. It wasn't some prophetic dream. It was me making sense of a lot of ideas in a dream."

We went back and forth with it for a while, and I could see that Chief Dudley was beginning to suspect I might be two turds short of a pile.

When I finished up the telling, Ronnie sat politely silent. Chief Dudley said, "I think we should go over and see the coroner."

When we came in, Shirley was sawing on her nails with a file. A bottle of pink nail polish was sitting on the desk along with other instruments that I didn't recognize but assumed were feminine cosmetic tools of some sort. It could have been a lock-picking set for all I knew.

Jay, it turned out, was outside, around back. We went out there and found him standing by a trailer truck and we could hear a large metal box by it humming. I realized it was a refrigeration unit.

121

Jay turned when he heard us.

"Ah, the law plus one," he said.

Chief Dudley said, "I assume that's been set up for the extra bodies?"

"Yep. Controlled temperature keeps the bones from falling apart. They're fragile. Had hell getting it approved by the city council."

"Why are you standing out here?" Ronnie said.

"Thought I needed some sunlight, but that's proving to be uncomfortable. Too much air-conditioning makes me feel uneasy and then too much of this heat makes me feel faint."

"Danny here has something that might be of interest, but we want you to hear it," Ronnie said.

"He had a prophetic dream," Chief Dudley said. "Or some such shit. A dream about all those bones."

"A vision," Jay said. "Really, Danny? A fucking spirit guide came to you?"

"Nothing like that," I said.

"Let's go back to the office," Jay said. "This heat is choking me and I want to be sitting down when I hear this."

In the office, we sat in the chairs near the coffeepot. None of us had coffee, and this time Shirley didn't offer to fix us any. She seemed to be at a critical point in her nail work.

"Long ago," I said, "when the flood that formed Moon Lake happened and the bodies were recovered from it, the only funeral home that would handle black bodies were black-owned and -operated. Ronnie's dad told us that when the bodies were recovered and taken to the funeral home in New Long Lincoln, there weren't enough clothes to be had to dress all the corpses. Most of what the families had owned—possessions, money—had washed away. This wasn't true of everyone. There were those who could afford suits and dresses for their dead, but for those who couldn't the funeral home provided the dead with blue burial gowns. This was done for several bodies that were buried in the cemetery on the hill above the lake."

"There's a graveyard up there?" Jay said.

"The dream reminded me. I realized my subconscious was trying to tell me something that was stuck in the back of my mind like an upholstery tack. Memories about the flood, about a junkyard near a sawmill where Mr. Candles worked. Remember all that, Ronnie?"

"Of course," Ronnie said. "The blue gowns being the shreds mixed in with the bones."

"Those pieces might be blue," Jay said. "Hard to tell at this point."

"I think over the years, maybe even recently, those bones were dug up and put in cars from the old junkyard up there, and then they were pushed off in the lake. The graveyard has holes where there used to be graves. Could have been like that a long time. The junkyard is locked down, but there's a new padlock on the gate, and I thought it might be the place where the cars came from. I don't know. Someone had been going in and out of there at will, perhaps for some time. Could be someone wanted that to stop. The owner of the property got a new lock."

"But why?" Chief Dudley said. "I mean, what's the point in digging up bones and putting them in car trunks and pushing the cars off into the water?"

"I'm not sure," I said. "I could be wrong, but it makes a kind of sense. Otherwise, too many coincidences. The dug-up cemetery. Bones, and what I think are parts of those shrouds in car trunks. Jay, can you check the bones, the scraps of cloth, determine if the bodies had been embalmed and if that cloth is from shrouds?"

"Bones aren't exactly fresh. Maybe I can figure something from the cloth. I don't know."

"But your father's car was already in the lake," Ronnie said.

"A body would have to have been brought to the lake and put in the trunk of the car, and until recently the lake was filled with water."

"Yeah," Chief Dudley said. "Makes more sense the body was already in the car. Who'd go to all the trouble to move cars out of a junkyard, dig up bones, put them in the trunks of cars, and push them off into the lake, then when it's dry, put a body in the trunk of your father's car? What would be the purpose?"

"It sounds somewhat ritualistic," Shirley said.

At the sound of her little voice we all turned to look at her. She was holding one hand up and filing a fingernail on it with the other.

"Reading in anthropology, I remember a chapter on rituals. People can do some odd and difficult things to fulfill rituals. And then there are sequence killers. Ones who kill as an obsession and can't stop. They have rituals they perform. I believe they call them signatures."

"Read that in a book, did you?" Chief Dudley said.

"Did," she said. "People like that, messed up that way, they frequently feel the need to perform murders in a certain manner, leave behind, maybe without knowing it, perhaps on purpose, signatures, little rituals, identifying it as their work."

"I don't think we're talking about murders," I said. "I still think the bones were from burials."

"Then we're still talking about rituals," Shirley said. "There's a group called Skull and Bones, they're just a bunch of Yankee college students, and way back they stole the bones of Geronimo. The skull is in their clubhouse, and they have ceremonies and rituals there using the bones. At least, that's how the story goes."

"We do have the junior college here," Jay said. "Could have been some college students, I guess. Part of an elaborate joke, maybe?"

"I don't find it very funny," Ronnie said. "My grandmother was one of those buried in that graveyard, along with my grandfather. My dad's mentor, the one who taught him boxing, he's there too. I never really knew my grandparents, and I hate to admit it, but I don't visit their graves. I remember Daddy saying he did from time to time but finally decided they weren't there. I guess a lot of people must have felt that way, or their descendants died off, and that's why the place had gone to ruin. Kind of feel guilty about it, now that I'm thinking on it."

"The dead do better in our hearts than in the ground," Chief Dudley said.

"What I'm thinking," Ronnie said, "is we find out about the land where the graveyard is, see who owns it, and get a list of who was buried there. We can see who owns the junkyard too."

"If it's all right, Jay, and you can do without me for a while, I can do that," Shirley said. She had put her file aside. "I can go to the Hall of Records at the courthouse. Beats sitting here and filing my nails, though I've done an excellent job on them."

"They look very nice," Ronnie said.

Jay said, "I was about to check the remains anyway. I'll do that, look at the cloth and bones, see if I can determine anything."

"Waste of time," Chief Dudley said. "Who can figure what some freak thinks? And, Danny, no offense, but your father still strikes me as more likely than someone digging up graves and sticking bones in car trunks and running them off into the lake. Some things can't, or aren't meant to, be solved."

"Might be some records about the flood that go beyond the stories I've grown up with," Ronnie said. "The library might have something on that if the Hall of Records doesn't."

"Why don't you do the library?" Chief Dudley said to me. "I got other work for Ronnie."

(21)

The library was a long, simple one-story building at the edge of town made of aluminum siding and cheap glass and an equally cheap glass door. When I went inside, I saw about half of the metal bookshelves were empty.

A very attractive woman about my age with blond hair and pink cheeks that matched a pink and full-lipped mouth lifted her head when I came in. She was sitting behind a desk and had a book stamp in her hand and a book open in front of her to use it on.

She wore a simple-looking green dress that wasn't all that simple really. She had on glasses with green frames. She took them off and placed them carefully beside the book she was stamping and came around the edge of the desk toward me. I could see the dress accentuated the fact that she had won the genetic lottery not only in facial appearance but in physical construction. She was short, under five feet was my guess, and that was counting the sensible heels on her green open-toed shoes. I should note that her blond shoulder-length hair might have been due to hair dye instead of genetics. Whatever the source, I liked it.

"Why, hello," she said, seeming happy to see me. Bored, most likely.

"Hello. I was going to ask about some research I'd like to do. Maybe you can point me in the right direction?"

"Tell me what you want, and if we have it, I'll give you a personal escort. I handle everything here, me and a few volunteers who come in to help occasionally."

She was close now and she had a sweet musky aroma about her. I didn't know if that was a hint of fine perfume or a lot of her natural hormones, but it was plenty all right either way.

I told her the kind of records I wanted. She paused and thought about it. She said she probably had what I needed and her name was Estelle. As she led me to the back of the library, I told her my name and where I was from. I said I was doing research on the original town and the building of the lake.

"Oh, heavens, why? Our town and the old one are hardly interesting."

"I think they might be."

"What's this research for?"

"A book I'm writing."

"Is it your first?"

"I've had a book published, a few articles, and a short story. I was a journalist until recently."

"A real-life author. Are you self-published?"

"No."

"A real publisher?"

"That's right."

"What's the name of your novel?"

I told her.

"I'll order it."

"Why, thank you. I was wondering if I could check books out as well."

"Are you a resident of New Long Lincoln?"

"As of the other day, yes."

"And writing another book."

"That's my plan."

"On New Long Lincoln?"

"I don't know yet."

She took a few seconds to let the idea of that sink in. "Sure. We can arrange a card."

As we passed a lot of the empty shelves, she said, "We're expanding. More books coming in. Lots of classics, but new stuff as well. We've got plans to put all the files on computer."

"That's nice. My father was a librarian for a time. Do you have a lot of readers in this town?"

"No. But don't tell anyone. I might lose my job."

In the back, past the empty shelves, there were full ones with lots of big volumes that favored black spines.

Estelle led me through the stacks, pulled a few books out just enough so that they were still on the shelves, but I could pick them out when ready. She put one in my hands.

My eye was drawn to one by someone listed on the cover as Natural Wilson. The book was titled *Moon Lake and Long Lincoln*. I thumbed it open, flipped through a few pages.

It was about the construction of the lake, about plots of land, deeds and such. It had foldout maps inside. They appeared to have originally been drawn by hand.

"I'll start with this one," I said, tucking it under my arm.

"It's not thought of too highly. A crank supposedly wrote it. I've even considered removing it. There's a table back there under a window, and it's cool in that corner. Might want to make camp there."

"Sounds good."

She paused, worked her smile on me. She knew there was power in it. "Decide you want to see our town, or maybe get some coffee, I'll be glad to give you my number."

"I'll be glad to take it."

"Of course you will."

*   *   *

Time flies when you're reading through books. What I was reading wasn't quite as exciting as paperback thrillers, but I still found it fascinating.

I pulled all the books Estelle had selected and read sections from them. Eventually, I borrowed a pen and a pad from Estelle for notes.

The residents of Long Lincoln drowning during the break of the dam was not mentioned in any of the books except for the one by Natural Wilson, which was large and full of facts but not particularly well written. It was only a little better than a monkey could do, but the information trumped the somewhat difficult composition, and the maps, though hand drawn, were good. Estelle hadn't thought highly of it, and I could understand her concerns, but it had a kind of heartfelt authenticity. It described the flood in detail based on the accounts of survivors, black and white. Black people were referred to as "colored" in the book. The cemetery was mentioned, and the sawmill, and how its importance declined after the demise of the original Long Lincoln. It said the land around the lake was sold to someone named Jack Manley Sr.

Manley was quite the real estate baron. Seems he was one of the big dogs behind the town of New Long Lincoln and had significance in the old town. He and some of the others had been the ones who had worked out the deal for the existence of New Long Lincoln.

Two of the others involved were names I had seen in the pages of the Natural Wilson book: Judea Parker and Kate Conroy. Other names of prominence popped up in the books, but Manley, Parker, and Conroy were always mentioned. One book had photos. I realized they were the three people in the office photo with Chief Dudley. In a few of the photos, going back to the time of the original Long Lincoln, they were young. The men were handsome and the woman was pretty. Later photos showed the natural progression of age.

Jack Manley Sr. and the others seemed like people I should know more about. Did Manley still own that land? I got the impression from Chief Dudley they were all still alive. Did they matter somehow?

In the back of the book there was a little section on the author. The book had been written in the early sixties, and it said the author lived in New Long Lincoln. When you thought about it, the author's information really didn't say anything. You knew no more about Natural Wilson from it than if you hadn't read it.

I eventually came out of my trance and sat there trying to decide if I had learned anything of importance. I could hear Estelle on the phone from time to time, and I heard her library stamp striking books now and again.

The window above the table where I was reading lost its light, and there were only the electric lights then, and they were comparatively weak. I couldn't believe how long I had spent there.

Estelle came back to the table, said, "Sorry, we're closing."

"No problem."

She handed me a library card. "You're set. I just need to put your address and phone number on record."

At the desk, I filled in my address and phone number on a form to make my library card "legal," and checked out three books. Estelle stamped them.

"Natural Wilson. Author of that fat book. Says he's from New Long Lincoln. Still live here?"

"No one knows of anyone named Natural Wilson, as far as I

can tell. Name is most likely made up. The book isn't held in high esteem, since mixing hearsay and legend with real events doesn't exactly make it a history book. If New Long Lincoln is the author's home, and he was an adult at the time of the flood, he might have passed on by now. Self-published that, you know."

"Thanks."

As I was heading out, Estelle said, "You have my number."

I had the books under one arm, but with my free hand I tapped my shirt pocket. "Right here. Close to my heart."

"Sure," she said and laughed in a way that sounded like a box of dishes tumbling downstairs.

(22)

I had no sooner reached my car than the lights in the library went out. I checked my watch and saw it was damn near seven p.m. Was that the usual closing time for the library, or had Estelle kept it open for me?

Course, if she had, that didn't mean I was anything special. It wasn't like New Long Lincoln was full of fun activities. She wasn't missing a night at the opera. But a woman her age who looked like that surely had more on her mind than overdue library books.

I closed my car door and sat for a moment, thinking about something I couldn't quite define—tugging at that damn string again. Whatever was on the other end of it remained there. I drove away.

I parked near the front of the Chandler house, and when I got out of the car to go inside, I saw two men coming up the sidewalk.

In the lights along the road and from the houses on both sides of the street, I could see they wore dark hats and suits like uniforms and seemed in quite a hurry. One of the men was short and stout; the other was tall and lanky. Even from a distance, their faces were strange. I stepped off the walk and onto the grass.

Due to all the boxing training I'd had over the years, I could tell from their body language the reason they were in such a hurry was on account of me. I was their destination. They had been waiting on my arrival.

When they were up close, I saw their faces were painted. The lanky one's face was darkened with cork, the way white minstrel performers used to blacken their faces. His lips were red with scarlet lipstick. Under his hat I could see what looked like orange clown hair. The shorter man's face was chalky white. They both wore black gloves.

I wondered suddenly if the circus was in town.

The short man with the white face said, "You wouldn't be considering staying, would you?"

"What?" I said, but they weren't interested in an answer.

The short man stepped in quickly. I dropped the books and pulled my hands up and tucked in my elbows as he hit me with a low left hook just above my hip. The shot caught me on my belt and clipped the bottom of my elbow, striking what is sometimes referred to as the funny bone, but it didn't feel that funny.

I fell to one knee as if to propose, and the tall one kicked me in the chest, a kind of a stomping kick. I rolled over on the grass and managed to get up when I would rather have stayed down.

They came swiftly toward me. I hit the little guy with a same-hand high-low combination, a left jab to the nose and a left hook to the ribs, finished with a right cross to his chin. It was his turn to go down.

The lanky guy tried to kick me again, this time a football kick, but I was ready for him. I scooped my arm under his ankle and lifted him high enough that when he fell, he cracked his head on the sidewalk. His hat rolled off but the clown hair stayed on.

The short white-faced guy was tough. He was getting up. Oddly, his hat was still on, though the brim was up in front. He raised his hands and advanced, bobbing a little. I had dusted some of the white paint off his nose, and I could see that beneath it, his skin was black.

I put my hands up, but out of the corner of my eye I saw clown-hair was getting up too. It was about to be messy at the circus, and most likely I was going to be the mess.

That's when the boardinghouse door flew open and Mrs. Chandler, in a blue nightgown, her hair tucked under some kind of blue nightcap, stepped out under the porch light for a moment, then came marching down the stairs and across the yard. She was carrying a single-shot shotgun about the size of a bazooka. Or so it seemed right then.

"You bastards get off my property now."

The men seemed like frightened chickens for a moment. Lanky guy grabbed his hat and put it on, and he and the little man started running down the sidewalk in the direction they had come from.

I took a deep breath and sat down on the grass and put my head between my knees.

Mrs. Chandler came over and laid the shotgun in the grass and knelt beside me. "You hurt?"

"Mostly my pride. But I've felt better. Like, before they hit me."

"Saw you put them on their butts. You did all right. I went and got my shotgun. If only I had a shell in it."

I gathered up the library books and we went inside the house, me limping. Mrs. Chandler surprised me and allowed me into her living room to sit on the sofa. I thought she ought to be careful doing that. It's like when you invite the family dog onto the couch for just one time, and then it becomes its home. She placed the shotgun on the floor next to the couch, and I tried to relax my side while Mrs. Chandler phoned the police.

Ronnie and Chief Dudley both showed up.

When they came in, I said, "Don't you have homes to go to?"

"I at least got my chicken and dumplings," Chief Dudley said. "Wasn't as good as I had hoped for. Heavy on the salt."

Ronnie came over and put her hand on my shoulder. "You okay, Danny?"

"This boy can really hit," said Mrs. Chandler. "I know hitting. My long-dead husband used to knock me down."

"Didn't he fall down those hall stairs there?" Chief Dudley said.

"Did indeed," she said. "Drunk. Broke his neck, some other bones that didn't count as much as that one. I look up those stairs, I remember that time fondly."

"He needed to watch his step," Chief Dudley said.

Mrs. Chandler went into the kitchen and started banging some pans or pots around. Chief Dudley and Ronnie sat and asked me questions about what had happened.

There wasn't much to tell.

"Were they white or black?" Dudley asked.

"They were disguised. One had burnt cork on his face, like in a minstrel show, and a silly orange clown wig. He was white, I'm sure. The other had white paint. He was black. I could see that because my fist wiped some of that paint off his nose." I held up my fist. It still had a smear of white greasepaint on it. "They wore black suits and black fedoras. They came to party."

"You been in town a day or so," Dudley said, "and you've already pissed someone off. Any idea whose feelings you might have hurt?"

"It wasn't like I went anywhere that I could actually make anyone mad, unless there's a library police, and if so, they're misguided. I've got two weeks on those books."

"Could have been an attempted robbery?" Chief Dudley said.

"Guess so," I said.

"You should go to the emergency room and be checked out," Ronnie said.

"Been hit in boxing enough to know all I got is a bruise," I said. "I'll be sore for a day or two, pee a little blood, and then I'm fine."

"Aren't you experienced for such a young man."

"I've really had the odometer running these past few years," I said.

Mrs. Chandler came into the room carrying a tray with cups on it. Steam puffed up from the cups. "Tea with honey," she said.

She sat the tray on the coffee table, picked up the books I had placed on the couch, put them on the coffee table, and studied the titles for a moment. Then she picked up the shotgun, said, "I'll put this away."

"Might want to be careful with that," Chief Dudley said.

"Wasn't loaded," she said. "Have some shells around here somewhere, but not in it."

"She ran a good bluff," I said.

When Mrs. Chandler came back, she said, "Let's drink it while it's hot."

(23)

When I woke up, sunlight was bathing my face. I climbed out of bed, not having been visited by my father's ghost, or if he had shown up, I'd been too exhausted to give a damn.

I discovered my side had swollen up like an overheated tire and my hip bone throbbed. Moving about was no more difficult than trying to drag a wounded rhinoceros off the sheets and dress him in footie pajamas.

I groaned and yipped a little as I eased out of my nightclothes, which was my underwear. Pulling those off was like removing my skin with rusty pliers.

I heel-toed to the bathroom, got into the shower, let the hot water run over me for a long time. I toweled off, took a couple of aspirin I had in my shaving kit, shaved, brushed my teeth, and put on one of my clean shirts. I combed my hair. Doing that felt like I was pulling wire out of my head.

I was limping my way to my car to get breakfast and had just reached the curb when I saw there was a blue current-model Chevy parked down the street from the boardinghouse. The woman behind the steering wheel was watching me.

She was too far away for me to tell much about her. She hadn't put burnt cork on her face or added orange clown hair to her head. She didn't get out of the car and come down to beat me up, so that was a plus.

Coincidence, maybe. She might have been looking for a lost cat in the neighborhood and it was standing next to me.

I checked. No cat.

I thought about walking down to ask her what she was up to, but didn't. She inconsiderately tossed a cigarette butt out the window.

I drove to the café, parked, and went inside. I found a booth, and no sooner had I settled than the woman driver came into the café.

She was fifteen to twenty years older than me, quite attractive in an "I'm going to give you playground suspension" kind of way. Her hair was black and almost to her shoulders. She had well-shaped bones. Her eyes matched her hair. She was nicely turned out in an orange dress, and she had silver bangles on her wrist and hoops in her ears and wore black open-toed shoes with low heels. A black purse only a little larger than a man's wallet was slung over her shoulder by a strap. If she'd broken a hundred-dollar bill, the change wouldn't fit inside.

She sat down on the seat across from me. Did it gracefully, like a woman who had been to a few bigwig soirees and didn't mind a local café either if they offered good service.

I didn't say anything. I had time.

Apparently, so did she. She smiled at me. Some money had been spent on those teeth. "May I buy you breakfast?" she said.

"May I ask what for?"

The server came over then, a young, freckle-faced woman in a white uniform that had the café's logo stenciled above the shirt pocket. She was smiley and crisp.

The lady ordered coffee and an English muffin, butter and strawberry jelly on the side. I had pancakes and sausage, and if I could remember what kind of syrup I asked for, I could die a happy man.

"My name is Christine Humbert. Ring any bells?"

"You know Saul, my old boss, right? You're the editor of the paper here."

The coffee arrived. A pot and cups, sugar and milk.

"That's right." She dipped her spoon into the sugar bowl and stirred the spoon-load into her coffee. She added a splash of milk to it from a tiny pitcher.

I sat and waited.

"I heard about what happened last night, Danny."

"From whom?"

"Mrs. Chandler called me last night. Kind of late. Said you were very brave. Saul told me you were coming, and if you came to me for a job, I should be nice to you. Mrs. Chandler is a friend of mine, by the way. I came to see you this morning, recognized you from her description, and since you were leaving, I followed."

"What happened last night—that's not going in the newspaper, I hope?"

"No. Mrs. Chandler told it to me in confidence."

"It's not that confidential. You're telling it to me."

"Mrs. Chandler is generally tight-lipped. I think she wants to put you and me together at the paper. She has some bones to pick with this town, and so do I. Husband of hers was a horrible man. Her high-school sweetheart. He was on the football team and she was a cheerleader. That was long ago. Cheerleaders wore more clothes then. I've seen the photographs."

"This the husband that fell down the stairs?"

"She just had the one. Bert. And yes, he seems to have lost a step.

Anyway, she told me what happened to you, and a few questions later I realized you're the one Saul asked me to give a job."

"I haven't asked."

"Not yet. Maybe not at all. But may I lay out a proposal for you?"

"I have a novel to write. Some affairs to settle in town."

"I might have an idea why you were attacked last night."

"All right," I said.

Right then our orders came out. They were placed on the table and our waitress went away.

Christine spread butter thinly on half of her muffin, added a touch of jelly, and took a delicate bite. A mouse couldn't have nibbled less.

"I think it's the town elders that arranged that business last night," she said.

"Why?"

"You're meddling."

"I didn't know I had meddled enough for anyone to know I was meddling."

"Someone decided you were. Discovering those bones. Wouldn't take more than fifteen minutes for the town to have that information."

"Ronnie really discovered the bones. I didn't even think to look in those car trunks. She did."

"I know Ronnie. She tries to do her job right. I know you lived with her parents awhile."

"Things you know, I'm starting to think you might just know Shirley or Jay at the coroner's office. And one of them could be the blabbermouth about all that. I haven't discussed that business with Mrs. Chandler."

"Shirley is my niece. Lovely girl. Thing is, she didn't gossip. She told me some of it because she went to the Hall of Records to do some research for you and Jay, didn't find what she wanted.

She asked if I could supply some of what she needed from the newspaper morgue."

"Could you?"

"She came and looked through some things, made some notes. I don't know exactly what she found. But you have experience in journalism. You know how to get results. You can probably find more than she did. Your old boss told me you were a real bulldog. I'd love you to come work for me."

"Did Saul tell you I'm writing a novel?"

"He mentioned it less than you have. But novel or no novel, you came here because of what your father did. It's a well-known event in this town. Story has been floating around, no pun intended, for years. Fact that you lived with a black family for a few months is curious to people. There are old-time racists here who think you doing that, a white child, would be the equivalent of your living with wild animals, like Tarzan being raised by apes. They might even think black would rub off on you."

"Those sons of bitches can kiss my ass," I said. "The Candleses are wonderful people. Better than my family ever was."

"Not everyone here is a bona fide racist, but there are a lot who prefer to go along to get along. Chandler said one of your attackers was white, one black. It's nice to see even here in East Texas we can have racial cooperation, a lack of prejudice among thugs. Here's what I'm thinking. They're afraid you're going to find things out they don't want found out. Things that might not have a thing to do with your father or him killing your mother."

"Part about my mother is unproven at this point. The bones found in my father's Buick are definitely not hers."

"Why are you sure?"

"Rather not say. I feel like I'm being interviewed for an article in the paper. You know more about me than I do you. I think you're using what you know as bait to fish for something bigger. I don't have anything bigger."

"Habit. I may run a small-town paper, but I'm an investigative journalist at heart. I worked for a large paper in Dallas at one time. But this place has its own hidden demons. And you, you're part of a town mystery. And the mystery is bigger than what happened to you. I know that. Lots of people know that, but no one knows the answers, and the real owners of this town, the city council, they are excellent at keeping secrets, some of which I suspect are dark and nasty. You are writing about this town, what happened to your father and mother, right?"

"I don't know," I said.

That was a lie. The other day, when I wrote my pages, they had been fictional but based on my experiences. It was highly possible I might retool them to make it more autobiographical.

"Want to research your book and at the same time dig into what goes on here in town while being paid? Write articles about it for my paper as you investigate? You can use those articles to put your book together. Get paid twice that way. Think about it."

She was smiling at me. Such a nice smile. She was like a black widow spider with investigative skills and an English muffin.

Still, regular money coming in could keep me from spinning out my advance, which wasn't all that significant.

I sipped my coffee, poured another cup from the pot. "I don't want a nine-to-five," I said.

"Okay. But I need some sort of reports from you so I can know where you are with things. First article within a week, and after that, one every week. They will be printed on Sunday. Latest turn-in time would be Fridays. You miss an installment now and then or the research doesn't pan out, we can recalibrate. That's a lot of liberty, Danny."

"What's it pay?"

She told me. It wasn't that good, and it wasn't that bad. Enough a mouse could pretend to be a bear for a while.

"Paper has a morgue with lots of research items about the lake and the old Long Lincoln. You might need that. It's much better than what the library or the Hall of Records has. Being a reporter for the paper will open a few doors. It's not going to be like the *New York Times,* but it'll help if you're on the staff. Add to that your natural good looks, which from this viewing seem plentiful, and you've got a double-barrel attack going."

"You know plenty about me. What's your backstory?"

"I grew up here. Moved off, went to college, got a journalism degree, worked for real papers for several years, then my parents got old. I came back here to help them about five years ago. Within a year they were both dead. I inherited some money. Went to work for the paper, ended up editor, then publisher. I always planned to leave, go back to the city, but I didn't. I'm a big frog in a small pond here. I like it, you want to know. Strange place. Missing people. Those bones in car trunks. The lake and people drowning in it. It's like that goddamn lake is made up of misery, pettiness, every mean, soulless act you can imagine, all of it wet with robber-baron dreams. This town is full of oddities, Danny."

"You make it sound almost supernatural."

"I'm not ruling that out. Not ruling anything out."

"What if there's really nothing to it and you're just paranoid?"

"Then I'm paranoid. But I'm going to bet you're paranoid with me. And if you're not paranoid, I'm going to guess you are at least curious, and maybe, just maybe, you're thinking you might turn this into a book that really makes you some money and puts you on the map. I know ambition when I see it in someone's eyes, because when I look in the mirror, besides seeing an excellent-looking woman with good bones, I see that same ambition in my eyes. So, question is, do you want to find out what the hell's going on or not?"

I only considered long enough to sip my coffee and put the cup down.

"I think I do."

(24)

Three days later, I was in the cold, well-lit morgue trailer with all the yellowing and graying bones from the car trunks, including those they assumed belonged to my father and mother.

The remains were lined up on two long, wide tables, and the bones had been shaped into skeletons to some degree.

Me and Ronnie and Chief Dudley were all in the trailer with Jay and Shirley. We had our arms crossed against the chill.

Jay led us alongside the long tables and pointed to this and that and finally said, "Some things have turned out, shall we say, interesting."

"How interesting?" Chief Dudley said.

"Yeah," Ronnie said. "Inquiring minds want to know."

Jay said, "I think these bones are from graves and that the bodies were embalmed, but even that doesn't keep a body forever. I think some of the cloth might be from burial shrouds, as you suspected, Danny. I think a lot of it is as you suspected. The only remains that don't fit are those of your father and mother."

"Shit, let's go to the office. It's cold as a witch's tit in here," Chief Dudley said.

We walked over to the office, and even that short stretch outside was stifling hot. When we were inside the office, it was cool but not freezing like the trailer. I felt as if I could have lived there, slept under the desk, had my coffee at the coffee table every morning.

When we were all seated, I said to Shirley, "I met your aunt."

Her pink cheeks turned crimson. "Sorry. I didn't mean to speak out of school."

"It's all right, considering the circumstances. I'm working for her now. Is there anything you found in the news morgue that's worth telling us?"

"I think so. I was looking for ritualistic connections. And I'm a bear for research."

Chief Dudley said, "I still don't get it, about the rituals. I can't see the sense of it."

"Rituals are important," Shirley said. "The Shriners with their hats and little cars, the Masons with aprons and swords and blood oaths, Boy Scouts with special handshakes and salutes, Girl Scouts with the same, the swearing-in of presidents, and the rising to acknowledge a judge. Thanksgiving dinner. Christmas presents and special church services. From eating black-eyed peas and cabbage for luck and money on New Year's Day to shooting off fireworks on the Fourth of July. Drinking grape juice and eating saltless crackers in the Baptist Church, wine and wafer in the Catholic. It's supposed to be the blood and flesh of Christ. Some believe it literally transforms to that when it's eaten as part of a religious ceremony. All rituals. You can slice and dice it to include other reasons, but the rituals themselves are the real reason. We like rituals. They please us. Crossing oneself against evil. Throwing salt over our shoulders. Wearing a graduation gown and becoming part of a parade of students to pick up our diplomas. All part and parcel of the same thing. Killers devise their own rituals. Not consciously but out of some inner need or past experience."

"You need to get out from behind this desk, Shirley," I said, "and go to work in law enforcement."

"Considered it," she said. "But even if someone is not murdering but stealing bodies, there's some ritual in that. Going to all that trouble to dig up corpses and put them in car trunks. Why car trunks? What's the personal connection? What are they trying to say?"

"Could just be an easy way of disposing of bodies after they've dug them up for whatever purposes," Chief Dudley said. "Bottom of the lake is a good hiding place, long as we don't have a drought."

"*Is* it that easy?" Shirley said. "Finding cars, putting the bodies in the trunks, pushing them off into the water. That's risky, and that's why I think it's ritualistic. And I found a series of suspicious deaths . . . here's the list."

She lifted a sheet of paper off her desk, handed it to the chief. He studied it briefly, placed it back on the desk. He said, "Okay. Enlighten us."

"Some of these people are survivors of that flood or, in some cases, descendants of survivors. Some aren't. Some are black, some are white. But there are more connections than differences."

"Over how many years did these deaths take place?" Ronnie asked.

"Since the lake came into being up until now," Shirley said.

"Jesus, kid," Jay said. "You should know from working here, people die, and some mysteriously, but that doesn't mean they're all connected. A killer would have to have been doing this since he was young and would now be old as the hills and twice as dusty."

"County here is big as some states," Chief Dudley says. "I think you're working too hard to make things fit, Shirley. Those deaths elsewhere in the county, what have they got to do with Long Lincoln, old or new?"

"I don't know all the answers. But there are a lot of similarities. Most of the deaths seemed due to strangulation, but some of the bodies were too far gone to determine how they died. The one that I think is the initiating death is Julie George. Elderly lady that died from what was listed as old age, but the coroner, the man whose place you took, Jay, he thought it was suspicious. Said she had petechial hemorrhages in the eyes and her hyoid bone was broken. That indicates strangling or hanging. Another thing was, she was reported missing from the rest home, and it was searched thoroughly. Next day they found her dead in her bed. Where did she go? The coroner wrote it up as suspicious because he thought she had been taken out of a window at the rest home for some reason, killed, and returned."

"That's crazy," Jay said.

"If someone did murder her, it's like they respected her and put her back due to respect. What separates her from the other deaths is she was directly associated with the city council. She wasn't one of the mainstays, but she was on the edge of local power and was close to the other members. She was certainly in their camp. She grew sick, and then she was dead. She left a sizable amount of money to the city council members in her will. Others associated with the council have done the same. Nothing fishy there—they had it put in their wills years before their deaths, as if it were some kind of tribute."

"Now you really are reaching," Chief Dudley said. "She could have wandered off, wandered back without being noticed, and died in bed."

"She could only get around in a wheelchair, and back then there weren't any motorized ones. That would have taken some wheel power, don't you think? Coroner back then certainly thought so, but the city council had the final say, as they still do in this town."

"Were there other bodies found in the lake?" I said.

"One or two. Maybe connected, maybe not. But with both of those, there was suspicion they died from strangulation. Coroner that kept having those suspicions was replaced after he reported suspicion on several deaths. There was one handpicked one, and then you, Jay."

"Are you saying the council controlled these things?"

"Or picked people who they felt they could influence."

"I wasn't handpicked," he said.

"They can't win them all," Shirley said. "But you've had a couple of deaths that were suspicious, right? What you thought might be strangulations."

"Doesn't mean they were ritualistic murders," Jay said.

"True," Shirley said. "Doesn't meant they weren't either."

"But it wasn't proved," Chief Dudley said. "Proof matters."

"No offense," Shirley said, "but some of these murders were on your watch, Chief. Their names are on that list."

"I noticed," Chief Dudley said.

"Unless you were looking for murder, a dead body in the woods could be someone who wandered off, had an accident, a misadventure. You might have to be looking for murder to know it was murder."

"Can I point out something?" I said. "If you're looking to make this about ritual, why weren't they in car trunks?"

"That's just it," Shirley said. "The bones in the trunks weren't murders. The others could have been. Are they connected? I don't know, but what a set of peculiarities. I think someone is digging up dead bodies, and someone else is murdering people. Or there's more than one murderer, and they're known to each other and are following the same ritualistic approach to murder."

"That's a lot of maybes and not a lot of facts," Chief Dudley said. "Again, I think if you work hard enough, you can make anything fit. Maybe some of those bodies found were murder victims, but it doesn't mean they're all connected. No offense, but it sounds like one of those nutty conspiracy theories."

"I don't know about all the deaths, if they're connected," Shirley said. "But there are a lot I believe that are."

"Is it okay I take this paper with the list of names on it?" I said.

"I have other copies," she said.

"You're buying this?" Chief Dudley said. "All these coincidences as related?"

"Just curious," I said.

"And for the record," Shirley said, "I want to emphasize that the bones in the cars and the murders may not be directly connected, but they are both ritualistic behaviors. It's no coincidence. It's patterns."

(25)

I was upstairs peeling my melted Baby Ruth out of the wrapper. I had forgotten to remove it from the sun-bathed windowsill. It looked like a fresh turd, and that put me off my appetite. I decided to rewrap it and place it on the edge of my desk where it was cooler and it might become more solid in a short time. This seemed deathly important in that moment, but then I heard the phone ring below, heard Mrs. Chandler trudging up the stairs. I heard her step on the creaking board near the top of the stairs. I heard her breathing heavily outside the door, and then she knocked.

When I answered, she said, "I'm not going to be your walking answering machine. You can get a phone in your room if this keeps up. I think it's that colored girl, the cop."

"I think the term 'colored' went out of vogue sometime back."

"Not with me."

I went downstairs and picked up the phone. "Ronnie?"

"Hey, want to go see my parents tonight? Have dinner?"

"I do."

"I'll pick you up at six. They eat early."

"I prefer it myself."

"Till then."

*   *   *

Ronnie drove me to the Candleses' house in her squad car. The house looked the same except smaller. It's the bane of childhood existence; all of your memories are subject to miniaturization.

Inside, the Candleses were much the same. Mr. Candles had put on some pounds, but he still looked as if he could turn over a truck and make it wiggle its tires. Millie, as I had been told to call her those many years ago, looked the same but with gray hair. The house smelled of baked bread and bacon grease. I loved it.

After handshakes and hugs, Millie commanded us to the table. She said a prayer, and when she finished, Mr. Candles said, "'Good food. Good meat. I'm hungry. Let's eat.'"

I had heard him do that before.

Millie's prayer and then Mr. Candles's playful one made me think of what Shirley had said about ritual. It was part of our lives and was so ingrained, we forgot how much of it there was, large and small, important and mediocre.

We ate, and the food was as good as always. When the meal was done, Millie put on coffee, and we sat and talked. We talked about the time I was there, and they caught me up on what they were doing now, which was still working, Mr. Candles looking forward to retirement, Millie saying never for her. She was still baking and selling her goods out of her house and so on. They praised me for becoming a writer so young and doing so well after a less than auspicious start.

Ronnie sat smiling and listening. When the coffee was ready, she got up and poured us cups. There was milk and sugar on the table, and they went about adding it to their coffee, and I kept my coffee black.

Conversation paused, and there was only the sound of their spoons making tinkling noises against the cups as they stirred.

Millie said, "I don't know why we quit writing each other. I feel bad about it."

"Life and getting on with things," I said. "It happens. I never quit thinking about y'all, though."

"He grew up so handsome, didn't he, Ronnie?" Millie said.

"Oh, he looks all right," Ronnie said.

"You don't look all polished out," Mr. Candles said. "I like that. A man ought not look polished out."

I wasn't sure what that meant, but I knew whatever it was, it was a good thing as far as Mr. Candles was concerned.

We were starting to sip our coffee when Millie said, "Oh, wait a moment."

She got up and pulled a pie from the oven. The oven was turned off, but when she opened the door the warmth hit the already warm room and was uncomfortable for a moment until the pie was placed on the table and the oven door was closed.

It was apple, and we all had a slice.

We talked some more. I told them how I planned to be in New Long Lincoln for a while, maybe a long while.

"You'll come see us regularly, won't you?" Millie said.

"That's the plan," I said. "Especially around supper time."

"You're always welcome," Mr. Candles said. "Maybe when you come by again, we could hit the bag a little. You and me and Ronnie, like the old days."

"I'd like that."

"That was some night when we went fishing and it came that big rain," Mr. Candles said. "Remember, Danny?"

"I do. Very well." I couldn't forget it. That entire night was one of the best in my life.

"Me too," Ronnie said.

"I was thinking the other day about the kid we saw on the bridge," I said. "Do you remember that?"

"Yeah," Mr. Candles said. "Winston. They call him Flashlight Boy. Poor kid. Been wandering those woods for years, ever since his father left him, like a stray cat. Some ways, that may have been the best thing that happened to him. His father used to beat him with a belt and was mean to him in a lot of soulless ways. I see Winston often when I'm out fishing. He knows me. Knows I won't bother him. He finds or steals flashlights and batteries from somewhere, rambles the woods with his light, shining it around. No one knows what he's looking for, if he's looking for anything. Hasn't got a home anyone knows of. There's been some mean-ass boys try to catch him, but Winston, he grew up fast and he grew up big. I think after his father, he decided he'd been pushed around enough. Heard some big-ass football players tried to chase him down, and Winston whipped them up one side and down the other, busted them up. Only thing got busted of his was the flashlight he bounced off their heads. But I've told you about him before."

"That's all right," I said. "I find it curious."

"Poor boy," Millie said.

"He doesn't ever speak," Mr. Candles said. "Might not be able to, might not want to. When I think of him and his light, I always think of Diogenes."

"Who's that?" I said.

"An ancient Greek that went around with a lantern, shining it on people, claiming he was looking for an honest man."

"Did he find one?" I asked.

"I don't think so," Mr. Candles said.

Our visit seemed to go swiftly, but we were actually there for three hours, and at least fifteen minutes of it was taken up with saying goodbye. This required moving from the kitchen to the porch, and then all of us walking out into the dark to the car. Eventually Ronnie and I ended up in the cruiser still waving at them and them at us.

Ronnie drove away slowly, the headlights poking at the night. "That was nice," she said.

"Like old times."

We tooled along for a while until we came to a nice neighborhood. I said, "We going somewhere special?"

"Thought you might like to see my house."

"Sure."

Ronnie's house was in a neighborhood filled with similar-looking houses, all of them nice.

"When I was growing up, black people couldn't live here. I don't think they love me being here now, since the rest of them are white, but I'm here, and I like it."

"Because they don't?"

"Partly. I was in before they knew I was black or brown or made of wheat straw. I don't have any social calls from the neighbors."

Inside, the house was nicely painted, and the lights were set just right to make things look even better. Ronnie asked if I'd like a drink.

"What you got?"

"Water, milk, and coffee. I have a couple beers."

"No more coffee. What are you having?"

"Would you believe a glass of milk?"

"Same for me."

We sat on the couch and drank our milk from small glasses.

I said, "Buying or renting?"

"Buying."

"This is nice."

"Think so?"

"Sure. My house, one I got from my aunt, I'm selling it. It ought to bring me some dough to last awhile. And I got a little from the novel, so I might even put some money down on a house here. I don't know yet."

"You got time to think it over."

I got up and walked around and looked at photographs on the wall. There were photos of her parents, and there was one of her at her high-school graduation, another where she had on her uniform and had made the grade in the police force. There were four people in the photo with her. Chief Dudley was on one side of her, grinning, and on the other was an elderly man who had a face only a dog could love, and then only if it was greased with a pork chop. There was a woman who had been beautiful once, not too horribly long after the Big Bang. The third was a blobby fellow who looked to have had his eyes glued open and seemed to be held up by a stick; he looked rough. Except for Ronnie and Chief Dudley, the others looked like hell's demons on a lunch break. I recognized those three, of course. They were the ones in the photo in Chief Dudley's office, in the books I'd checked out from the library. Jack Manley Sr., Kate Conroy, and Judea Parker.

In a moment, Ronnie was standing beside me, holding her glass of milk in one hand, pointing at the photo with the others.

"See those other people, not counting Chief Dudley?"

"Yeah. City council, right?"

"They're acting all glad I'm a cop, but that was just their way of dealing with change and trying to turn it into a photo opportunity. They didn't want a black woman on the force, but there I was. Just five years earlier they wouldn't even have considered me. They were filling a quota, but I like to think I'm more than that."

"Of course you are."

"I believe you believe that, Danny, but I may never rise above a basic officer due to my color. Chief Dudley was all right about me being on the force, got me the job, but he didn't crow too loud about it. He's afraid of the city council. Everyone is. They own nearly everything, and what they don't own, they soon will. When they die, they have their own replacements picked, or at least Jack

Manley Sr. does. His son, Jack Jr., is just like him. A nasty piece of work he is. Big, handsome, looks strong as Hercules and probably is. Cold as a dead penguin on an iceberg. The others don't have kids, and my guess is they don't want them. Parker has a nephew. Maybe he'll be a replacement. He's a cop. Dumb as a bar of soap, so maybe not."

"Everywhere I turn, they pop up in photos or in conversation," I said.

"They would. If ever there was a secret government, it's them. Let me show you the rest of my little place."

We put the milk glasses in the sink. She took me through a gap that led to a short hall with a bathroom door that was open. She turned on the light in the bathroom. The porcelain was as bright as the sun. Unlike my place, there was plenty of room in there.

"You have no idea how long I cleaned in here so it would look good when I brought you over. I wanted you to see how I've done, that I had a very nice place to pee."

"You've done good. And it is indeed a very nice place to pee."

As we stood there, I was reminded of that moment long ago in her parents' hallway when she had kissed my lips and made my stomach flutter. I felt it more when we stepped out into the hallway again.

She showed me one of the bedrooms. It was simple, occupied mostly by a large bed, with an adjoining bathroom. There was an open closet and I could see two uniforms hanging there, some other clothes. There was a chest of drawers.

"Comfortable," I said.

"Enough."

"Show me the other bedroom."

"Looks just like this one without the extra bathroom. Bed has different-colored sheets and I have a desk in there. I mostly use it as a kind of office when I need it. You know what I was thinking a moment ago, Danny?"

"I don't think so."

"About that time."

"That time?"

"I want to know if a moment ago when we were in the hallway you thought about something I remember pretty well."

"I'm scared, because if I tell you what I remember, I'm afraid you'll have meant you remember a song playing on the radio or some such thing."

"I can assure you that's not it."

"Would it be about a kiss?"

"Happy you remember."

"How could I forget."

She was close to me. I had the sensation of greater warmth in the room.

"You want to see if the kiss is still good?" I said. "You know, experiment?"

"Thought you'd never ask."

It's impossible to adequately describe how soft her lips were. It would be like trying to describe the touch of a butterfly's wings, the taste of fresh honey. We kissed and held each other next to the bed for a long while, and then somewhere between our kisses, she turned out the light and we ended up in bed, hastily pulling off our clothes, then finding each other, soft and wet and warm and in motion.

When we were satisfied, we held each other and made sounds like purring kittens, and then our need built up again, and we were at it some more. Then it was over, and we were spooning, the curve of her sweat-damp back against my sweat-damp chest. She was like a puzzle piece I hadn't known was missing, and then she said, "That was good, wasn't it," and I said, "Sure was," which seemed like a damn inadequate remark for what had just happened, but it was all I had the energy to say.

Eventually I could hear Ronnie's slow and steady breathing, and there was still the sweet smell of her in my nostrils. I listened to her breathe for a long time, delighting in her closeness, and then I gently kissed her on the back of the neck near her hairline and drifted peacefully off to sleep.

My father's ghost, thankfully, didn't show up.

(26)

Daybreak brought us another sweet moment, then we showered together, laughed while soaping each other up. Ronnie had her hair under a shower cap. She shampooed my hair for me. Who would have thought a hair-washing could be so erotic? We made love again, the hot water from the shower beating down on us, and then we were out and dried and dressed and on the road.

We didn't kiss when she dropped me off, but we wanted to. We thought it might not be smart to have me kiss a police officer at seven thirty in the morning in her cruiser. I didn't think right in that moment that Ronnie might have other reasons connected to race, though I would realize it when I gave it time. Ronnie was always more alert than I was, and that alertness had made her a good boxer. It bothered me, though. It shouldn't matter, but I knew for some in that little town of New Long Lincoln, it would. She had her job to think about. White and black were still colors a lot of people thought didn't and shouldn't mix.

We had skipped breakfast, so without going to my room, I got in my car and drove over to the café and ate. Then I went to the hardware store and bought myself two nice ax handles. I left one in the car, and when I got home, I put the other beside my bed. It wasn't exactly high-tech, but after the encounter outside of the house the other night, I felt it might be necessary, if for no other reason than psychological assurance.

I started to work on my article. I looked through the library books and made notes. I folded out the map in the Natural Wilson book, studied it closely. I found the spot where the old town had been before there was a lake, and then I found the hill where the sawmill was, the junkyard, the cemetery, and on the other side of the hill was a notation for a building that looked like a castle. There was a name written above it: LONG LINCOLN COUNTRY CLUB. I, of course, had already seen all of this, the club from a distance, but it helped to see reference to it. To pause and put it all into perspective.

Using my notes, I began to write my article for the Sunday edition of the newspaper.

*   *   *

The editor, Christine Humbert, pointed me to a chair in her office, took my article, sat behind her desk, and read it while I twiddled my thumbs. I saw her face crease a few times, her mouth twist, and it made me wonder if I was hitting a chord or stepping on her editorial toes somehow. Finally, she finished. She placed the article on her desk as gently as if it were a Fabergé egg.

"It's good, Danny, but anecdotal stories won't cut it. You need some actual people saying these things are true, that they witnessed it. I've seen most of this before; it's popped up over the years, but the way you've laid it out, it's really good. Still, the stories about the dam and people murdered by flooding them out, people on the city council knowing this, condoning it, perhaps instigating it, needs justification."

"It's a general piece. As it continues, week to week, I'll reveal what I find. I'm only reciting common stories to build the framework, the legends, not actually pointing the finger at anyone directly. By the second piece, I'll be writing it more like a mystery, and the idea is to reach some conclusions when I get to the last piece. I think it will take six issues."

"And the mystery will be, was the town flooded with the knowledge people were there, and were city bigwigs behind it? Or was it an accident?"

I had mentioned the bodies in the trunks of the cars, which by now was commonly known, but I hadn't mentioned the murders Shirley told me about, her having found information about them inside the very building where we now sat. I wanted to be a bit more certain about that business before I started spinning that web.

"I think the city council knew people were in the old town when they had workers set the water loose," Christine said. "Too many have told me over the years, old-timers, that you could see the lights in the town and some people moving around, and they let the water in anyway. I believe the council didn't care if people died. That bunch are ruthless and without a conscience. They don't even pretend to be democratic. They even have their meetings in private, out at that big social club or whatever they call it."

"Long Lincoln Country Club," I said.

"Article comes out, it could be a little too close, even if you say clearly that at this point these are legends, not proven fact. I asked you to write the articles, but seeing it in black and white, it hits harder than I thought. And this is only the first installment. I think, legends or not, it's more than implying our town was founded by murderers. That's not new information, Danny. But the way you've laid it out, the way you're airing out their shitty drawers, it's powerful stuff. That said, I'll run it, but if we run more articles, we need more facts."

"I'll have them."

"That's confidence for you," she said. "You're certain you can reach those conclusions beyond hearsay?"

"Reasonably. But now you're making me nervous."

"We have words, and they have money."

"Words are powerful."

"Powerful enough to get our asses in a crack. That Jack Jr., he's a real estate man, helps run the only insurance company in town, and he's a lawyer to boot, a crack one, like his father. He's beat a lot of lawsuits over the years, many brought by relatives of flood victims claiming they were owed money from a settlement, but he made that settlement go away, or at least put it in limbo."

"Your niece thinks there may be more nefarious connections."

"She was born curious. Sometimes, I fear, too curious. Please keep her out of all this. Council reads this, Jack Jr. may make plans for us, free press or not. If the council did in fact drown people, they might even have more in mind for us than lawsuits. Those two that visited you wearing disguises—you don't think that was a random mugging, do you?"

"I don't know what to think about that," I said. "But what I wrote about, it's not a new idea. This guy called Natural Wilson mentioned this conspiracy in his book. I admit it's hearsay, but sometimes hearsay can turn out to be truth."

"Natural Wilson was a pen name for someone in this town that had an ax to grind over the whole lake business. Book was self-published. The printer is unknown. It was sold in grocery stores, feed stores, souvenir shops, and our one bookstore. There was a lawsuit, and though the council members didn't have a way of finding out who to sue for writing it, they did sue the people who handled it. It worked. Stores quit carrying the book. But a few copies got out there. It made a stir in some places, but eventually the stir settled down."

"How could the author hide? Natural had to get the books in those stores somehow."

"The author hired people from out of town to distribute. People who the author worked with through third parties. No one knew anything other than they had been hired to deliver books, and if the stores wanted them, they could have them and didn't owe Natural a red cent. Natural Wilson, whoever that is, just wanted to do that stirring I mentioned. Could have been a personal vendetta. Weren't really that many of the books, and it's believed the city council bought up most of them."

"Sounds like you should have written this article yourself," I said.

"I don't have the skill. I can edit, but I can barely write a grocery list. No one else here was willing."

"So you picked me as the goat?"

"You picked yourself," she said.

"Do we print, then?"

"We do. For your next article, you might want to get closer to the council members. Research Jack Manley Sr. He's still around."

"I mentioned him in the piece," I said.

"I said research him. He's not only on the city council, he's the mayor. Not an elected official. The council picked him. And then there's Judea Parker. He's no spring chicken either. And Kate Conroy. She's the council's mouthpiece. She gives meanness and spite a good name. Keep in mind, airing the council's shitty drawers could get them rubbed in our faces."

*   *   *

It was still daylight when I got back to the Chandler house, and though no one menacing was around, I decided I should be prepared in case the clown show turned up again. I pulled out the ax handle I had in the back seat, carried it upstairs with me, placed it next to the other one in my room.

I thought about calling Ronnie, but after what Christine had told me, I wasn't going to be good company for anyone, and I didn't want her to feel I just wanted to meet up so we could have sex, though I won't lie, it crossed my mind.

Upstairs in my room I ate the candy and fruit I had left, and it was the worst thing you could eat for supper. I guess it was why I slept so miserably. I would feel as if I was easing off to sleep, and then all of a sudden, I was wide-eyed. I made several trips to the bathroom and back to bed, and that helped a little.

Eventually I did sleep, but I dreamed dark and heavy. In the dream, I saw a body lying on the floor. It was covered in shadow and it was in a room with a small open window. Starlight came through the window and fell across the body and gave it shape, but I couldn't see the face. I had an uncomfortable feeling I might know who it was.

And then the shape on the floor rose up, and there was a buzzing so loud it was a roar—the roar of the flies that cop had told me about.

The shadow shape weaved and went straight for the open window, then out of it, and it was gone. I caught a glimpse of its face—my face. The light faded. The room fell solid dark and all my dreams fell dead on the floor.

PART THREE

THE MOONSHINE CASTLE

Hidden places hold dreams, and secrets both good and evil.

— Anonymous

(27)

Ronnie and I saw each other a couple times in the next few days, and we took trips out to the dry lake to look it over, as if at some moment there would be a revelation. None came.

We made love at her place. It was better each time, but we didn't see each other much due to her work, her hours having been expanded to deal with domestic squabbles, drunks, petty robberies, and too much paperwork. But I felt good with her and she with me. Seemed to me that love was blossoming or, in my case, had already arrived by jet, the blossoms on board.

As for what the law found out about the bones in the trunks of those cars, it was no more than what we had already determined. The remains lay cold and silent in the morgue, their deeper mysteries so far unanswered. Chief Dudley didn't seem to have any thoughts or words of wisdom on the matter.

Some nights my father came to me, his ghost both real and unreal, clutching my ankle. Occasionally I could swear he spoke to me in his wet voice, his words as cryptic as Sanskrit to a squirrel. I always awoke upset and a little frightened, but when I turned on the lights or bathed in the light of the rising sun, the spectral feelings faded away as swiftly and easily as cotton candy melts in the mouth.

And then on Sunday, my first article came out in the newspaper.

It sold a lot of papers, and fast, not only in New Long Lincoln but in satellite communities and small towns all around.

In my article, I didn't mention that there might be a killer roaming East Texas, as that had already been suggested by the discovery of the bones. I didn't mention my father was a suspect, but at some point in the article series, I intended to. I didn't try and suggest what Shirley thought, that the bones in the trunks had been exhumed and weren't murders. I didn't know enough to agree or disagree with her theory.

Tuesday morning, I had been up only long enough to shower and get dressed when Mrs. Chandler, not wishing to come up the stairs every time the phone rang, yelled up at me that I had a phone call. It was Christine.

Christine said I should bring myself immediately to the newspaper office as something important had occurred. She didn't tell me what, but I had no doubt it had to do with the article I had written. A certain amount of fallout had been expected. That was all right. I had hoped to stir both the sympathetic reader and the flies.

When I got there, Christine's office had three people in it that I didn't know. There was a cool, clean man about the size of a half-track. He was in his forties, wearing a dark blue suit that didn't come from any store in East Texas. He wore it with a hot-pink tie that lay crisp against a blue shirt several shades lighter than the suit and fastened to it by a stickpin as white-silver as a star. He was seated where I had sat the day before. Christine, wearing gray and blue, was behind her desk looking as if she couldn't decide if she should dissolve into a puddle or leap over the desk and go for the man's throat.

The other two people in the room were attractive women who were somewhat interchangeable in appearance and dress, their outfits being dark, man-style suits with equally dark open-at-the-neck shirts and no ties. Their shoulder-length hair matched their suits. They were long-legged and eager-looking, cautious scavengers waiting to eat the scraps that the seated man might leave for them once he had made his kill.

When I closed the door behind me, the man looked at me. It was like watching an owl turn its head; it unsettled me, but his eyes were not owl-like at all. There was something feral in his glance, as if he were anticipating the slow devouring of a helpless field mouse. His black hair was slightly oiled and shone in the light like a lubricated mop. His feet were flat on the floor. His spine was stiff and his shoulders were squared. A painting or photograph of him might have made him look handsome, but his actual presence gave you the impression that he was somehow not quite fastened together right.

"Danny," Christine said. "This is Jack Manley Jr."

"The lawyer," I said.

"Exactly," she said. "Insurance and real estate as well. Ladies, I don't believe we've actually been introduced yet."

"No need for that," Jack Jr. said. "You don't need to know them. They're not major players." He had a voice as flat as Kansas and simultaneously as sour as old milk.

The women had leaned forward at Christine's offer of introduction, but now they rocked back like bowling pins resetting. They seemed neither insulted nor disappointed. They hardly seemed real. I think he scared them even more than us.

"Only person you need to know is me. Mr. Russell, you and Miss Humbert have written and printed some rather vile stuff about my father and other members of the city council, and they find it disturbing. Disturbing enough for them to consider legal action."

"I don't remember saying they did anything," I said.

"It was easy to read between the lines."

"All kinds of things might be between the lines—turds and flowers, depending on perception—but it's the lines themselves that count. I merely said what has been said about the town council for years about what happened the night the lake filled. People were drowned, that's a fact. As for the city council, or the city dictatorship, I didn't say that the things said about the council were true, only that they were said. I quoted from a book."

The new look Jack Jr. gave me made me feel less like a mouse anticipating consumption and more like I had already been consumed whole and was lying in his stomach being dissolved by digestive juices.

"That rubbish by Natural Wilson?" he said. "I certainly doubt Natural is his name, and he hasn't come forward to explain himself or that book. And it's years old. Lies then, lies now."

"Might be rubbish, but it's part of your city's lore, and the article made it clear it's lore, not facts. The facts are being researched and may come out over time, and they might not fit the legend. Or they might. Way I saw it, so many years have gone by since the new town was built, it was high time for a retrospective, including bits of lore, which, again, my article makes clear."

"Walking the line, aren't you?"

"I don't think so," I said.

"Well, I don't like it. The city council doesn't like it."

"Sounds like a personal problem," Christine said. "But not a legal one. Tell you what, Jackie, why don't you pack up your ladies, taking care to maintain the creases in your pants, and heel-toe yourself and your Italian shoes on out of here. When you have a true legal matter, then you can come back. Bring the ladies again, pull the plugs out of their asses, and bring their names with them next time."

"Miss Humbert," he said. "You don't want to get on my wrong side."

"That was really scary," Christine said. "The little sneer when you finished, that capped it off. I might even remember it five minutes from now. But, so we're clear, you and me, we were on different sides before we ever met. What I think is, if you're bothered this much by quotes from a book that contains regional folklore, then it might be more than folklore you're worried about. I'll even say this—you're really going to shit your knickers full of stinky when the whole story gets out. We might mention how you came here to threaten us over something you feared we might say. That will sell some fucking papers, won't it, you well-dressed piece of dog shit. Pardon my language."

"You are coarse, Miss Humbert."

"What can I say? Someone drags dog shit into my office, I'm willing to say it stinks."

"It's the innuendo of the article we're discussing," Jack Jr. said. He turned those feral eyes on me again. "And your mention of the bodies in the trunks of those cars. I think it's a distraction from the obvious thing here. Your father was a serial killer."

"You think that, do you?" I said. I wasn't surprised that came up. New Long Lincoln's word of mouth worked faster than the telephone wires. It hadn't been in my article. That had been a short piece in the paper the day before, and there wasn't any mention of my father being responsible for anything other than driving off a bridge ten years back with his son in the car.

"I do think that," he said.

"We can talk about what might be said or what might be true for hours," Christine said, "but nothing in that article gives you the right to bring yourself in here with your two pull-toys and aggravate me at my work or have me call in one of my reporters when he could be home writing the next article for next Sunday's paper. Even pulling his johnson would be a better use of his time than this."

"I was, in fact, in the middle of that," I said.

"Saddle your bitches and head out, Jackie," Christine said.

"Don't call me that," he said.

"It's better than what I want to call you."

"I'll throw in a nickel and two cents and ask if you know a couple of boys that like to play dress-up," I said. "One with white greasepaint on his face, the other with cork and orange clown hair. Sports red lipstick. Not really his color. One of those guys totes around a mean left hook. Both like to wear hats and dark suits and strut like gangsters high on hog tranquilizer. Ring any bells?"

"What in the hell are you talking about?" Jack Jr. said. He was almost convincing.

"It's just a quiz I'm giving everyone. Ladies?"

They didn't say anything. They didn't even look at me.

"You may be a little too smart-ass for your own good, Mr. Russell. And you, Miss Humbert, you call yourself a lady."

"I wouldn't dare," she said.

"You know," I said, "you strike me, Mr. Manley, as one of those people who see everything around you as something to consume. I get the idea a lot is not enough for you. I also get the feeling that my article is stirring something full of blood and shadows."

"That's supposed to somehow make me feel bad, guilty? I'm a capitalist, Mr. Russell. If it's there to consume, I consume it, and smack my lips when I finish. I eat and eat until I'm so full, I think I'm going to blow, and yet I keep eating. There are those who can, and those who can't, those who do, and those who don't."

"I'm a capitalist too," I said, "but with a small *c*. A comfortable portion for me is enough."

"Everything in life is a banquet. That's the kind of nutrition that makes you big, Mr. Russell. I can tell by the way you stand, the way you wear your clothes, you'll always be small. A little man close to the floor yelling up to his betters, wondering why he too can't be tall."

He smiled at me, and it was like something you might see in the tiger cage at the zoo at feeding time.

"I suggest both of you consider what you write next. If it continues in the tone you've set with the first article, you will hear from me."

"Don't let the door hit you in the ass on the way out," Christine said. "You too, ladies. Nice suits, by the way. Who says crime doesn't pay?"

Jack Jr. stood up so slowly an entire new species of humans could have developed, invented fire and tools, and died out. The creases in his pants were not in any way wrinkled as he rose. He took a moment to show me how intense he could stare, then started for the door.

I stepped aside and opened it. The three of them, without saying a word, went out in single file, him smelling of Brut cologne, them hinting of different perfumes. The cloud of mixed scents made my nose hairs twitch. I closed the door gently behind them, let out my breath, went over to the visitor's chair, and collapsed into it.

"It's like the devil and two of his imps have left the room," I said.

"Oh, hell, Danny," Christine said, it being her turn to let out her breath and collapse deeper into her chair. "I nearly messed myself. You have stirred the hornets' nest, and they are eager to sting."

"You didn't seem that afraid."

"I do a bit of community theater, so you'd be surprised how I really felt. My legs were trembling under the desk."

"They sue me, all they get in return is the remains of a not overly impressive book advance, a typewriter, and two ax handles."

"I'm worried about me, not you. Listen, be damn sure whatever you write next isn't an execution warrant for the both of us."

(28)

Late that afternoon, after buying some clothes and shoes at a JCPenney's and a few more bananas and candy bars, I arrived home. Clasping my good friend the ax handle in my right hand, carrying the bag containing my new clothes and shoes, bananas, and candy bars in my left, I went up to my room.

I put the ax handle next to the other one so they could keep each other company, though I was uncertain what two ax handles would talk about. I put the new clothes away and started toward my desk. I wasn't sure what I would write, as I really didn't know anything new that could be printed in the newspaper, but I still had a few days to organize my thoughts and put together an article.

Truth was, that creepy Jack Jr. had upset me. His threat of legal action seemed to conceal another threat as well. I almost expected another visit from the circus clowns.

I wondered what life might be like in Bora-Bora, provided I had enough money to get there. If I did and found a tree to live under, about all I could get out of it was a swinging weekend, a pineapple, and a sunburn.

I hadn't sold my aunt's house yet—my house—and it might be time to pack up my small bit of goods and go back there. It wasn't

Bora-Bora, but it wasn't here. Ronnie was here, though, and the thought of being even two or three hours from her unnerved me as much as Jack Jr. and his threats.

I was thinking on this when I saw the folded piece of paper on my desk that the librarian had given me, the one with her phone number on it. I had pulled it out of my pocket and put it there before I consigned my shirt to the dirty laundry.

It wasn't like I was going to chase her down for a date, not with what Ronnie and I had going, but I unfolded the note and looked at it.

It said what it had said before. Estelle Parker, and below her name was her phone number.

Sometimes you have to be slapped in the face to see what's right in front of you. Right then, I was slapped hard.

I had filled out a form with my information on it. Estelle had given me her number with a smile, and that smile had flattered my ego and swollen my dick enough that I had let down my guard. My biology makes me easy that way.

Estelle's last name was Parker. Same last name as one of the town fathers. She knew I was an author and she knew I was researching. The thugs showed up not long after I left the library. They'd had just enough time to put on their burnt cork and white face paint and go to the address she had given them.

As Shirley said, it was a pattern.

*　　*　　*

I brought my ax handle with me to the car. I didn't think I'd need it for a less-than-five-foot-tall librarian with a delicate manicure, but it traveled with me nonetheless. When I arrived at the library, it was with great reluctance that I left the ax handle in the back seat, went inside.

One of the volunteers was working that day. She was young and perky. She told me Estelle was going to be out all that week and weekend. She was taking some personal time.

I left and found a phone booth and called the number she'd given me. She didn't answer. I took the phone book and looked up her name. Her address was there.

I drove down the block to the drugstore, asked for directions to the street she lived on.

It was a short drive. When I got there, the sun was so bright that the idea of there being a kind of darkness moving through this rather all-American small city seemed as unlikely as discovering a talking pigeon with a recipe for hot-water corn bread.

I kept feeling as if I were being watched and followed. If I were, they were as sneaky as the Invisible Man. By that time, I was imagining someone behind every tree and bush and in every alley. It's funny how people wanting to beat your ass makes you cautious.

The block Estelle lived on was cute as a puppy. It reminded me of the block Ronnie lived on. It looked like a movie set of a small town in all those old Hollywood movies I loved. A place where the milk was delivered early morning in bottles that were left on porches, and a kid on a bicycle threw newspapers. On weekends, husbands mowed the lawns and wives made pot-roast dinners for their families. It didn't seem like the kind of place where good-looking librarian ladies called in thugs to beat the shit out of a new resident for doing research. It also didn't seem like the sort of house and yard and location a librarian could afford.

I went up the walk and knocked on the door. For a moment I thought she might not be home, as she hadn't answered her phone, but I was damn certain to give it a try anyway. I was looking over the flower beds next to the house, as precise and neat as a botanical garden, when the door unlatched.

And there she was. She was wearing a blue and white sundress and she was barefoot. Her blond hair was a little tousled, but that made her look all the more appealing. She had a magazine in her hand. It was rolled up, as if to correct a dog.

"Daniel," she said.

"Yep. I looked you up. Thought if you had a moment, I'd like to talk to you."

She tried not to look bothered, but her pretty mouth did a bit of involuntary gymnastics at the corners. She finally decided on a smile bright enough to read by in the dead of night.

"Come in," she said. "I was sitting on the patio."

She led me through the house making sure to keep a couple paces in front of me so I could take note of how well she walked. The house smelled of cinnamon air freshener.

We went through a sliding door made of glass and into a back-yard. A sprinkler was sputtering water over the emerald blades of close-clipped grass, and the sun shining on the wet beads caused them to shimmer like pearls.

I viewed all of this from under a striped awning that draped over a nice little patio and coated it in comfortable shadow. There was a metal table under the awning and there was a yellow-striped pitcher on it. The pitcher was filled with ice and had a milky-looking liquid inside that I took for lemonade.

With the water sprinkling, the perfectly trimmed grass shimmering, a cool wind sighing over the wooden fence that surrounded her backyard, and a bird singing in a luscious green elm, it seemed like I had stepped into a little slice of heaven with its own resident angel who preferred a sundress to a gossamer gown and wings.

Estelle placed the magazine on the table and took a seat and gestured for me to do the same. The cushions on the metal chair were not as comfortable as they looked.

"I thought I might have lost my allure. I expected you to call well before now. But come by? I didn't expect that. But I'm glad you're here. Would you like some refreshment? I have lemonade. I could get another glass."

"I'm fine. I thought I might ask you something. Are you kin to the Parker on the city council?"

"Why, yes, I am. Judea is my uncle."

"I think the best way for me to do this is to get right to it. I gave you my information for a library card, and when I said I was writing about the old lake and what had happened there, you got nervous and called your uncle, or someone connected to him, and they called some muscle, and the muscle came to visit me."

"I have no idea what you're talking about, Daniel."

"I think you called to let someone know that I was snooping around, and they sent two jokers with stupid disguises to rearrange my ribs and innards."

"You were hurt?"

"I managed to hurt them back a bit, and I had some assistance from my grumpy landlady and her shotgun."

She let her mouth do the gymnastics again, then she lowered her chin for dramatic effect.

"I didn't think that would happen. Them hurting you."

"But you did make that call, right?"

A fly came into the picture and hummed around the lip of her striped lemonade glass. She watched it hum for a second, then brushed at it with the back of her hand. "I owe you an apology."

"At least."

"I didn't mean for you to be hurt in any way. Not at all."

She sounded sincere and looked so adorable in her little sundress, I wanted to hug her. Bears are like that too. They look adorable, but if you move in close, they'll bite your face off.

"It was a knee-jerk reaction. All those books on Long Lincoln and the lake. I've been taught to look out for the family. I was letting my uncle know you might be digging into the past a bit, might write a book about it, and I didn't want him to be blindsided."

"By what?"

That was left unanswered. She said, "I just made things worse."

"For me you did. Why would you keep the books in the library if you don't want them used for research?"

"It's not the research, it's the intent of it. People know the story of the flood and the drowning of folks who lived there, one of those unfortunate accidents."

"Damn unfortunate for the people who got washed away, I'm sure."

"But school papers are one thing, and the books do give a kind of legacy to the town—"

"Difference being I might really dig in and look out beyond the books."

"Just didn't want the council to be surprised. My uncle and the council, they've always had a thing about the Natural Wilson book especially. Lies, you understand. The part about the city council being involved, I mean. But it's one of those old stories that won't go away. I was just letting my uncle know a book might be written, and I thought he might want to talk to you about it, see if he could discourage you from writing it or have his side of the story told too. But that wasn't the sort of discouragement I meant. I thought he might send Jack Manley Jr. to see you, threaten legal action, that sort of thing."

Had she been standing on my neck pressing my windpipe with her foot and told me such a thing, I would have almost believed it right then. She was so cool and sweet, ice cream wouldn't have melted in her mouth.

"I did get a visit from Jack Jr. He put on a nice suit and took a moment to squirm out from under a rock to threaten me with a lawsuit. He brought a couple of female bookends with him. I think he might also have been subtly threatening me with a concussion."

"I think that was due to your article in the paper. Having so much of the history laid out like that. More people saw that article than ever saw the Natural Wilson book. No one checks that town history stuff out. Jack Jr. is a bit of a stiff-neck, for sure. And on the slimy side. I feared he was going to ask me out once. Thought I might have to fake leprosy to avoid him, but it didn't happen. Thank goodness."

"You're working too hard," I said.

"Whatever do you mean?"

"Too hard to convince me. This is where you turn angry, isn't it? Trying to make my being attacked all my fault. You damn well knew you might be putting me in jeopardy when you made that call."

"Some things don't need to be known, Daniel. They really don't. Especially if their veracity is debatable. May I ask you a favor, Daniel? May I politely ask that you drop this whole thing and that you not tell anyone you came to visit me? Can you stop digging a hole so deep you won't be able to climb out of it?"

"You can ask," I said.

"I hate intrepid people. I can never be that way. I hate living here in this town and ought to move away, but I don't. I hate a lot of things, but I don't hate the inheritance I have, and that comes with a major proviso. I stay here and I stay quiet about certain things, and by me telling you even that, I've already gone too far. I won't talk any more on the matter, so you might as well go."

She shifted in her chair so the backyard with its sputtering sprinklers was in her view and I was not.

"You don't have to be all that intrepid, Estelle, but I have a feeling there are things you'd like to get off your chest. The inherited money and this nice house and a bullshit job at the library won't help you carry that around for the rest of your life. Want to take the weight off, call me at the boardinghouse. You have the number." I slid open the back door, closed it behind me, went through the house and out to my car. The sun was much harsher out there without the sprinkler and the cool wind and the awning shade, but despite the heat, I was beginning to have a permanent coating of ice on my spine.

(29)

Ronnie joined me for late lunch at a burger joint. She only had about thirty minutes before she had to get back to it. We found a table at the rear that offered us a reasonable bit of privacy, and we kept our voices down. I told her all of what had happened with Jack Jr. and my talk with Estelle Parker.

"You think it's more than the article you wrote?"

"I think my coming to town and the bones being found due to the drought are all connected somehow. Wouldn't surprise me to find that we're only looking at a few of the puzzle pieces, and maybe it's less like a puzzle and more like those Russian dolls where you remove one, and there's another inside, and then another, and so on."

"Yeah. Shirley is right, I think. This isn't just a bunch of coincidences. The drought. Your father's car and the bones in the trunk, and then us finding the others, your article. It's stirred the rats, that's for damn sure."

More like those flies the cop had told me about than rats. I could almost hear their wings beating in a loud echo.

"Jack Jr. is a key in all of this, as he's their enforcer," I said. "I don't know if he does it himself, but he has it done, and I have the feeling he's perfectly capable of doing it if the need arose. Way he looked at me in Christine's office today, I think this goes deeper than the threat of litigation."

"He's good at what he does," Ronnie said, "but he's not well liked. Very sociopathic, narcissistic, but totally without the charm it's claimed they have. He's the kind of guy that could throw a puppy out of a moving car, is what I think. I guess that's what makes him such a good lawyer and insurance salesman."

"Why would anybody buy insurance from him?"

"Lot of people in this town, they want insurance, they go to him. Someone new comes in, tries to set up shop, something goes wrong for them, and they give it up pretty soon, leave town. I never thought of it as being nefarious until right now. I just thought that it was hard to beat Jack Jr. because he's so established."

"This town has been like this so long," I said, "I don't think people know that not every place is like this, with a city council you don't vote on and an appointed mayor, neither of which likes to be asked questions."

"I agree."

"You know, Ronnie, people still turned their heads when we came in here, a couple, black and white. This town smells of the Confederacy more than any southern town I've been in, and I grew up in the South."

"I admit passing Jefferson Davis's statue doesn't make me cheer up when I think about it. But it and that flag have been there such a long time, it's become part of the scenery. It's surprising what we can get used to."

"It's not there for scenery. This place has a nice veneer, but underneath I can smell rot. I have a feeling that the Long Lincoln Country Club might have some of those rotten answers."

"The law isn't even allowed out there without permission, and they don't get permission."

"If the council is outside the law, or believes itself to be, that's a whole different can of worms."

Ronnie reached across the table and touched my hand. "I have to go. Be careful. This worries me for you. I think you may have opened a den of vipers instead of a can of worms."

*　　*　　*

I drove over to the newspaper office and looked through their morgue for a while and mostly turned up what Shirley had turned up. I kept looking for more, but all I found were more articles that talked about murders, possible murders, mysterious deaths. I made a list of the names and checked the list I had taken from Shirley.

Most of the names I found matched her list. There were a few I had written down that didn't. I couldn't be sure there was any connection between the others, but I thought there could be. A couple I felt certain (one from her original list) didn't seem convincing as part of a pattern, but the rest did. It felt like confirmation. Maybe Shirley and her rituals had gotten into my head.

When I left out of there, the sky had turned a persimmon color and a piece of moon was starting its tour rising from a corner of the sky. By the time I drove off, the persimmon sky was turning blue-black.

On the way home, I thought a copper-colored Ford that showed up under the streetlights, visible in my rearview mirror, was following me. I was nervous enough about it that I didn't go home straightaway. I drove to the police station and parked out front beneath their night-lights where I could see their front door. I could see movement behind the glass, a cop in there, and that almost reassured me. Nothing really assured me. Not in this town.

The Ford had rolled down a side street. I chalked it up to me being foolish. I was becoming paranoid but consoled myself with the old idea that just because you're paranoid doesn't mean they aren't after you.

I didn't get out of the car but sat in the parking space at the police station for about fifteen minutes, then pulled out and drove home without seeing a copper-colored Ford.

(30)

As I was about to ascend the stairs, my trusty ax handle in hand, Mrs. Chandler came out of the kitchen and started across the living room. She said, "Come sit with me awhile."

"I thought that area was off limits."

"You've been in here already."

I thought about my dog-on-the-couch analogy. Bark, bark.

"You can come in when invited," she said. "You're invited. And you won't need the ax handle. I won't hurt you."

She had taken a seat on the couch by this time and she patted a spot next to her. I saw on the coffee table in front of her there was a large book. I recognized it. Natural Wilson's volume on Long Lincoln.

I put the ax handle on the floor and sat by her. "Not going to ask about the ax handle?" I said.

"I know what it's for," she said, and she touched the book on the coffee table. "Read your article. It was good, but it's only got a part of the truth."

"It's one article. A series of them will follow."

"I know. It says so at the bottom of it. I read all the way through and even understand what I read. This book you mentioned. I know it well."

"Okay," I said.

To emphasize, she patted the book again. "I know what's not in the book that the author would have liked to be there but was too frightened to write. I know it's not very well written, and I know most copies were bought up when the book first came out, and I know the one in the library is one I donated."

"I have that one upstairs."

"Yes, and it's been gathering dust in the library for a long time, but my guess is after you turn it back in, it will never be on the shelves again. It will cease to exist. They were foolish letting it stay there."

"They?"

"You know who I mean." She pursed her lips. "Now that I'm old, and I have cancer—"

"Hell, I'm sorry. I had no idea."

"I don't talk about it usually. It's what it is. It's a bad cancer too. Eating me from the inside out. Wish it would go away, but as the old saying goes, wish in one hand and shit in the other and see which one fills up first. Prayer has been suggested, but you could modify that saying to pray in one hand and shit in the other and see which one fills up first. You would have the same results."

"Isn't there something you can do to treat it?"

"It's a done deal. I have a bit of time, the doctor thinks, and I feel okay. He says it'll come on fast, and suddenly, I don't want to do a damn thing. He says by that point they'll have me so full of morphine or some such, I won't know if I'm flying to the moon or trying to slice it up for a wheel of cheese. I've come to terms with it, and I've decided it's about time I let loose the badger in the angel cake. I don't really want to discuss my cancer. I want to tell you what I know before I can't. I want to give you some things. I think a lot of dead bodies are surfacing, just like when someone drowns in the lake. They go down, but in time they come up. And recently in car trunks."

Technically, they hadn't come up, but I let that go. I got the symbolism of it. "I'm intrigued," I said.

"Of course you are. Listen to me. I want to give you some information that might help you, or it might make you go upstairs and pack and move on. And I wouldn't blame you. Let's start with this. Once upon a time I had a husband, and I found out too late he was a malicious, unprincipled asshole who would screw a knothole in a tree in case a squirrel was bent over inside picking up an acorn. I married young, as that's what girls did back then. My plan was to have a family and go to football games and ice cream socials with my husband and children, do the wife thing, the local-citizen thing, maybe bake a cake or pie for some county fair, die old and happy surrounded by my children and not too bad-looking for a hundred and ten. But that part of my plan didn't turn out so good.

"Bert, he was nasty as the scum on pond water. His inability to run with a football was etched into his past like a thorn. He was smart and well built, kind of pretty, but physically he was slow. He ran like cold molasses on a winter morn, had all the blocking ability of a fog on the road. So his football ambitions were just that, ambitions.

"Our bedroom used to be the one you're in at the top of the stairs. My husband, Bert Chandler, was a hitter, and he liked to correct me, as he put it. Meaning I wasn't supposed to disagree with him even if he said sewage was the food of the gods. Some years ago, he was standing there on the stairs. He had just corrected me and raped me, which he called 'having fun,' and he was expecting me to go downstairs like a good little girl and make his breakfast. I came out of the bedroom, having adjusted myself to a bit of normalcy, having dried my tears and combed my hair, and there he was at the top of the stairs, all showered and dressed.

He was straightening his tie. Blue with gray stripes. I remember it perfectly. He was a fine-looking man, standing there, though I noted he had missed a spot while shaving and some hairs stood out from his chin like little spikes. Odd thing to remember, huh?

"For him, what he had done to me was nothing important. It was how he thought things should be, a slap and hump when he felt like it. He was going to eat the breakfast he expected me to fix for him, go off to his lawyer job, working for Jack Manley Sr. At that time, Manley's boy, Jack Jr., didn't work there in either law or insurance. That was to come.

"Quiet as a dream, I came up beside Bert and shoved him with both palms, knocked him down the stairs. I can't say I planned it, and I barely remember doing it, the actual pushing, I mean. He landed on his head on a middle step, and there was a popping sound like someone stepping on a crusty bug, and then that great big body of his tumbled the rest of the way down and lay on the floor at the base of the stairs, one shoe having come off his foot. His hair had slipped and there was a lock of it on his forehead, like an old bopper might wear. His head was set funny on his neck, and he was looking up at me. If he had been able to see, he would have seen me doing a little happy dance at the top of the stairs. Just came out of me, dancing like that. Like I was leaping up and down on burning coals, but I was ecstatic.

"Near everyone in town suspected I pushed his ass, but no one could prove anything, and the only person I've ever admitted it to is you. I did collect a good amount of money, though. He had a lot tucked away. And since Jack Manley Sr. also sold insurance, Bert had put together a comfortable life insurance policy from him for the both of us. I always suspected, just a feeling, that Bert had a policy on us both to remove suspicion that would be there if he decided I might could have an accident. One policy was just too obvious. Surprised that bastard. Got him first.

"I got the insurance money and the money that he had tucked in places around the house that he didn't think I knew about, and I got this house and a car. Jackpot.

"Jack Manley Sr. came around shortly after Bert was in the ground, buried in a cheap particleboard coffin in the suit he died in, same tie, same stickpin, not embalmed, as I wanted the worms to get to him as fast as possible.

"Jack Sr., who was tighter than Dick's hatband, offered me a regular monthly check, quite generous, as a way of honoring my husband's memory, as he put it.

"Reason for those checks wasn't about Bert's memory or my widowhood. It was just in case I might know something Bert told me that could be harmful to Jack Sr. or, for that matter, the city council, this town's own little Gestapo.

"Bert worked for Jack a long time, had grown up with him, Parker, Kate, all of them, knew their kids and so on. When all of them were little, they had a secret society. They still do. Back then they made up their own little god and had a wooden statue of it and everything. Carved out of a piece of an old creosote post. They called it Creosote Johnny. Kid stuff, but you know what Bert told me they used to do? They had a monthly meeting and a ceremony in the woods somewhere, sacrificed a little animal to a successful future each time. Squirrels. Cats. Dogs. Strangled them with a garrote. And you know what else? They have had successful futures. Money. Power. Sex. They know what's going on with everyone in this town, and they have their thumbs on the scales. They own New Long Lincoln, heart and soul. They owned the old town for the most part, engineered the flood for a new and better place they could control as the city council. When some people wouldn't move, they took it on themselves to eliminate the problem."

"You're not suggesting these ceremonies worked? That they were some kind of black magic?"

"No, but maybe they thought so, and maybe it doesn't matter now. They are what they have become. Dedication. Hard work. Ruthless acts. That's what got them there. The main three, anyway. The others were just assistants, really. Now it's Judea Parker, Jack Sr., and Kate Conroy. Some, like Jack Jr., well, he's important, but he's still just a worker bee waiting for Jack Sr. to go tits-up so he can slip into his place. I think they are now not too unlike how they were as kids, but with more power and money.

"People you would never suspect owe them allegiance. That's why I would be careful with Dudley. He's all right, I guess, but they have things on him."

"What sort of things?"

"Come on. Think about it. He's been living with a man who brings him lunch and goes to restaurants and travels on trips with him. He and Duncan aren't just good friends. They're butthole buddies. I don't give a shit, but members of this town would if it got out. You can't exactly call a place like this broadminded."

I understood then.

"It's insidious," Mrs. Chandler said. "Someone with money or power has a kid who gets in trouble with the law, runs over someone while drunk, rapes a girl at the junior college. Well, for the right faithfulness to the council, the right donations, the problem might go away. A slap on the wrist, or maybe nothing at all. Someone well positioned in town needs help with something or other, like maybe you think colored people moving into your neighborhood brings down the property value, the council can be there if they decide to be, and like a miracle, the folks who don't fit will be loading their goods in a pickup truck and leaving town. City council may have photos of someone, like, say, a fat chief of police and his boyfriend doing the midnight backstroke. Those photos could go away. For certain concessions, of course. Favors to be given in the future when needed.

"There are people and businesses all over town that are indebted to the council in one way or another, big and small. Like the insurance company Bert worked for and is still run by Jack Sr. and Jack Jr. It's the only one in town and it's financed by the bank here, and if for some reason the city council, who might as well be the company and the bank, don't want to pay out, they don't, and they know how to get away with it."

"One tongue licks the other," I said.

"Exactly. Being married to Bert, the city council suspected I knew all this. Bert, you see, for all his faults, was a talker. And a good one. He could be entertaining that way, but he was a blabbermouth. They knew that, and when he had his unfortunate fall down the stairs, they wanted to make sure I was beholden to them. I think Bert at some point, for his own protection, let them know he had records he had kept, and they feared those records might come to light. Not long after Bert was in the ground, I had the feeling, more than once, that someone had been in the house searching, trying to find out if there were records."

"If they're as dangerous as you say," I said, "couldn't they have just . . . well, taken you out?"

"Believe me, I thought of that. But for all they knew, those records were squirreled away someplace where they could be accessed by people outside the jurisdiction of this town, maybe upon my death. They don't fear New Long Lincoln, but outsiders could make it tough on them if they dug deep enough."

"That would be me," I said.

"It would. Thing is, Danny, there are records, and they never found them. I know that, because if they had found them, the records would be gone. They are extensive, and they are well hidden. This house used to belong to a man who sold bootleg whiskey and had what you might call a speakeasy and what some used to call Moonshine Castle. When Bert bought the house, he redesigned it so that the hidden drinking room became a depository for all the damaging records and—get this—reel-to-reel tapes he had dealing with the city council. He secretly recorded a lot of business that went on. Even Bert knew he was walking on eggshells, so at some point, he must have told them what he had for his insurance policy, and they had to assume he had it stashed away someplace safe, which in a way he did, but not the way they might think. But those records? Now I'm giving what he had to you."

(31)

"Come with me," Mrs. Chandler said.

She rose and I followed her through the kitchen and finally through a thick door about the size of a drawbridge. Mrs. Chandler turned the big metal knob with both hands, put her shoulder to the door, and swung it open.

When Mrs. Chandler flicked on a weak overhead light, dust swirled and the air tasted like a dirt sandwich. The room was small and seemed smaller in that it was tucked tight with a bulky desk that looked to have been built about the time Calvin Coolidge was in office. There were stacks of papers and books resting on it. A rolling chair with a hole-pocked leather seat was pushed up in the leg well. More books and files were mounded precariously on shelves that ran five high all around the redbrick walls. There was a reel-to-reel machine on a smaller desk that looked ready to fall over and burst into a thousand pieces. The little desk and recorder wore a coat of dust like an old wool blanket.

She said, "I knew they weren't giving me money for nothing, so there had to be a reason they wanted me on their side. Bert spent a lot of time in his office downtown, and when he was home, when he wasn't kicking my ass and raping me, he was in here with the door locked. Now and again I could hear him playing a reel-to-reel, but the door was far too thick for anything to be understood outside of this room.

"I got to thinking if he was hiding something—and he was always bringing in papers—it would be here. But then again, if they came and looked, which I suspicioned they did, they would have found this place, and anything here they could have taken easily. They kept paying me, so I felt if there was something, they hadn't found it.

"Then I remembered the Moonshine Castle. It was supposed to have existed in this house. I looked everywhere for it, specifically in this room, which is what made the most sense to me. One day I'm sitting at the desk here, drinking coffee, trying to figure where the goods might be, maybe in storage somewhere, or perhaps Bert was running a bluff all along, and I heard a squeak, looked down, saw a mouse at my feet. I have this thing about mice and rats. One of them could run me a mile and make me jump over hurdles. I lifted my feet quick and the wheeled chair rolled out from under me and flipped over and tossed me on the floor. Mouse ran right past me and was gone.

"So I'm thinking I'll poison that little disease-carrying son of a bitch, and I put the stuff out in this room, and about a week later I smell something like an elephant has died under the house. The odor goes all through the place, but in here, that's where it stank the most.

"I determined it was in the wall. I took a hammer to it, and behind the drywall I found bricks. That's why the wall is all bricks now. I took out all the drywall eventually, working a bit at a time. But while I'm taking it out, looking for that dead mouse, behind the desk there, close to the floor—do you see that little iron loop? You'll have to look under the desk."

I looked. The loop was sticking out of the wall close to the floor and a four-foot-long patch of wainscoting.

"Help me slide the desk aside," she said.

We moved it.

"Now," she said, "go pull the loop, then lift."

I pulled. I heard a clicking sound like a big cricket sawing his legs, and then I lifted. The wainscoting came out of the wall a few inches, and now the floor, right in line with floorboard cracks, lifted. It was a trapdoor. I pushed it back. The gap was about three feet wide all around.

"Fit right in, didn't it?" she said.

I looked down into the dark gap and could see some wooden stairs, and then I couldn't see much of anything.

"We'll need a flashlight," she said. Mrs. Chandler took one from the desk drawer and, with the beam leading her, went down the steps, and I followed.

I could quickly tell in the scanning beam of the flashlight that it was much larger than the upstairs. The room ran most of the length and width of the house. It was stuffy, as there was no cooling from the house unit.

There was a long bar, and on it were metal and plastic see-through containers with files and reels of tape in them. Shelves behind it were also stacked with files and loose papers. There was a long table and a few chairs in the room. Beyond that, there was very little.

"There's a light on that wall," she said. "There's a wire that comes out of it, and it's a little threadbare, so I wouldn't touch it. Just give the switch a quick flick. First time I turned it on, I managed to touch the wire instead of the switch and got lit up well enough I damn near sucked my panties up through my asshole. I could taste them in my mouth. Pardon my language, but I'm dying of cancer, so what the fuck."

She stepped back from the switch she had set the light on, which didn't encourage me.

I flipped the switch with a deft and swift touch. The room lit up, and not in fire, as I'd feared, but in a golden light that came from rows of raw bulbs fitted in bare ceiling fixtures.

"Had to buy new bulbs to get some light on the subject, but this room, or something like it, is what they were looking for. I know. I looked through it."

"When did you find this?"

"Years ago. It's why I believe they haven't had me have an accident of some kind. They think Bert had the goods, and he did, and they fear something happens to me, the records will end up being released to the world. Everything he thought mattered, he copied, boiled down to the essence—he was good at that— and stashed it here. Over time, I've read a lot of this stuff, listened to some of those reels, the hidden recordings of conversations Bert had in his office. No doubt he had enough to have them by the wing-wangs. I liked that monthly check, so I didn't do anything about it. Just like they hoped for. Well, I didn't do anything directly. I didn't have the courage for that. But I did put a kind of message out in a bottle once, telling some of it, hoping someone else would come forward that knew something so I wouldn't put my tit in the wringer, but they didn't. I was trying to feel bold and at the same time keep my payment and my safety. But my message didn't do much. Now and again the bottle pops up and someone reads the message, but you're the first to make something of it, you and Christine."

I smiled. "You're Natural Wilson."

"I am," she said.

(32)

Mrs. Chandler brought a small rotating fan down and set it on the end of the bar to blow a bit of dust and dry air on me, and then she brought coffee and sandwiches and even a cookie while I went through the files.

The files were plentiful and dusty, but well organized. I found lists that were reminiscent of other lists I had seen: The one Shirley had made about murders. The one I had made at the newspaper that mostly matched hers. The list was of people who had insurance policies during the time of the older version of Long Lincoln. There were some that came later. According to Mrs. Chandler, most of the people on the list were black families or poor whites, though not exclusively.

"The policies are to provide payouts to beneficiaries who lost people in the flood due to negligence or right-out malicious activity. They've been altered so the payouts, much of that money provided through different insurance companies under Jack Manley's insurance umbrella, don't go to the families at all. The other companies pay Jack Manley himself. It's hidden, and cleverly finagled, but that's who ends up with the money. Him and the council. Many of the policies were issued without the owners of the policies even knowing they had a policy."

"Damn."

"Yeah. The council owns this town.

"Discussions about how to do what they did are on the reels. Bouncing multiple insurance companies under Manley's umbrella."

"They stacked the deck."

"The gravy trickled through a few rocks before it got back to the council, but they were getting paid for the people they drowned, for policies they made up for dead people or people who would soon be dead. By their hands."

"No doubt in your mind the council is responsible for the deaths?"

"It's not about my mind. It's all in the files and on the reels."

"Son of a bitch," I said.

"I should have come forward, but I kept thinking that in the end, if I did, they'd be forging and cashing a new policy made out for me. I know how it sounds. But read the files, listen to the reels, and write your articles."

She left me there, except for bringing me fresh coffee from time to time. I spent a few hours reading, listening to reels, but finally, due to the heat, the dust, and the overwhelming mass of information, I had to climb out of there. I closed the place up and enjoyed sitting on the living-room couch for a moment taking in the cool conditioned air.

"What do you think?" Mrs. Chandler said.

"I think it's a real-life Gothic nightmare."

*   *   *

Upstairs I took a long hot shower and dressed and sat down at the typewriter and began to write up some of what I knew. A basic draft for my article. As I wrote it, I was overcome with this sense of unreality. How could this be?

And then something dark occurred to me. I hadn't seen any insurance policies with Mr. Candles's or Millie's names written on them, but what if those forged policies existed? What if they were in the wings? And maybe there was one on Ronnie. Maybe there was one for me.

I went downstairs and called Ronnie. Said I had some serious things to tell her. She was a little hesitant, like I might be asking for her hand in marriage.

"It has to do with the deaths Shirley talked about. And that can of worms you were worried I was opening that might actually be a nest of vipers."

"Oh?"

"It is a nest of vipers."

(33)

Driving to Ronnie's that night, as soon as I was away from the downtown lights, I could see ragged clouds blowing over the fragment of moon and the scattering of stars like wraiths.

In my eagerness to see Ronnie, I had left the house almost an hour early. I was adrenaline-fueled on what Mrs. Chandler had told me, the revelation that she was Natural Wilson, the information that she was dying of cancer. The stacks of papers, the reel-to-reel tapes sequestered behind that big block of a door and down under the floor in the Moonshine Castle had added to my nervousness.

Before I left to see Ronnie, I made sure the most important of the files were safe. I went to the Moonshine Castle and packed them and the reels into a couple of large plastic containers from downstairs. Then I went outside into the shadowed alley between the Chandler house and the Judson house. I peeked through a window into the Judson home. I couldn't see much. I tried the window. It was locked.

I went out to my car and got a flashlight out of the glove box and pushed it into my back pants pocket, grabbed the tire tool out of the trunk, went back and stuck the end of the tire tool under the window, and popped it up, breaking the latch. I pushed the window up, then put the tire tool back in the trunk.

In the Moonshine Castle, I grabbed one of the file boxes and toted it out. It was pretty heavy. I pushed it through the open window, and then, trying to look casual, I headed back to the house and grabbed the other container and did the same. After peeking in both directions, I determined no one was looking and climbed through the window.

I coughed some dust, pulled the flashlight from my back pocket, and used it to look around. I found a hall closet and opened it up. I wondered if this was the closet where Judson had shot himself. It just looked like a closet. No blood. No brains on the wall. The paint seemed old. I put the two boxes inside the closet, then slipped out the window and pulled it down.

I felt pretty clever. I hadn't taken all the files, but I had plenty, the best stuff. That was insurance, just in case someone did figure out the Moonshine Castle.

I was thinking about all of that when I arrived in the well-lit section of houses where Ronnie lived and parked at the curb. I thought I might sit there until it was time but then felt like an idiot. I decided to drive back into town and buy myself a soft drink, then motor on back. By that time, she would be expecting me.

Before I drove away, I noticed, due to her porch light, that a note was pinned to her door. I got out and went up the walk on cat feet and, in the light, read what the note said.

Danny. I called Mrs. Chandler, but she said you had left. There was a big accident out on Highway 59. I have been called out. I'm so sorry. I must cancel tonight. Such is the life of a policewoman. I know you said it was important. Forgive me. Call me tomorrow at the station. Ronnie

I won't lie and say I wasn't disappointed, but there was another part of me that felt okay with it. I was perhaps too wound up to be good company anyway, and it was possible I was worked up because Mrs. Chandler had worked me up. But the more I thought about what I had found, what Shirley discovered, what we knew about the bones, the more I believed I had in fact taken a can opener to a nest of vipers.

I took the note with me, and before long I was on my way to the lake. I wasn't sure why I was going there, but sometimes a drive could clear my head or line up an article in my subconscious so that it would come out of me with a near explosion of beating typewriter keys. I passed shapes of country houses with yellow glows in their windows that didn't make them seem warm and illuminated but made them appear more isolated, like luminescent fish in a great, deep ocean.

Finally, there were trees and no houses, just a clay road that became a two-tire rut, and that came to an end at the massive dead hole in the ground that was Moon Lake. Out there, there were no lights except my head beams. I cut those and sat with the motor on, the air-conditioning humming, my foot on the brake, the darkness gathering around me as clouds smothered the moon and the stars. It was like being in the belly of an anaconda.

My mind had so much debris floating around, I had forgotten to worry about that copper-colored car that I had seen before, but now there were headlights behind me. They lit up the inside of my car like a spotlight performance in a cheap bar.

I still had my foot on the brake, and in its red glow, by view of the mirror, I saw the car's lights go out and I could then identify that copper-colored car for sure, gently coated in brake-light red.

I didn't have room to turn around without going off the road into precarious areas of mud and brush, so I killed the engine, picked my ax handle out of the back seat, and climbed out of the car.

Me and my ax handle decided the best course of action might be to walk away swiftly, so I did, along a straight stretch toward the lake, then down a hill, then I turned along the shoreline, stepping swiftly and not very safely on the dark, brush-cluttered trail.

I heard car doors slam, and then I could hear the soft slide of shoes on clay behind me. At first the sound was slow and then it sped up, and so did I, struggling to identify the trail in front of me. I started to trot. I could hear them behind me, breathing loudly, nothing soft about their shoes now.

There was a crack in the sky, a rolling away of clouds, and in that temporary piece of dull light, I saw the trail had a split-off that went to the right and up a brushy hill, so I went that way. I made it just as the clouds regrouped and smothered the light. The air was as thick as wool socks.

I was making damn good time up that hill and thought I had outpaced them when I heard their breathing practically on me. Turning, I swung my ax handle, catching only the empty dark, and then the dark wasn't empty.

I could see two shapes clambering up toward me, one short and stocky, the other tall and lean. The short one had that white crap on his face again, and it glimmered greasy-wet even without much light. The other seemed a golem of tar and orange clown hair that had shifted to one side of his head. They had left their hats at home, though they were still wearing dark suits.

I took a backswing and the ax handle whistled through the air and caught the short one on the jaw as he was working his way up. I hit him so hard, I heard the change in his pants pocket rattle. He did a kind of backward frog leap and went tumbling down the hill in a cluster of clay dust.

That's when the tall one made his lunge. I swung again. I connected alongside his neck with a meaty sound that jarred the ax handle and sent vibrations all the way up my arms and into my shoulders. He fell over on his side like a plank someone had dropped.

The stout white-faced one was up again, using his hands to help him scramble up the hill. I broke and ran, but they had both recovered enough to chase me, and it didn't take long before they were on me.

I went facedown under a tackle from behind. The ax handle flew from my hand, and fists began to clobber me in the kidneys. I managed to roll out from under my main attacker a little, enough to see it was white-face. I swung a fist and it caught him under the ear.

He grunted. I could feel him grow weak on top of me. I bucked up my body, and off he toppled, went rolling down the hill like a log. The tall one was still in play, and he was kicking my head football-style. I tried covering up with my arms. Then the tall one appeared to jump backward into the air, and I heard him scream. A shadowy shape only a little smaller than a rhinoceros in platform shoes stood over me. I couldn't tell much about him besides his size, but it was obvious he had nabbed my attacker by the back of the neck and thrown him backward into the night like he'd been made of pipe cleaners. The wig the goon had been wearing spun off his head and fled into the night like an alien spider.

The thing that walked like a man grabbed me and swung me over his head and settled me on his back, where I clung like a baby monkey, my arms around his pillar of a neck, my legs around the barrel of his body. Then, with me riding piggyback-style, away we went, faster than seemed possible. My rhinoceros continued up the hill, smashing us through brush that scraped me and him, but if he was bothered, he didn't let on. By the time we reached the top of the hill, I was feeling sick from having been knocked about and also due to the fact that my rescuer smelled like donkey shit under a heat lamp.

Just to maintain the tone of the night, it started to rain with vicious intensity.

The rhino wore a too-small suit coat, and he pulled a flashlight from one of its pockets and turned it on. It was a heavy, rubber-coated thing and the light showed lines of rain in its beam. What it was pointing at was a split between two large trees. In that split was a vine-covered red-clay hill with a patch of lichen-coated concrete in the side of it. To know it was there, you would have really had to be looking for it.

Big man grabbed one of my arms, swung me off his back as if I were a swizzle stick, and pushed me through the split in the trees against the concrete slab. The great slab moved, and when it did, it revealed a slice of deeper darkness than the night.

He poked the flashlight in there. I could see a bit of dust moving around. A foul odor climbed out of the gap. A lot of uncomfortable ideas crossed my mind. Big man grabbed me by the shirt and yanked me inside. He heaved the slab of door to, and with the flashlight in one hand, he threw a big metal bolt lock with the other. It made a heavy clacking sound, securing the door in place.

The rhino grunted, pointed the light into the darkness. There was a short flight of slime-covered concrete stairs that led down into a run of scummy water that looked no less inviting than the river Styx. The smell had grown so bad by now, it made his personal aroma seem like French perfume.

He poked the light at the stairs a couple of times, made a noise in his throat like gargling glass.

Taking the hint, I started down them, careful as I went.

(34)

Down in the stink, the big man moved swiftly and I followed his bobbing flashlight, assuming now that the person who had saved and was leading me was none other than Flashlight Boy, though there was nothing boyish about him. He was no longer the strange young man who had leaned over the old bridge looking down on me and Ronnie and Mr. Candles. He was part of the forest and the lake and the drowned world.

The tunnel was long and we splashed through a trickle of water and then went up some steps and into a wider tunnel that turned off to the left. As we went, I saw there were other tunnels now and again. Many had been bricked over and a few of them leaked water, but the flashlight only touched on them and then moved on, so my evaluation of them wasn't the best. The flashlight swung back and forth, but it was clear to me that he could have found his way around down there without that light.

We came to another tunnel that opened wide enough for a train to have gone through. Flashlight Boy began to move swiftly about, and then there was illumination. The light came from flashlights hanging from metal spikes in the wall and from sagging metal racks and some were tied on strings that were fastened to exposed rebars in the ceiling. He went from flashlight to flashlight, and soon the room was bright enough to perform heart surgery.

There was an old panel truck sitting in the middle of the big room, and the slats that had made up the panels in the back had collapsed. What little remained of them appeared to be held together by nothing more than the stink of the tunnel. The truck was mostly rust, and the tires were gone. It rested on corroding wheel rims.

There wasn't a trickle of water running through the raised center of this section, but it still had a dampness to it, and the walls were coated in a velvety-green moss. Rats squeaked by us as Flashlight Boy moved about. In some of the old racks were the remains of large barrels. What was left of them were rotting staves and the rusting metal bands that had held them together.

In the light, I could see Flashlight Boy clearly. His face was dirty white with a nose that appeared to have been broken at some point and healed crooked. His cheeks, chin, and forehead had lots of scars and some fresh scratches from going through the brush. I was pretty cut up myself.

He was wearing under that black suit coat a blousy, pull-over blue shirt stuffed into too-short black pants with cloth so thin at the knees you could see his flesh. The zipper was sprung on the pants, and I could see the blue shirt through the gap there. He had on big shoes that were stuffed with cloth and paper that poked out of the sides. His teeth were not in good shape and appeared to have the same moss on them that covered the walls. He was built like a block of concrete on legs, with a head that sat almost neckless on shoulders wide as a beer truck. His hands were the size of lunch boxes with fingers. When he looked at me, he smiled his greenery, and the light from the flashlights made his eyes appear unearthly, like he was by birth an underground denizen.

Now the rats were gathering and moving toward him. They climbed on him and made a coat of themselves from shoulders to ankles. They clung and squeaked; some went into the pockets of his coat or under it to who knows where. He took one in his hand and petted it. It was an unnerving and beautiful sight simultaneously.

I prowled around in my memory for the name Mr. Candles had called him that night, and I found it.

"Winston," I said.

He leaned forward and looked at me. It was as if he were processing and translating the word from English to some other unknown language and back to English. A noise came out of his mouth, but it wasn't a word. It was loud. His rat coat abandoned him with an explosion of squeaks, hit the floor, and ran off into the darkness beyond our well-lit section. Winston may not have been able to speak or maybe he was out of practice, but he nodded his head. My saying his name seemed to energize him.

There were concrete shelves built out from the walls between the racks. On the shelves were hundreds of what we used to call tins. Containers for things like fruitcakes and assorted nuts. He had found them over the years, I suspected. He took one and opened it. What was in it was a foul-smelling odor and chunk of something brown. He scooped it out and poked it into his mouth and chomped it. It was food he had scavenged, and I was glad I didn't know what it was. He held the tin toward me. I looked inside. More of the same. He grunted, and I shook my head.

Pushing the lid onto the tin, he studied me with suspicion, then leaned in close to me as if to examine my face for some sort of message. He was so close I could smell his breath, could damn near see it. It smelled like sour milk, moldy leather, and damp newspapers with just a hint of dead animal. But that was all right; the rest of him still smelled like donkey business.

He set the tin aside and opened others, showing me his treasures, which included more food, lots of flashlight batteries, pins and rubber bands, screws and marbles and all manner of gewgaws, even a scratched-up I LIKE IKE badge and some baseball cards, including a Mickey Mantle that looked as if it had at one time been pinned to bicycle spokes to make an engine sound when the wheels rolled.

Once again, he grabbed me and pulled me along and flicked on more flashlights and gave the tunnel even more light. He showed me treasures hanging from sticks and string that had been made into hangers of a sort. These were dirty, rat-chewed suits and shoes and white shirts turned yellow, men's dress ties, all black. There was a blue robe hanging on a wire rack that was fastened into the wall. I recognized it immediately and a hot chill, like dry ice, shot through me. It was a burial robe and it had been there for a while. And now where the suits and shirts and shoes and ties came from became obvious.

Even as I put it together, Winston grabbed me again and dragged me along through a dark gap in the wall, eased in ahead of me, and turned on the flashlights there. The room was smaller than the one we had been in, and there were a lot of barrel remains and neat stacks of bones and some skeletons that were mostly held together by leathery strings of viscera and sheets of darkened flesh that looked like ancient beef jerky. One of the skeletons was wearing a rat-chewed fedora and a shirt that had become part of his flesh. A black tie with a silver tie clip was pinned to the shirt.

All those bones we had found, the fragments of burial shrouds, what he was wearing—it was clear now who had dug them up and taken them away to use for himself on some future day. And he had been at it for a long time, and most likely all these had come from a variety of cemeteries when the one up the hill was played out.

One piece of the mystery explained.

(35)

It was cool down there and my nose had acclimated to the smell, and though my body still hurt, the throbbing had passed.

I was worried Flashlight Boy might see himself as a kind of Batman and me as his newly acquired sidekick, Ass-Beaten Boy, and here in the rat or bat cave, depending on choice of name, we would dwell forever.

We were sitting on concrete blocks that jutted out of the wall, him across from me, his mouth sagging open, full of that ugly greenery, studying me like a cut of meat at a butcher shop. I was studying him as well, keeping it friendly with smiles. He had, after all, saved my life. I remembered the story I had heard about him being bullied, about those football players Mr. Candles had mentioned. Because of how he was treated, maybe he felt I was being bullied by those two clowns and had come out of the dark and saved me. I had no doubt he was proud of himself. I was proud of him too. Had it not been for him, I might well be in a shallow grave in the midst of a dry Moon Lake, waiting for the water to come back, cover me over, and forever hold me down.

Though this was our first up-close meeting, Winston had been around me a lot; maybe he even recognized me. That light I had seen the night of the deep-water plunge, him on the bridge, and then the flashlight beam moving through the shadowed woods the day Ronnie found the other bones.

I was trying to figure how some of his bone collection had ended up in the car trunks while we sat there looking at each other. I didn't come up with any answers. But it was obvious to me that this was part of the tunnels that had been built during Prohibition, the ones Mr. Candles talked about. It had been an ambitious project indeed, but the liquor business then had been lucrative enough to warrant it. This room had stored barrels and even contained trucks for hauling across the South and maybe beyond. Trucks like the broken-down one in the other room.

I took a chance and pointed to a large corridor that led off from where we were. Winston leaned forward when I said, "Over there?"

He grabbed the flashlight that was on the concrete block beside him, sprang up suddenly, dislodging a few rats that had been trying to climb back on him, rapidly came across the gap between us, grabbed me up, and started pulling me toward the dark gap where I had pointed.

Me and him were the best of pals.

*   *   *

The corridor was dark, and his light was like an enormous firefly. Flashlight Boy moved so rapidly, I had to be on my game to keep up with him. He was fast as the rats who loved him, and they squeaked along in the dark as we went. Roaches blackened the floor of the tunnel and the walls, some of them damn near big enough to own a motorcycle.

Water reentered the picture as we bounced down some stairs and along a wet, mossy trail that led to who knew where. I wasn't sure I was glad I had asked about what was down this dark tunnel.

There was some debris in places, mostly barrel staves where the goods had been stored or perhaps at some point abandoned. Then we were going upstairs again, and finally we came to a wall and our progress stopped.

Flashlight Boy, Winston, turned and put the flashlight in my face so that all I could see was that blinding light. Then he snapped the light off, wheeled, and put his shoulder against the wall.

The wall screeched slightly and moved. When it moved there was faint illumination that oozed into the darkness, and then we were in a massive cellar, and in the cellar were rows of racks stacked with bottles and barrels. Spiderwebs, cobwebs, and dust coated the goods. A few rats came out of the tunnel and ran between our feet and among the barrels.

Winston took off his damp, muddy shoes, and, copying him, so did I. We left them on the dark side of the tunnel. Obviously, Winston wasn't going to win a spelling bee or a job teaching calculus, but he was shrewd in his own way. He had experience in this kind of business, and being here appeared to be something he had done numerous times.

As we stood in the center of the room, I saw the source of the light was a block-style window high up—built just aboveground was my guess—and the light was artificial. It couldn't be late enough, or early enough, to be sunup. Across the way was a big double wooden door with big pull rings on it. I went over there and out of curiosity pulled at one of the rings. The hinges were well greased and the door came open. Inside was a large room full of trucks and cars, wheelbarrows, gardening tools, and automotive parts. A garage and storage area, obviously, and a well-furnished one. The automobiles and trucks looked as new and shiny as a child's first Christmas.

I pushed the door shut. I turned and looked up.

There were some stout stairs that led up to a platform perched before another large door. Winston grabbed my shoulder in a viselike clutch and propelled me to the base of the stairs, stopped there, and put a finger to his lips.

Then up the stairs he went, and I followed. He put his ear to the door and listened. From the platform, I could see out the small, square window. I saw a light on a pole. It was the source of the slice of dusty yellow light in the cellar.

Gently, Winston opened the door. When he did, the air turned fresh, cool, and crisp. It was softly lit in there; the lights glowed along a lengthy, white-tiled hallway that blinked with polish. There were a lot of photos on the walls, and at the far end of the hall was a wide and tall mahogany door with a big black handle on it.

I didn't have to figure on where we were at all.

We were inside the Long Lincoln Country Club.

(36)

When I had been living with my aunt for a couple years, me and some kids I shouldn't have been running with, a group of boys already prepping for their future arrest photos and a series of warrants, broke into a big washateria in downtown Tyler, Texas.

It was night and there was no one around, and it was easy. A back window slid up and we went inside. The floor was smooth tile like the tile in the country club's hallway. The washers and dryers were like big, stout, polished cannons.

It occurred to me in some strange way then that all the people that came there came with dirty laundry and a pocketful of quarters to wash away dirt and blood and, in some cases, social sins that had stuck to their clothes. A wife's dress with semen on it, semen that didn't belong to her husband. Blood on a man's shirt that was due to a fight, maybe even a murder, perhaps of the wife with the wrong semen on her dress. Shit in undies from too many fresh vegetables or a touch of ptomaine, sweat of hardworking people, spittle and urine, clothes worn by the prosperous, the blue-collar slogger, the dignified, and the insane.

I imagined I could feel all the people that had worn those clothes. Their ghosts filled the air, or at least they filled my head, and it made me sick to realize how fragile we were as human beings. I didn't really understand that feeling right then; it was just this uncomfortable sensation I experienced in the moment. I turned and went out the window, and that was the end of my association with my hoodlum friends. I ran out into the night and all the way home. I showered for a long time, hot and soapy, until I felt almost clean.

I'm sure there were good stains and good dreams in those clothes as well, love and affection, peanut butter from enjoyed sandwiches, fabric containing stains made by happiness and the best of intentions, but over time I came to feel what I had sensed in my hoodlum moment was the knowledge that humans were a pitiful and, in the greater scheme of things, insignificant lot.

That awareness scared me, made me soul-sick. The feeling would pass eventually, but sometimes on dark nights when I thought of my father, it came back. His ghost was their ghost, and we were all pitiful. Even those powerful assholes in the photos on the country-club wall were not free of it.

There were photos that had been taken at different times in their lives. In some they were young, in others middle-aged, and some of the photos were more recent. No matter what age they were, in a way they always looked the same. Smug and arrogant, eyes like glass beads, sour manipulators, small-town royalty with golf carts and permanent memberships to the country club.

The door at the end of the hall was opened by Winston and we stepped into a ballroom of enormous size in height and circumference. It was brightly painted with lots of lights and lots of tables, all of them stacked against the wall, one on top of the other. Only a few of the lights were on, and the others awaited the touch of a finger to illuminate them. There was, of all things, a disco ball in the center of the ceiling. I found it hard to imagine the members of the city council getting down to Donna Summer or the Bee Gees, considering their current age.

Winston seemed excited about his position as tour guide. He hustled me through another door and into a room not as big as the ballroom but still impressive. In the center of the room was an obsidian-black triangular table. There were three seats on two of the sides, one at the broad end, and no chair at the point of the triangle. On a raised dais was a tall chair with an ornately designed back and a large hole on either side of the headrest.

I walked around the table, looking at it, running my hand over it. It was a large chunk of wood, and it had been polished smooth as a baby's bottom. The chairs were made of wood too, but with soft cushions in their seats and other cushions hung on their backs.

On the walls were bookshelves that ran around the room in a horseshoe shape, and there was a ladder for rows of books near the ceiling, which was high. The shelves were filled with thick tomes. No airplane reading there. There were a series of tall, curtained windows on one side where there were no bookshelves.

More interesting were paintings on the wall of nude men and women, and it took me a moment to recognize, due to having seen photos when they were young, that they were of the city council's big three when they were young. They were tasteful in a carnival painting kind of way. Kate Conroy had been a looker in her early days, if the painting of her didn't lie. She still had those cold button eyes, though.

There was one set of closed cabinets behind the chair on the dais. I opened them and stepped back at what I saw. It was crude and made of scorched-black wood. It was like a totem, two feet high and crudely carved, a piece of creosote post that had been whacked into a squatting statue with wide, flat feet, knees spread, arms tucked between its legs, hands holding an erect oversize penis. Its face had been sculpted so that it had a wide smile full of black pointed teeth, and the eyes were almost like skull sockets, but deep within them were little red pupils that looked like chinaberries but were blobs of red paint. The ears were large and donkey-shaped. Its nose was long and had crude nostrils drilled into it. So this was Creosote Johnny. It was simultaneously silly and disturbing. I took hold of it. It was heavy and you could smell where the wood had once been scorched and you could smell the creosote as well. I felt as if I were handling a venomous reptile.

I turned it in my hands. On the back of it were a lot of small marks in several rows, like someone had been keeping score of something.

Winston came up behind me and thumped the penis and made that gargling-glass sound he used for a laugh. It startled me. I carefully put the statue back and closed the cabinet doors. I wiped my slightly black-smudged hands on my pants and took a deep breath of refrigerated air.

Winston led me to a locked door and did something with a key he had gotten from somewhere, most likely lifted at one time from this very facility. He jiggled the lock, opened the door, and switched on a light. There were chairs all around the room, a couple of velvet couches that looked as if they had been stolen from a Jane Austen novel, a long table between the couches, and some large cushions on the floor. The room swirled with dust and there were cobwebs in the corners; it looked not to have been used in ages.

Behind the chairs, many of them facing the walls, were metal file cabinets. They were large cabinets built into the walls, and each had little paper markings in slots on the file drawers. Every paper slip had a year written on it. They went back for many years, long before anyone on the council today could have been involved. I tugged on a few of the file drawers, but they were locked up tight.

This place gave the vibe of being more a lair than a country club.

I thought there might be more to see, but my guide was all out of enthusiasm, and truth to tell, I was feeling spooked.

Winston turned out the light, grabbed me by the sleeve, and yanked me in the direction we had come. We ended up in the beer and wine cellar damn quick.

Winston had left the door open. We slipped in there, and he pulled the section shut, careful to save his fingers. It fit tight enough that it would be easy not to know the wall entrance was there.

With his light on, Winston led the way until we reached his inner sanctum with the stolen funeral clothes, the rotting food, the hordes of rats, and the disintegrating truck.

It seemed in some way nicer there than in the country club. I felt as if I had escaped the confines of hell.

(37)

I hung out there for a time because I wasn't sure I could walk off without Winston unscrewing my head from my neck. I was trying to read the situation carefully before I made what could be a fatal false move.

Winston sat across from me as before, with his mouth open, and in all those flashlight beams, I could see that half his tongue was gone. It looked to me like it had been cut out, or perhaps it was a birth defect. His rats were crawling on him, making a carpet of squeaking gray fur. A few of them were gathering around my feet. I gently toed them away.

Winston couldn't carry on a conversation, and I wasn't in the mood for one even if he could have. In time, I decided to find out if his level of understanding was greater than it seemed. I said, "Winston. You dug up graves for those clothes, right?"

He pondered my words like a dog that had been asked to perform a certain trick it hadn't done in a long time.

He nodded.

I was putting more and more of what I had seen down there together. The bones stolen from the graves had to lead to the car trunks. Had something to do with that lock being put on the gate. I took a flier. "Did you ever put bodies or bones in car trunks?"

He gave this question less consideration. He nodded.

I didn't know how to ask a man who couldn't speak why he'd done that or how the cars ended up in the lake. There was no way for him to explain, but that didn't keep me from trying.

"I was wondering why," I said.

He looked down and shook his head. Then he rolled on his side and pulled his knees to his chest. He was demonstrating what seemed to be the position of the bones in the car trunks.

I sat awhile longer, then finally stood up. "I need to go, Winston. Thank you for protecting me and showing me your world. But I need to go."

His mood changed. His eyes narrowed as if he had stepped out into bright sunlight. He ran a finger across his throat, then put it to his lips.

"No. I won't tell where you are if you want to be left alone."

He nodded and grunted. I hoped that was an agreement.

Picking up his flashlight, he stood so fast he shed quite a few rats. He started for the tunnel that we had used to enter his sanctuary. I followed him, which, like before, took some work. He was swift and knew the small geography of his world quite well.

By the time we came to the exit, I could feel my blood sugar dropping like an anvil off the Empire State Building. When we came to the door, he threw the latch, pushed it open, and let the wet night come in. He grabbed me by the shoulder and with no more effort than it takes to remove a dust mote from a windowsill, set me outside in the rain.

I held up my hand in a "stop" motion, then reached into my pocket and took out the knife Mr. Candles had given me, the one with everything on it but a tommy gun and a concrete drill. I gave it to him. It seemed like a small thing I could do for being rescued and shown the inner workings of the Long Lincoln Country Club.

He examined the knife under his flashlight, then looked at me and smiled. Without so much as a grunt or a lingering fart for me to pass the time with, he closed the door and left me there. He seemed a firm believer in having a time limit for guests.

It was still night. It was still raining.

Typical.

The night was so dark I couldn't see which way to go, so I leaned against the concrete lichen-covered door and let my eyes adjust a bit. I was successful enough with that to at least see the brush-lined rain-beaten trail we had used to arrive at the door.

I carefully started down the trail, eventually coming to the spot where Winston had tossed the tall man. The man was gone. So was his clown hair. The stocky man was gone as well. I looked around and found my ax handle.

Using it like a cane, I worked my way back to my car, saw that the tires had been slashed.

No harsh notes had been left under my windshield wiper. In fact, they had twisted the wipers off. They were sore losers and held a grudge.

Their car was gone.

I unlocked my ride and sat behind the wheel for a moment. Then, metaphorically girding my loins, I got out and started walking back toward New Long Lincoln in the dead dark and the pounding rain.

(38)

It was a long, hard, wet walk for a hungry man whose blood sugar was in the basement, but I kept at it. The rain grew in intensity and made things darker, so the flashlight wasn't doing me a lot of good. I was glad for the ax handle to support me and give me a mild sense of security.

Most likely, though, way I felt, if the duo came back, I'd be easy as cake. They'd take the ax handle from me, shove it up my ass, and leave me gathering flies and ants in the bushes.

I watched carefully for headlights and listened for sounds of thugs coming out of the bushes or leaping from trees, because by that time I was paranoid to the max.

The rain thinned a little but not before I was soaked to the bone and had covered a few miles with water squeaking like Winston's rats in my shoes.

Then it was like someone exploded a silent strawberry bomb. There were streaks of red light against the dark sky. The light widened and the dark shrank, and abruptly it was morning. In short time, the strawberry sky began to turn the color of a lemon. Birds began to sing. I felt like I was in a Disney movie.

The rain continued to wane. The air was beginning to toast, and little clouds of steam rose up from the ground. When I arrived at the edge of town, Buck Rogers and his tow truck came by, stopped, and waited on me. When I caught up to it, he reached over and rolled the window down on the passenger side.

"You look like you been run over by a truck, then maybe mistreated by wildlife."

"I feel like it. I think I can give you some business, by the way."

"Well, hop in."

"I'm soaking."

"Plastic seat covers. You're fine. That's an ax handle you have there, is it not?"

"Observant. May it ride too?"

"I got nothing against ax handles."

"You're out early," I said.

"Towed a car this morning. Someone ran into a tree last night. On my way to colored town for breakfast."

I told him where I needed to go; did he mind taking me? He didn't. I told him where my car was; could he tow it? He could. I asked about tires. He said he most likely had some that would fit at his garage.

"I'll pay you when you're done," I said.

"No troubles. I was wondering, I mean, I know the black/white thing would probably mean it isn't happening, you know, the stigma, but I'm thinking you and Ronnie looked pretty cozy out there the other day."

"She told me you used to date her."

"Yeah, and I'd like to again."

"She told me you liked the women pretty good."

"Don't you?"

"Not more than one at a time, and I mean only one relationship at a time."

"You are evolved."

"You sound like you might have gone somewhere other than high school."

"College up north for a while. They call us Negroes up there when they know we're listening. At least here, I know where I stand."

"That bad, huh?"

"Jim Crow rides in the back now, but he still gets plenty of trips around town and rests his forearms on the back of the driver's seat. I can see his very white face in the rearview mirror."

"You got that car imagery going," I said.

"Deal with cars day in and day out, it's easy to have that connection. They call it a metaphor, Danny."

"Do they now?"

"Twice today and four times on Sunday."

"What do you know about New Long Lincoln's city council?"

"Curious question."

"I'm a curious guy."

He looked at me out of the corner of his eye. "You thinking of running for mayor or any other city-big-ass position, you're not getting out of the chute on that one. Way they get voted in is they don't. Unless you count three votes between them, for each other, and that means one vote for themselves."

"I know that much. I'm just looking for certainty."

"They're self-appointed assholes so old you'd think they'd have died by now, but they're like fucking Boris Karloff in *The Mummy*. They're sturdy. Have the constitutions of cockroaches. Back to what matters to me more than the city council. About Ronnie?"

"I like her."

"How much?"

"A lot."

"How does she feel about you?"

"I get the impression she likes me too. And about the black/white thing, I don't give a shit."

"I was hoping you did."

"I bet. No hard feelings."

"Bullshit," he said and smiled.

(39)

It was still raining when we got to the Chandler house and Buck let me out.

"Save the galaxy," I said before I closed the door.

"I'm waiting for the day where no one makes a Buck Rogers joke."

"Today won't be that day."

"I suppose it won't."

As he drove off, I went up the steps with my ax handle, with which I was developing a close and loving relationship. I felt as if we had moved beyond the courting stage and perhaps a ring was in order.

I took off my shoes and socks and left them on the porch. When I went inside, Mrs. Chandler was sitting on the couch. She had a nice silver coffee service on the coffee table in front of her. She had her finger through a little hole in a coffee-cup handle and was raising the cup to her lips. She lowered it and gave me an expression that told me I looked as bad as I thought I did.

Good Lord, she looked to have worsened since I saw her last. She looked as if her spirit were slowly dissolving and her bones were collapsing. Hours before, she had pretty much seemed like herself.

"I wondered where you were this morning," she said, "but from the looks of you, I'm going to say you've been out."

"To put it mildly. Let me change, and I'll tell you."

"Please do, and when you finish, I'll have a mop for you to use in the hallway."

"Fair enough," I said.

I went upstairs and took a couple of aspirin from my shaving kit, popped them in my mouth, and then ran water into my cupped hand and used that as a chaser.

I looked at myself in the mirror. My head was swollen and one ear had ballooned up at the bottom. My eyes made me look like an earnest raccoon. The expression on my face made me think of a man who'd decided to jump out of an airplane at ten thousand feet without a parachute and hope for the best on the way down.

I took a shower in water so hot I almost scalded myself. I combed my hair and clipped a few nose hairs, got dressed, and went downstairs in sock feet.

The mop and pail with soapy water were waiting on me. I nodded at Mrs. Chandler and mopped up my mess, hurting all over as I did. I took the water outside and dumped it on the lawn, left the mop and bucket on the concrete porch. I brought my socks and shoes inside and put them on the bottom step of the stairs.

I moseyed into the living room like I didn't hurt anywhere near as bad as I felt and sat on the couch. I had to do that gingerly so my innards wouldn't fall out. Mrs. Chandler poured me a cup of coffee.

"Same friends?" she said.

"Same ones. My, how they've grown. I also made a new friend. He's six five, at least, and larger than the frontier. He can't talk, because part of his tongue is gone, and he lives out there in the woods around the lake and underground with rats and rotting beer barrels, and he steals a lot of flashlights."

I had already broken my word to Winston about not saying anything about our little visit, but truth was, after the night I'd had, I needed someone to talk to, and Mrs. Chandler was it.

"Do you mean poor Winston?" she said.

"He sided with me when my original friends decided to kick my head in."

"I wasn't even sure he was still alive. He's young enough to be alive, but the way he lives, I'd have thought they would have found him dead in the old junkyard by now."

"Why the old junkyard?" I said.

"His father worked there for the original owner. As a child, he used to hang out there all the time. He wasn't too bright, bless his heart. Bert told me Winston liked to play in the cars up there. He's actually rather mechanical-minded, or he was when he was a child. Now the only mechanical thing he might do is put batteries in a flashlight."

"He has a lot of flashlights."

"Steals them, batteries too, food from houses when he can. A few little colorful things that catch his fancy. He's stealthy, seldom seen. He's become a kind of legend. Some people think he's made up, like Bigfoot. But he's no legend. He can get into anywhere, like a rat, and out before anyone knows it."

Winston certainly knew rats. Maybe they had given him a few breaking-and-entering tips. "Is he mechanical enough to repair old cars and put bones in the car trunks and drive them off into the lake?"

"That's quite a question."

"Well?"

"Cars up there now can't be repaired without parts and money. Most of them probably can't be repaired with money, they been there that long. But back in the day, yes. His father wouldn't let him learn to drive. Feared he was too simpleminded, but he wasn't, really. Just sort of strange and antisocial, subject to moods."

"What happened to his tongue?"

"I don't know when that happened, but I knew it happened. Some say his father did it to stop him from crying when he was young, but that could be an apocryphal story.

"Winston would fix up old cars in the junkyard and steal them. He'd go joyriding. And if they didn't run, he'd push them down the hill and drive them into a tree or some such just for the hell of it.

"Poor boy wasn't right in the head. Bert told me that Winston took a grown-man beating when his father caught up to him. Said he was there one time on council business, getting parts for a truck or some such, when the kid got a whipping. I think Bert thought seeing the kid getting held by the collar and taking a beating with a belt was funny. Bert was the kind of guy that would laugh at an autopsy of his own mother. Winston would take lickings, and then his father would lock him up in a car trunk as punishment. Leave him there overnight. It was like being in an oven in the summer, a refrigerator in the winter. Bert said the kid learned to like it. A metal womb."

All of a sudden, Winston stealing clothes from graves, then putting the dead's remains in car trunks and driving or pushing them off into the water made sense. I understood the source of his ritual. I also understood why Mrs. Chandler pushed Bert downstairs.

"How could the law let that happen?"

"They didn't let it happen; it just happened. Winston's old man didn't care about the law. He was friends with the city council because he fixed their cars for free. They helped him out in return in a variety of ways. Back in Prohibition, he was a mechanic on their trucks. He got a free ride from the law. Law is where you buy it. That way then, that way now."

"Chief Dudley in on all that too?"

"I think he tries to do right. But they can keep him from doing certain things if they decide to. They have tentacles in everything. He kind of has to go along to get along, I suppose. And then there's that blackmail business. Poor Dudley. He and Duncan are just trying to be happy. In this town, rape would come second to merely being different in that kind of way."

I thought then of the murders Shirley had discovered. I didn't see Winston doing that, and I didn't feel they were connected to him in any way. Winston was trying to survive. He was even a protector. He had damn sure saved my bacon.

"You look rough," Mrs. Chandler said. "I'll make some fresh coffee, some toast, because I'm not cooking anything serious. After you eat, I've something to tell you."

*   *   *

By this time, I was sick from hunger and exertion on top of not sleeping all night and having had my body tenderized like hamburger steak. I drank the coffee she gave me and had four pieces of toast with butter and strawberry jam. My blood sugar settled, but the coffee didn't stimulate me at all. Normally, as many cups as I drank would have wired me to the point of being able to enter a jitterbug contest and win.

"You look a bit more alive," she said. "Maybe you should go to the doctor."

"My bones aren't moving in odd directions, so I think I'll be all right. What I need is rest. And then I'm going to write this Sunday's article. You said you had something to tell me."

"Estelle, the cutie librarian. She called and said they want to see you. Want you to meet them at the library at three thirty."

"I'm not sure I want to do that."

"One way or another, you'll have to deal with them. May I again suggest leaving town?"

"Estelle didn't say something like 'Come alone,' did she?"

"No. She said come. Like it was an order to be obeyed. I can help you pack."

"I'm going to see them, and I'm going to see if Ronnie will go with me."

"They don't respect the law in this town. They can get around it on most anything."

"Yeah, but Ronnie has a gun."

"One moment."

Mrs. Chandler got up, went to a closet between the living room and the kitchen, opened it up, pulled out a cardboard box, brought it over. She placed it on the coffee table.

She opened the box. Inside was a cloth wrapped around something. She opened that and I could see a shiny snub-nosed revolver with a handful of shells. "You might want to have this for yourself."

"I don't like guns."

"And the city council doesn't like you. I doubt you'll need it, but when the law isn't the law, you might."

"I don't think I'll be having a shoot-out in the library, but I'd like Ronnie there. She at least represents the law."

"I keep telling you, Danny. There is no law."

*   *   *

I called the station for Ronnie, said it was an emergency. They said they'd look for her. I had no more than hung up the phone and was halfway upstairs when it rang.

I skipped back down and answered. It was her.

"I know you're on duty, but if you could see your way clear to come by and pick me up at three thirty, take me to the library, that would be a relief for me. I don't have a car right now. I'll tell you about it on the way there."

"You called me, said it was an emergency, so you can go check out a book."

"I have been asked—that's the polite word—to meet with the city council there."

"They only come out, like the groundhog, now and again, so that's something, and maybe not a good something."

"That's why I want you there. You're the law."

There was brief silence before Ronnie said, "I'll be by at three fifteen."

Upstairs, I locked my door and put a chair under the knob for insurance, just in case the city council decided to send my buddies all freshly greased up in face paint to finish off what they had tried to do at the lake.

I went to the bathroom and found my aspirin and palmed some water from the faucet and swallowed a few of them. When I looked in the mirror this time, I didn't so much look like a man about to jump out of an airplane without a chute anymore. I looked like a man who had already jumped.

I set my alarm clock, which until now I hadn't even removed from my suitcase, for 2:00 p.m., closed the blinds, and then, naked, climbed under the sheets.

I felt a little feverish, like my skin had been stretched too tight and that something was inside the knots on my head trying to work its way out with a hammer and chisel.

Even in pain, I went to sleep. But I dreamed.

Dreamed about Winston and his tunnel full of rats. Dreamed about those cold, plastic-looking faces in the photographs on the wall of the country club. The nude paintings.

The council leaned forward from the frames and looked at

me. They began to climb out of the photos and paintings, flop to the floor in my little room. There were multiples of them. On their bellies, they slithered toward me like serpents, leaving slimy snail trails behind them. Their mouths were open. They had dripping fangs.

I was too tired to give a damn.

Even when my father showed up on the edge of my bed and looked at them and they crawled away, I wasn't particularly moved. I found him a confusing figure even in death.

I hadn't met anyone in this town the right age to have known him or my mother or my aunt. My family seemed as if they were ghosts long before they were dead.

PART FOUR
HOW THEY GOT HUNGRY

The moon, the moon,
They danced by the light of the moon.
                    —Edward Lear, "The Owl and
                                the Pussy-Cat"

The truest things are often outright silly.
                    —Anonymous

(40)

I awoke to the alarm, and by the time I had turned it off, I was thinking more clearly.

I didn't really need it, but I took another hot shower to keep my body lubricated and to warm my brain. The warmer it got, the more my brain thought the right answer was to pick up my car at the garage and go home. If it wasn't ready, maybe I should take a bus.

That thought didn't go away, but I pushed it to the back of my feelings, got dressed, did the aspirin trick again, and at three fifteen picked out the more attractive of the ax handles and went downstairs.

I didn't see Mrs. Chandler and decided not to bother her. With the worries she had, way she must have felt, she might be taking a nap.

I thought about the gun in the closet but stuck to my decision not to take it. Truth was, I had shot a gun only a few times in my life and was more likely to shoot my dick off than hurt someone else. Besides, how nasty could three octogenarians be?

Nasty as the help they hired. Who said there would only be them? Still, I didn't get the gun.

When I stepped outside, the rain had passed, but the clouds were threatening more, and I could see webs of lightning behind them, and hear distant thunder.

Ronnie was already parked at the curb in her cruiser. I climbed in and she said, "Let me start with I've missed you."

"You too."

"My God, what happened to your head?"

"You're going to love this story."

"Before I hear it——" She leaned over and we kissed quickly. It wasn't anything fancy, but it felt good. On the drive over I capsulized my adventures. I violated my promise to Winston again, told her the location of his hideout. I told her about the materials from Mrs. Chandler, that the most important of them were stashed in the trunk of my car. I left out the part about how I feared for Ronnie's parents. I would save that for when I could take more time to explain.

She listened as she drove, giving me the sort of sideways glance you might give someone who had arrived at a formal wedding wearing a rabbit costume with a hole in the ass end.

"So, two men in disguises in a copper-colored Ford chased you down to the lake, and Flashlight Boy saved you. He lives underground with rats and clothes from graves, and you and him went prowling inside the country club by a secret entrance?"

"Sums it up. Also, did I mention he's the one putting the bones in the cars and that Shirley was right when it comes to ritual, how it's connected to life experience?"

"You left that part out."

"That little ritual doesn't include the bones in my father's Buick. That part I'm not so sure about. The murders are separate too."

"It sounds like a Gothic gumbo."

"Yep. Oh, there's a creosote god named Johnny involved as well."

"What the hell, Danny?"

"Know how it sounds, but I think I know now what goes on in the clubhouse, how it's connected to the murders. But I need to check something first before I lay that out. I could be letting my imagination run away with me."

"I hope you are."

"So do I."

We were already at the library. There was a big black car parked outside, but no copper-colored Ford.

When we got to the glass door there was a Closed sign on it, and there was shadowy movement behind it. The lock clicked, and Estelle let us in. She was dressed in a baby-duck-yellow dress and matching high heels and her hair was almost the color of her dress. She had been in the hair dye again.

She studied Ronnie a moment but didn't say anything. She led us to a back room without speaking, opened the door like a theater usher, and in we went, with her following after.

It was a conference room and not all that large, but it had a stage for kid performances and civic events up front, and here was a long table on the stage, and there were three figures sitting behind it. The cooling unit growled behind the walls and the air inside was a little chilly, considering outside it was as warm as a fat man's ass crack.

Estelle took a seat in one of the chairs at the back of the room. A woman's voice from behind the table called for us to come up. Her voice had a foghorn quality. We walked to the stage. I decided I didn't like looking up at them and took the steps onto the stage, and Ronnie followed.

We stood in front of the table and the three wizened creatures that ruled their small world with iron fists and a magnolia fart looked about as threatening as concrete yard gnomes.

The woman, who had to be Kate Conroy, was sitting between the other two in a motorized wheelchair. She looked like a large bird that had broken its wings. Her arms were thin as sticks in her black suit coat. The sleeves hung slack around them. There was enough room in her ivory-white shirt for two children of moderate size, one of them riding a pony.

Her face was all bones and white parchment, but I could envision the woman she had once been, the one with the high cheekbones and the heavy lips, the one who could easily have been the model for the painting I had seen in the country club. A woman with power in the head, power in the body, and a heart like a block of ice.

The man to her right was a big sag of a fellow and seemed to have been placed in the chair as if he were a beanbag, with most of the beans collecting in his stomach. His head was large and his shoulders wide, though they sloped dramatically. His face looked to have enjoyed the sun too much and there were more spots on it than on a pinto pony.

I knew him immediately. He was a white-haired, well-cured version of his son, Jack Jr. They both had those feral eyes and exuded all the warmth and animation of winter roadkill. He had both hands wrapped around the knob of a cane and was leaning forward on it. If someone had snatched it away, he might have collapsed onto his shiny black shoes in a puddle the color of his blue suit and his fire-red tie.

The man on Kate Conroy's left was a ball of clothes with a head stacked on top. A plastic oxygen mask covered his face and distorted his ancient features. The mask had a hose and the hose ran to a small oxygen tank with a Dallas Cowboys logo pasted on the side. The tank fitted into a silver pull-along rack. It hummed pleasantly, like a drunk in church.

It had to be Judea Parker, Estelle's uncle. His eyes were closed and his mouth was drooling. He seemed to be napping deeply or recently dead.

It was strange to think these were the powers that be. The ones who, through money, connections, and intimidation, had created their own fiefdom in which their subjects mostly existed without awareness of just how much a part of it they were.

"Mr. Russell," Kate Conroy said, and her voice was surprisingly strong, even a bit lusty.

"Kate Conroy, I presume."

"You presume right. And I see you've brought a little friend from the affirmative action pool."

I felt Ronnie grow stiff beside me, but she didn't respond to the remark.

"Let's cut right through the shit," I said. "Tell me what you want."

"Commendable. I like cutting through the shit. What we're here to tell you is we need you to go home, wherever that is."

"I can't be the first person ever to complain about how you do business. And suspect how you do a lot more of it."

"No, but you're the first person that has the skill to make what we do sound more interesting than it is. You seem to be trying to turn simple business opportunities we've taken advantage of into some sort of crime. Like that nonsense about the dam so many years back."

I'd been planning to play it clever, but I was feeling a lot less clever today. Last night they had tried to kill me, of that I was certain, though by proxy.

"Here's cutting through the shit. I find your rituals interesting."

"What?"

"I find Creosote Johnny hilarious and silly, and when I think about it, the three of you seem like three ancient children with a thick wallet and a big club. Bullies that never outgrew being assholes."

It was like the lights in the room shaded, the air-conditioning dropped a few degrees.

"You seem to have been prying where you shouldn't," Jack Manley Sr. said. His voice wasn't as strong as Conroy's. "Sometimes you can dig a hole so deep, you can't get out of it. And you've misunderstood a lot of what you've found. Rituals. That Creosote Johnny stuff. That was from when we were kids."

I decided to hold back that I had been in their lair, but I said, "I got it from a good source. I admit there are some holes I need to plug, but I'm starting to feel like the material to do that is out there, and all I have to do is reach for it."

"Reach too far," Manley Sr. said, "you might not like what you grab hold of."

"I'll have to have a long reach either way. You guys go back a distance."

"We dined with dinosaurs," Kate Conroy said, and she showed me a lot of her dentures, "and yet we're still here. Now and again, don't you know, others have tried to rock us off our thrones, and we didn't rock. Things turned unfortunate for those would-be usurpers. But we'll give you this. You are determined, and, worse, you seem to be driven by some sort of self-righteousness. You haven't figured out yet that the world is already owned, and certainly this little piece of it, and the owners are not like you. The careful, kind, considerate, and fair-play jokesters aren't the ones who will out. They don't seem to understand that to make things happen, to make the big things work, the oil that runs the gears is nasty. Has to be."

"And you're the oil?" Ronnie said.

"Ah, it speaks. Yes. We are exactly that. And let me tell you what you both are. You're insignificant. You're caught in a trap of morals and ethics and platitudes. All of that is window dressing for life. Let me tell you what life is. Life is nothing more than survival. Darwin didn't discover that empathy helped us survive;

he discovered being the strongest and the most determined helped us survive. We aren't that strong anymore, but we got here through strength and lack of sentimentality. There's those who would like you to believe that the ones who haven't made it, who haven't made their way to the top of the food chain and accrued power and money, didn't because they didn't have the breaks, didn't have the opportunity. That's bullshit. We are here and have been here and have run things and controlled things because we are the best of the best. Some people are just born better. Some people, they come from inferior stock. You can take your sympathy and your Social Security and your Medicare and your welfare and stick it up your ass. Let those who can rule, and let those who can't manage as best they will. I've nothing against throwing a bone to them now and again, but they live off the bones and scraps, while we live off the meat, the hearts, and the lungs of the universe. It doesn't matter if you understand or don't understand; that is the way of Darwin, the way of the universe, and you two, you're like most, you're down there in the scrap heap."

"There are people richer and more powerful than you," Ronnie said. "So doesn't that make you inferior to them?"

Jack Manley Sr. made a croaking sound, like a frog that had tried to leap too far. Parker was still immobile. Kate Conroy lifted one side of her mouth and showed a few teeth.

"Girl," Jack Manley Sr. said, "we don't need your sass. You are at the very bottom of the heap. They can dress you up in all manner of uniforms and clothes, give you a banana and put a hat on you, hand you a banjo, same as a monkey, and you'll still be what you and your kind always were. The bottom of the heap."

For a moment, I thought Ronnie might go for her gun and see how fast and accurately she could shoot all three of them, but instead she grew silent.

"If you're the top of the heap," I said, "you're like that little swirly on top of fresh shit." I nodded at Parker. "And what's with him? Is he training to be third base?"

"It's not like I expected you to understand," Conroy said. "I suppose I wanted to warn you is all."

"That shows some sympathy, doesn't it?" I said.

"It shows we'd rather do this easy than hard. Whatever you find, whatever you do, we can explain it away—"

"Or pay it away," Jack Manley said.

"It's just a lot easier for us if we don't have to deal with inconveniences," Conroy said.

"I've enjoyed our time in the air-conditioning," I said. "But not much else. We'll see ourselves out."

"You'll let it go, then?" Conroy said. "We could give you a bit of financial incentive. You and your little piece can go somewhere up north and screw and leave things as they are. As they ought to be."

"Highly unlikely," Ronnie said.

"I take money, I agree to what you want, I wouldn't trust you to let it be, even if I was willing to do that," I said. "One day I might find myself with a garrote around my throat."

I didn't think Kate Conroy could turn any whiter, but the last three ounces of blood in her seemed to drain into her shoes.

"And I'd check that sucker's pulse if I were you," I said, indicating Parker.

"Goodbye, now," Conroy said. "You've had your warning."

As we started out of the conference room, Estelle rose and accompanied us to the exit. When we were all three just outside the door, Estelle's face looked cold and sad and ghostly. She said, "For God's sake, Danny, the both of you. Run. You have no idea."

(41)

In the car, as we rode along beneath clouds as thick and nasty-looking as curdled milk, my emotions raw and throbbing more painfully than my sore ribs and knotted head, Ronnie said, "I don't know about you, but on one hand, I look at those three and think they're about as tough as my dead aunt, and on the other, they give me the chills. I think we need to go to the FBI."

"Good idea, and I have some perfect evidence in the trunk of my car for them. And I know where there might be more. The country club. We need all we can get, because like they were saying, they can explain it away with money and position. But then again, they don't know what I've got so far and what I could add to it."

"I think they plan to get rid of you, Danny. Me as well."

"Seems as if they might. And in their own special way, they might even profit financially from our deaths."

"You sure there's more in the country club?"

"No. But I think I'd like to find out."

I explained about the insurance then, my fear for her parents as well as us. Told her how we could all be future targets of their insurance scam, sacrifices to Creosote Johnny.

"Do you think they believe that statue is some kind of god or demon, that Creepy Johnny—"

"Creosote Johnny."

"You believe they think it has powers, gives them powers?"

"I believe it's their totem. That to them it represents all they ever wanted to be. I doubt they believe it's supernatural. It's like an old pocket watch from a cherished relative. A lucky rabbit's foot. It's ritualistic, like Shirley said. And it's eerie. When I picked it up, I felt like it did have some kind of dark power. Reading about it in Bert Chandler's notes set me up for that, even if I knew it was bullshit. I got to thinking about this story I read once, about how what a person feels is part of what he creates, and on one level it becomes real. They created Creosote Johnny out of their own beliefs and designs. That thing is them in a way. If they ever had souls, that damn thing has absorbed them. Metaphorically, of course. I hope."

"Now you're creeping me out," Ronnie said.

"I'm going to take what I have in my car, soon as I get it back from Buck, and leave town, go to my house. I'll give you an address. Here's the key. Tell your folks to go there. Beg them to go there. No matter how wild it sounds to them, convince them."

"I suppose telling Chief Dudley isn't a good idea."

"I wouldn't. I don't know he's bent like they are, but they couldn't be as powerful as they are without influence. My understanding is the law doesn't even apply to the country club. And I don't know about the sheriff's department, but my guess is they have their own infiltrators. Might not be that they're out to help the city council directly, but they are willing to do it indirectly."

"By staying out of their affairs," Ronnie said.

"Giving them free rein to make things float smooth."

"Well, I wouldn't trust the sheriff's department as far as I could launch them out of a catapult. We'll meet at your house later?

Then we'll plan on getting those files you talked about, see what's in them."

When we stopped in front of the Chandler house, I wrote down on her pad the address of my home and told her where I would place the key in case she got there before me.

Ronnie leaned into me and I held her, and this time the kiss was not quick. I hated to let her go.

(42)

I looked up Buck's garage in the yellow pages, and though he said he didn't like being reminded of the legacy of that other Buck Rogers, his advertisement for towing, mechanic, and body work had rockets sketched on it and were used in part to form the letters of his name.

Recognizing the address as being on the western side of town not far from where Buck had picked me up, I decided to walk over and not bother calling. The day had heated up under the heavy cloud cover and the threat of more rain. A slight warm wind was sighing, carrying with it the satisfying aroma of damp earth.

Though it was late afternoon, and it might seem strange for a man to take his ax handle for a walk, I can't say as it worried me much. I already had a target on my back. Being out of the library and away from the crumpled rulers of their little world, it all seemed a bit dreamlike and silly.

I went along and didn't see any copper-colored Fords or goons in white- and blackface. Though I suspected they were the sort that confined their activities and colorful disguises to the nighttime.

When I got to Buck's garage, I was steamed but still felt a lot better than I had earlier. Only the knots on my head still throbbed. The warm walk had loosened the rest of me up.

Buck's garage was a good size. My car was parked out to the side. It had new tires on it, and though I had forgotten to mention it to him, he had replaced the windshield wipers that had been twisted off.

Inside the garage there were tools on the wall and some inflated car inner tubes on hooks and a calendar with a long-legged black model dressed only in her skin. It drew my attention immediately, and I would be a liar to say otherwise. I didn't look at it too embarrassingly long, but what drew me away from it wasn't my sense of modesty. In fact, the calendar had kept me from focusing on something that should have been immediately obvious.

There was a car in one of the stalls that made me tingle to see it, and not in the same way the calendar had. I immediately found Buck's office, which was in the back with the door partially open. I could hear a small fan whisking the air in there. I went in.

Buck was sitting at his desk. He looked up at me with his good face and his nice smile.

"I see you got me some tires and wiper replacements," I said.

"Just making you out a bill. See you still got your ax handle."

"Never leave home without it."

I sat in the hardwood chair in front of his desk. The little fan was on a windowsill and it was struggling with the heat like a child trying to pin a professional wrestler. Still, it was a smidgen of comfort after my walk.

I lay the ax handle on the floor. Buck gave me the bill. I pulled a check out of my wallet and wrote it out and gave it to him.

When I passed it across the desk, I said, "I see you got a car in there up on a lift."

"Observant."

"It's copper-colored and a Ford."

"So it is."

"Crashed out near the lake?"

"That's right."

"May I ask who it belongs to?"

He lifted an eyebrow, opened his center desk drawer, placed my check in there, and closed the drawer.

"Jefferson Davis," he said.

"President of the Confederacy. He's still alive?"

"That's funny, Danny. That must be some of that writerly wit. If it was that Jeff Davis, I'd kill him on general principle. No, a black guy named Jefferson Davis. Why do you ask?"

"This Jefferson Davis have a tall white fellow come in with him?"

"He did."

"They walked in, right? Were roughed up, like me? Like maybe someone had hit them with some punches and an ax handle?"

"That's quite a list you have there."

"It is."

"Would the ax handle in question be the one you've been carrying around?"

"One of two. I've lost track of which is which."

"Yeah, they were banged up. Faces were stained with something. You could see they had tried to wipe it off."

"It was burnt cork and greasepaint," I said.

I hesitated to do what I was going to do next, but then I thought, Well, I've already jumped out of the airplane without a chute.

"Let me tell you a little story," I said.

"Will it have bears in it? I like stories about bears."

"There's at least one bear with a flashlight."

I told him what had happened to me last night. I told him I thought the city council was behind a lot of not-so-good things. I told him about some of those things, but I didn't mention my evidence. I left most of it out. I did add that Ronnie might be in danger, then I watched his expression.

He perked up. "You think?"

"I may have told you too much, but I wanted to tell you because I might need any information you have about Jeff Davis, about the other man with him. And Ronnie seems to trust you."

Using Ronnie's name to pull Buck in was perhaps a bridge too far, but if Buck was working on Jefferson Davis's car, was Buck his friend or just a businessman doing a job? I had begun to suspect everyone had connections to the city council, even a tow-truck driver and mechanic. I wanted to chalk it up to excess paranoia, but I was too paranoid to totally do so.

Buck leaned back in his chair, pursed his lips, said, "And you think this is the same car that followed you?"

"Copper-colored. You picked it up near where I was last night? Wet night. Slid off the road. They walked in. Yeah, that's the car."

"Jeff has always been an Uncle Tom. But I don't know. That stuff about the tunnels. You sound like a man that might wear an aluminum-foil hat to keep the aliens from reading your brain waves. Jeff, though, he's sketchy. His grandfather's slave master was a Confederate. As a joke, they named one of the slave children Jefferson Davis. White folks frequently named black kids in slavery days if they chose to. Hell, maybe one of the white folks was his father. How's that sound? You have a kid and someone else names it? That's got to be some shit. The name got passed down, though. You'd think it wouldn't. Not after slavery ended. But Jeff's family has always worked for and kowtowed to the Parkers. It's a family tradition, like black-eyed peas on New Year's Day."

"That right?"

"Jeff would wave the Stars and Bars and sing 'Dixie' if the city council asked him to. He'd eat shit and hope to get some gravy on it. Eat shit enough, you can learn to like it. With or without gravy. He likes it. Of course, sometimes you eat so much of it, you can't eat anymore."

"Like you?"

"Came back here, didn't I? Went off, got some education, but came back like a goddamn homing pigeon. What's up with that, huh? I'm back here eating shit again. Smaller amounts and farther apart, but I still got the taste in my mouth, and I don't even get any gravy on it. Scared to death I might learn to like it the way Jeff does."

"Who's the white guy with Jefferson Davis?"

"Coolie Parker. From the family of Judea Parker. A cousin. He's low on the totem pole, but he's on the pole."

"That makes him kin to Estelle Parker too?"

"She the babe at the library?"

"She is."

"Yep. They're kin. Here's something to love: Coolie is a cop."

"Oh, hell."

"Exactly. Now you know how we black folks feel when we deal with the cops. Shoe is on the other foot, hoss."

"Not all of us white folks were born with silver spoons in our mouths. Chief Dudley? What about him?"

"He's friendly enough, but he's been around too long not to have their fingers up his ass at least some of the time. Listen here, we can call Jeff, have him come around, and have a polite talk with him. Ronnie's in danger, I'd do that. Just a chat."

"No need to pee in your own soup. I've told you more than I should."

"Let me ask again: Why did you?"

"Maybe I'm looking for allies. I'm making a guess with you and hoping it's a good one."

"That's almost it, but I think it's more that I got Jeff's car here, and you're thinking I might know something about him, right? You told me some stuff, but you told me just enough stuff, not all of it. Some of it you want to know if I already know it. You're fishing for information about who is who."

"Maybe."

"I haul and work on cars. That's it. I'm not inside a nefarious secret organization. I'm not sure yet there is an organization to be inside or outside of. But I believe there are a lot of assholes out there, that the town's full of them. But I get into this, I may have to leave town with what's left of my tail between my legs."

"You've done enough. Told me what I needed to know."

"You're still leading me along, aren't you, Danny boy? Sure I'll regret it later, but you may have picked your man right. All goes sideways, maybe you and me can move away. Open a garage any-where but here. You could have a stall to write in, and you could bring me coffee and cook for the rent."

"Would we snuggle at night?"

"Why wouldn't we?"

"Would I have my own desk?"

"Why not? And your very own rotating fan. I'm going to phone Jeff."

(43)

Buck made the call while I went out and pulled my car into the garage and into a walled stall with a sliding door, which I pulled down. Unless Jefferson Davis had X-ray vision, he wouldn't know it was there.

I went inside the office for some more of that fan.

Buck had his legs stretched out, his feet on his desk, the fan blowing air on the back of his neck. "Son of a bitch is coming around in a few minutes. Said he's getting dropped off. If he's with someone that stays with him, we'll play it as it lays. I'd like you to stay back here in the office out of sight at first."

"I don't want you taking this on alone."

"You have a blue-black knot on your head, and you're moving like a spider missing four legs. I'll leave the door cracked. You can listen. There'll be a time for you to come out."

"All right," I said.

"I might say some things that sound like some bad things, but don't panic. Some of the bad things may in fact turn out to be as bad as I say, but most of them won't. I don't think."

"Is that some kind of pep talk?"

"Could be."

"It's not working," I said.

*　　*　　*

I had a curtain in the office split a little, and I was standing there looking out the window at the front lot. The fan wasn't doing me any good over there.

Next to the window was a row of framed photos. They were all of Buck in army duds, and other soldiers were with him, along with a German shepherd about the size of a moose.

A blue Chevy Impala with a scrape on the door showed up and let Jeff out. Jeff came across the lot with his shirttail out and flapping, walking like one leg was a pogo stick. Good. Either me or the car wreck had given him that limp.

I dropped the curtain and eased over to the door. It was open but slanted, and I could hide behind it and see into the garage through the crack near the hinges.

Jeff came in and Buck smiled and spoke pleasantly. I was waiting for Buck to say those bad things.

Buck said, "He's in the office."

I had been set up. I went for the ax handle on the floor, but they were already through the door by then, Jeff holding a little revolver on me that had to have been hidden under his shirt, probably stuck into his pants at the base of his spine.

"Put the ax handle down," Buck said. "Better yet, hand it to me."

I hesitated, then gave it to him. Ax handle versus revolver had an obvious outcome.

"Why don't you sit your ass?" Jeff said.

"Don't shoot him in my office if you can help it," Buck said.

"We'll take him back out to the lake on account of he likes it out there so much. No more fucking around then. I'm just going to shoot you full of holes, nosy. Where'd you and that retard go last night, to butt-fuck in a ditch?"

"Didn't need a ditch," I said. "I dropped my pants and leaned on the ax handle. I would have called your name while he did it, but I didn't know it then."

He cocked the hammer on the pistol.

"The lake is less messy," Buck said.

"You rotten bastard," I said to Buck. "All that bullshit you fed me."

"Told you how I might learn to eat shit. It's on my breath right now. Damn, for a reporter, you talk way too much."

"Can't argue that," I said.

"You call anyone else, tell anyone you were coming here, Jeff?" Buck said.

"Called my sister to give me a ride, drop me off. She don't know nothing."

"Car's not really ready to pick up," Buck said.

Jeff's face puckered. "On the phone you said it was."

"I lied," Buck said, and swung the ax handle against the top of Jeff's arm so hard, I thought it might have broken bones. Jeff yelped and dropped the gun. Another swing of the ax handle, and Jeff was on his knees with blood coming out of his mouth.

"What the fuck?" Jeff said, and a tooth tumbled out between his lips, bounced once, and lay on the floor like a Chiclet.

"I wanted to be sure Danny was telling me true about how you tried to kill him."

"I won't forget this," Jeff said.

"Might ought to, you want to keep the rest of those teeth." Buck looked at me, smiled a little, said, "Think about it. Me in my office and some honky I met once comes in and tells me that shit. I had to be sure before I put my neck on the chopping block."

"Are you sure now?"

"Absolutely."

*   *   *

At Buck's direction, I went out in the garage and pulled down the sliding doors to all the stalls and locked the back entrance.

When I came back into the office, I drew down all the blinds as he instructed, and Buck had me hold the gun on Jeff while he used some rope and tied him to the chair where I had sat. When he was finished, I gave the gun back to Buck and he pushed it into his waistband and then together we lifted Jeff and the chair and carried him out of the office and into one of the empty stalls.

"What you doing?" Jeff said.

"Going to see you get washed down, Jeff," Buck said.

I had no idea what Buck was talking about. I was just following his lead.

Buck got a bucket at the far end of the stall and filled it with water from a sink there, then he found a large, ragged-looking towel that was stained with grease, threw it over his shoulder, and carried the bucket over.

He sat the bucket down at the side of the chair. He took the towel off his shoulder and dunked it, kept hold of it with one hand, dipped it in and out of the pail a few times. Some of the water dripped on the floor. Buck took the towel and wrung it out between his big hands over the bucket.

Without so much as a "Shit, look out," he swung the wet towel and cracked Jeff with it on the side of the head over the ear. The wet towel sprayed water over all of us, made a sound like a beaver tail slapping water, and turned the chair over with Jeff in it. Jeff let out a noise that made me sick to my stomach.

"Damn, Buck," I said.

"You keep cool and quiet," he said to me. He looked down at Jeff in the overturned chair, said, "Listen here, Jeffy. Done that to get you set for a question or two I got. Better answer right.

I got a built-in bullshit detector, and I got this towel. Set him up, Danny."

I took hold of the chair and rocked it upright. There was a little trail of blood coming out of Jeff's ear.

"Going to go around on the other side now, so I can talk in your good ear," Buck said.

"Jesus, Buck," Jeff said. "Ain't never done nothing to you."

"You hurt my feelings, sucking up to the man like you do. The Parkers. City council."

"Just getting by, Buck. You know that. You know how we all got to do?"

"You like doing it more than the rest of us."

"It's how things is, man."

"Here's how things is, Jeff. I'm going to ask you questions, and every time you don't answer me or throw out some honey, I'm going to whack you with this fucking towel. You'd think water on a towel wouldn't do much, but it's quite the load. I learned this bit from some cops in Tyler. Before that, I was a tunnel rat in Vietnam, you know that, Jeff? I had some bad events happen there. Joined the rats to keep them from sending the dogs down, which is how they first did it. Dogs didn't deserve that, considering what happened to them down there. Made me sort of mean, doing that work. And I can be damn mean when I need to be, Jeff."

"Done seen that mean side," Jeff said.

"Have indeed. I thought what I did in Nam was worth noting, but where I learned this little trick with the wet towel, well, that was those Tyler cops I was saying about. They picked me up and cross-examined me in a jail cell with a weak overhead light for a couple days before they figured out I was the wrong man."

"That's some shit there, Buck," Jeff said, trying to get on Buck's team. "Way they treated you."

"They got the man they wanted because he came in and

confessed. Heavy conscience, some shit, felt he had to get it off his chest. Didn't even look like me. Shorter, slope-shouldered, had an ass like a cheap bleacher cushion. You know what was really special after I'd had me a wet hard time for two days? He was white. They picked me up, brought me in, put me in a jail cell tied to a chair, same as you, with a bucket of water and a towel and a big ol' cracker that could have thrown a shotput from first base over the home-run fence. He did some work on me. First fifteen minutes I'm there, I shit myself, confessed to two robberies, animal fornication, and car theft, and I hadn't done any of them. I mean, shit, I told them a story about fucking a chicken or a duck or some such. I think I threw a sheep in there. I thought about adding in a whole herd of cows. You see, it hurt when they whacked me with that goddamn wet towel, so I fibbed. But Jeff, I know you. Know how you are. You lie to me, I'll know it. You feeling me here, Jefferson Davis?"

"Don't do me like this, brother."

The towel whirled up and came down on the top of Jeff's head, hard. Beads of water flew, made glowing blobs in the light. The blow caused Jeff's chin to drop to his chest, and then it sprung back up like an accordion.

When Jeff had gathered himself, he said, "Fuck, man. Jesus, Buck. Jesus."

"You're going to see him soon," Buck said.

"You ain't even asked me a question."

"You know, you're right. Thought I had."

"I don't know about this, Buck," I said.

"Yeah, well, it bothers you so much, go in the office, stand in front of the fan, and wait until I get tired or finished. Get the calendar off the wall there, take it with you. Got some tissues on the desk."

"This isn't even your problem," I said.

"You made it my problem. Hearing what you told me, I'm full up with it. Realized I'm eating a lot more shit than I thought I was."

Jeff hadn't been hit but twice, but he looked within two more blows of a cheap funeral.

Buck said, "Before I go farther, Jeff, before I ask that first question, something goes wrong here, that sister that brought you, is she your best pick for next of kin? I'm already coming up with some kind of accident you might have had, like getting caught in a fucking car wash."

"What you want to know?" Jeff said. "Come on, man. Ask me."

Buck had gone back to the bucket and was soaking the towel again. He carefully twisted it out between his fists and kept the roll in it. He widened his stance and stood in front of Jeff and let the towel swing back behind him.

"Ask me, man. Ask any goddamn thing."

"All right," Buck said. "And think your answer over carefully. I want to see a fucking light bulb above your head glowing with thought. Danny, he had a talk with the city council today. They had some plans for him last night, didn't they? Don't even think about pulling my wing-wang on this. Talk to me."

"Me and Coolie was supposed to break him up a little, maybe just wipe him off the map. Then that big son of a bitch showed up and juked on us. Put the towel down, Buck. I'm talking."

Buck looked at me. "Got another question for him?"

"You know what's going on out there, don't you?" I said to Jeff.

"Naw, I don't know all that close-up shit."

Buck swirled the towel in the air and cracked it like a whip and it hit Jeff under the jaw and knocked the chair over.

"Fuck," Jeff said.

"Would you mind setting that up again," Buck said. "Next one. Going to see I can flip him over twice."

I set the chair up. Jeff coughed, and when he did a fine mist of blood flashed from his mouth and colored the air. A moment later the mist was on the floor in tiny drops.

"That last part, that was some bullshit pulled fresh from the bull's ass," Buck said, leaning over and placing his face close to Jeff's. "I know you."

"Man, we done been fishing together," Jeff said.

"Yeah, but I didn't enjoy it. I've known you all my life, Jeff, and I got to tell you, I've never liked you."

Jeff leaned over and spat blood on the floor. "That hurts my feelings, Buck. You used to fuck my cousin. You remember her—Jill . . . Jenny."

"Jessica," Buck said.

"I ain't got no more to say," Jeff said. "Go on and finish me off, but don't use that fucking towel no more."

"I like the towel. Do I like the towel, Danny?"

"Seem to."

Buck leaned back and flung the towel out behind him, gritted his teeth.

Jeff said, "All right, now, white man. Ask me that question again. One I answered wrong."

"He's talking to you," Buck said.

"White man part clued me in," I said. "Insurance policies, Jeff. Tell me about it."

"I don't get up in their business. I just do what they need when they need it. Pay me good to do that."

"I didn't hear you mention insurance," Buck said. "He asked about insurance."

Jeff's face was popped with streams of sweat and beads of water from the towel, droplets of blood. "I'm down on the edge already. I tip off it, I got a long way to fall."

Buck moved and the towel whirled out and popped the air and

a rain of water sprayed on all of us. The sudden pop of that towel almost made me scream.

"You aren't as close to the edge as you're about to be," Buck said.

"All right, all right . . . shit, tell you this stuff, I got to leave town and keep going."

"I'm okay with that," Buck said.

"They got them this ceremony. Bring out this fucking creosote log got a face whittled on it. Set that up, that means its insurance-money time. Got this chair with holes in the back of it, and they bring out a doped-up guest to sit in it. They slip a rope through them holes in the chair and around the guest's neck, and then this stick gets twisted, slow-like, while them farts sit at a table and watch it done. Take photographs, film the whole thing with a home-movie camera. Them old dead eyes start to glow then. One time, they didn't have nobody in mind, so they insured a stray dog, strangled it, and you can bet that policy paid off. Ain't nobody can get to them. They got a wall of protection, they want it. They say a stick is a pickle, then you might as well put it on a sandwich. Not like the law is looking to know anything. They are the law."

"Your buddy Coolie being some of that law," I said.

"We work together, but we don't hang together. Comes down to a get-together at the club, I just serve drinks and try to act like what they're doing isn't all that nuts. All in a day's or night's work. I got bills, and the council's got steady dough. Beats digging potatoes or wiping asses at the old folks' home or mowing lawns. You get used to that money, and you can get used to money right easy. It's a happy habit. I might as well stay as happy and helpful as I can, 'cause I figure somewhere they got a policy on me. I'm just not wanting them to collect it just yet."

"Between the three of them they couldn't turn a doorknob," I said. "Who does the strangling?"

"Mr. Jack Jr. these days. He'd beat a baby to death with a baby rattle for the fun of it. They're all that way, every one of them, but Jack Jr., he's only one young enough to turn that stick and tighten the rope these days. He's like a big ol' bear. Only time I ever seen him smile is when he's turning that stick. Let me tell you something, white boy, they got them a policy with your name on it, and you done signed it and don't even know it."

"I'm finished with the questions," I said.

Buck dropped the towel in the bucket, splashing water.

"What about me?" Jeff said. "Gonna leave me tied to this chair?"

"Could be your new home," Buck said.

(44)

It could be a lie," Buck said. We were in his office, him behind his desk, me on a stool he brought out of the closet. Jeff was still out in the garage, still tied to the chair, but now with a shop rag stuffed into his mouth. An oily one. "A creosote post with a face. A fucking lair. On top of that, you got your story about your man Flashlight Boy that lives in a tunnel with rats and steals clothes from graves, puts bones in trunks. And then we got that whole strangle-the-shit-out-of-someone-in-a-chair thing. I said I knew when Jeff was lying, but I don't know I do. You believe any of that shit?"

"I not only believe some of it, I believe all of it. I've seen Creosote Johnny. I didn't tell you that creosote-post business, about the ritual strangulations, because I wanted to hear that from someone that knew about it. I keep expecting to wake up, but things just get odder and odder."

"I knew the council were greedy fucks, not on the up-and-up, but shit, man."

"You get used to doing whatever you have the urge to do because you keep getting away with it, then you just keep doing it, no matter how outrageous. What about Jeff? What happens to him now?"

"He's all right."

"In what way?"

"In the way I decide. Don't ask me any more questions here, Danny. Look, I'm going to put him in his piece-of-shit car, which will run a bit, and get him out of town and leave him with a threat. I might even give him an ass-beating before I let him go, but I'll take care of him."

"You think he'll leave and stay gone?"

"He'll know what the alternative is. Don't get your panties in a twist. He and Coolie, they'd have killed you or dropped you off to sit in that strangle chair. No need to sweat Jeff."

"They'll be looking for him."

"I don't think they'll look that hard."

Buck put his hands behind his head and gave one of those looks that makes you think he might have forgot something in a public restroom somewhere.

"You put me in this, Danny. Now don't try and put it on me."

"You did more than expected. But yeah. It's my fault."

"Only time I was ever sorry is when we let a big old beautiful German shepherd named Bobo go down in a hole in Vietnam, a tunnel. He got two of them Cong, ripped their fucking throats out, but they killed Bobo. Then I got them. What was left of them was small and imprecise in structure. After that time, Danny, and I say this without one fucking word of apology, I'm all out of sorry. Step on your foot. Walk in front of you. Sorry and excuse me. Mess with me with bad intent, I got some bad intent to give back. Dogs are ten times better than people. Not real picky eaters either. Of course, there's Ronnie. I could like her a lot, but so far, I haven't worn her down enough. Might be she's just looking for a better class of human being. You go on home and let me finish up here."

I collected my ax handle, left the office, and looked at Jeff tied to the chair with a rag in his mouth. He watched me with hope.

Ignoring him, I took my car out of the stall and drove it out to the curb and sat behind the wheel, clenching it the way Jack Jr. must have clenched that garrote.

I wasn't all that fond of myself right then. I was just good old Danny Russell, assistant to a wet-towel expert. Merely asking a few little questions and leaving a man tied to a chair with a rag in his mouth.

All I needed were some flies to pull the wings off of, a kitten to kick downstairs, an orphanage to set fire to on Christmas Eve with the kids asleep in their beds and presents under the tree. I wasn't going to think about Jeff. He'd be like the parakeet your mother said got free and flew out the window when in fact the cat had eaten most of it and the rest of it was tucked up under a rosebush.

I felt sick to my stomach. I felt overwhelmed. I felt as if I were a minor star in a melodrama. I felt as if I were plunging through that bridge on my way to the water. I felt all manner of things, but the one thing I didn't feel was good.

(45)

When I arrived at the Chandler house, because my mind was so scattered, I uncharacteristically left my ax handle in the car.

Inside, Mrs. Chandler and Christine Humbert were sitting on the couch. Mrs. Chandler had started to look like her skin had been removed and stretched over wire hangers.

Christine looked less poised than usual. She wore jeans and a loose shirt and tennis shoes. Her hair had been tied back in what appeared to be a quick fashion, as a number of strands were poking out randomly.

They were both looking at me.

I walked in without an invitation. I was starting to be that bold dog. I put the files on the coffee table. Christine looked up at me. Her eyes were wet. She had her hands resting on her knees. Her thumbs and forefingers were in splints wrapped with white tape.

"Hoped I would see you," Christine said. "I was leaving a good-bye message with Mrs. Chandler. I'm selling the paper and moving. I got a good price."

"What?"

"I think it's best."

I looked down at her hands. "Who did this?"

"I had an accident."

"What kind of accident was that?"

"Stupid one. Sometimes, Danny, being right isn't enough. I wanted to see you before I went away."

"Ah, hell," I said.

"No more articles," she said. "Write the book. Do it somewhere else, but write it."

"They had a talk with me, and now they've had one with you. Jack Jr. do this?"

"I prefer to say I had an accident."

"But when you get past your preference, did Jack Jr. do this?"

"Go home, Danny. I thought some things could change. I thought I was a brave crusader. Seemed so simple and they seemed so obvious. But evil wins out more than we like to admit. It has a stronger agenda than the rest of us. Goodbye, Danny."

Christine stood and came over and kissed me on the cheek and carefully moved past me toward the door. I thought about giving her a pep talk about how we could get it done, but I was all out of pep. I listened to her go out the front door and close it.

Mrs. Chandler said, "Let it go, Danny. She's scared and has a right to be. She knows what you have. I told her about Bert's files."

"We wouldn't make a very good secret organization."

"There have been enough secrets. The light needs to be shone on these cockroaches, but Christine, she needs to go. It's best. Maybe she's right, and you need to go too. Write that book the way she said. Far from here."

"I admit it crossed my mind. But I think they wouldn't let that happen in the long run. They offered me a way out, but my guess is that was just an attempt to make me think I had one. Relax a bit, then they can make sure I disappear or turn up in a ditch somewhere. A victim of misadventure."

"Sit beside me, Danny."

I sat.

"Listen here. She wouldn't say who, but someone put her hands in her desk drawer and slammed it closed. Whoever did it made it clear that if she continued publishing your articles, it wouldn't end well. The whole newspaper staff decided on new careers. Christine is tough, but not that tough. No one has to be that tough. I feel like I started all of this with that book long ago. Perhaps I shouldn't have."

"I want to go back to where I lived and put new and serious locks on all the doors, bars on all the windows, and climb into bed and stay there. That's what I want to do."

"But?"

"Do that, I might as well be mistreating and murdering people myself. My silence will do that."

"I suppose that's true," Mrs. Chandler said.

"What about you? You're in danger too."

"Figure by the time they decide to get any kind of vengeance on me, they'll have to go out and pee on my grave."

I picked up the files. "I think you might trick that ol' cancer."

She smiled at me. It wasn't a smile that said I was particularly convincing.

*   *   *

Upstairs, I sat down and wrote the next article just as if it were going to be published, and when I finished, it was late in the evening.

The weather didn't encourage it, but I decided then that I had to get away. It was a crazy thing to do, but I took my article and put it in my suitcase with the rest of my stuff, packed up my typewriter and all my gear, and carried everything out to the car. I drove two hours back through blinding rain to the home I had inherited from my aunt.

Neither Ronnie's nor her parents' car was there. They hadn't arrived or weren't coming. Ronnie trying to convince her mother and father to run away on what they would consider hearsay might not be an easy task. And I don't think either had a tendency to run.

I used the spare key that was hidden under a rock in the dead flower bed to let myself in. The house felt strange, as if the place had abandoned all hope. It smelled stale, or maybe that was me.

I turned on the central air and locked up. I don't know how safe I was, but I felt more secure than I had in days. Away from New Long Lincoln and all that I knew. Here, that world, what was going on there, seemed as distant as another universe.

I went to bed then but didn't sleep well. I didn't get a visit from my father's ghost, but my memories of Buck Rogers working over poor old Jeff Davis made me toss and turn. I could hear the sound of that wet towel on human flesh.

Next morning, I read my article over. When I considered the evidence, the people who had been killed for insurance payouts, my feelings about Jefferson Davis adjusted a little. I wasn't ready to hit him with a wet towel myself, but I was slightly more thankful that someone had.

(46)

'd awoken to the battering of the rain on the house, and though it was solid morning, the light through the split in the curtain was slim to none and seemed to have been painted blue-black. Outside, my yard was flowing with water and the wind had blown limbs down from the trees and they looked like the skeletal remains of a dead giant.

My phone was no longer hooked up, so after eating some stale cornflakes wet with water instead of milk, I managed to drive through the rain to town to find a phone booth. Going from car to booth I got so wet you could have wrung me out and used me to beat Jeff Davis to death.

I scrounged some change from my pocket, called Ronnie, and asked her if she was going to come.

"It's been strange. I worked on convincing them all night, and only this morning did they agree to go, but I'm not sure for how long they'll stay. I gave Mom the key. They are leaving before noon. Maybe a little later. They're waiting for the rain to pass, though the weather report doesn't look good for several days. Rain might keep everyone inactive, including the city council."

"Don't count on it. Council has you in its sights now, and I believe they are a spiteful bunch who would put your parents in harm's way to get back at you. Not that they wouldn't harm you outright, but I think that's how they think. Sadism is their personal connection. What about you? You coming?"

"I can't run, Danny. I'm the law."

"Thought you might say that."

"There needs to be some kind of law in this town, and right now, I think me and Chief Dudley are it."

"You haven't told him anything, have you?"

"If I told him, how much of it is he going to believe?"

"They have blackmail goods on him."

"That doesn't mean he's in on all their shenanigans or even knows what they are."

"That's part of their strength, us not knowing who's in with them and who's not. It's like a vampire cult, only besides lives, they drain money and power. Who's going to believe that? The host isn't always aware of being drained."

"Coolie Parker came to work looking like he had been in a fight with a badger and had done it with one arm tied behind his back."

"I hope he hurts bad."

"Said he had a car accident."

"He would. He got those marks from me and Flashlight Boy."

"If you're calling me from home—"

"Phone booth."

"I suppose you've decided you've had enough."

"Last night, for a while, I thought so. Christine is leaving town like she's riding a missile. Told me to write the book from home. Someone, Jack Jr. is my guess, broke her thumbs and index fingers and, before that, had her sign a bill of sale for the business. No way she would have sold it had she had a choice."

"My God."

I almost told her about Jefferson Davis, what he had said, but that didn't put me or Buck in a particularly good light, so I thought it might be best to hold that back for the time being.

"I was going to stay here and write the book, but I decided I need more evidence. There are files in the country club, Ronnie. I think they are keepsakes, trophies of those they have dispatched for insurance money and a happy dampening in their shorts. I get those files, then I have absolute proof. Like Shirley said, it's all about ritual, and my guess is part of that is collecting trophies or records of what they've done. That could be solid proof."

"That sounds iffy."

"Everything sounds iffy. I keep thinking I'll wake up from all this. Listen, I've turned the air on in the house, so your mom and dad will walk into the cool. There's no food here, unless you count half a box of cornflakes and no milk. I'm going to grab a few things, fill the car up with gas, and head your way. I'm going to put some money on the kitchen table so your parents can buy food. Anything to make it easy for them to be here. And be careful at the cop shop. Figure there's more leaks there than a sieve."

"Trust me, I'm being careful. I'm a little frightened."

"That's a good thing. I'm a lot frightened. I try and find someone to tell this to, some law outside of town, I think I could make a case, but I could make a real solid one if those files at the country club have what I think they have in them. Add that to the files I have from Mrs. Chandler's dead husband, Bert, I think even their contacts would have a hard time supporting them, keeping them out of the soup. Can you meet me at the Chandler house late afternoon?"

"I have some duties first, and I want to do them and not cause suspicion. But I should be there before sundown."

"Good enough. Might want to not wear your uniform and come in your own car, not the cruiser. Nothing says something is going on like a cop car at the curb."

"All right."

"But bring your gun."

(47)

The lightning danced along the sky and sizzled among the trees, reverberated with butt-clenching snaps and crackles, and strobed briefly through the limbs and leaves.

Lights burning late morning in houses along the way blew out and went dark as I passed. Transformers on poles sputtered and hissed, and pole lights winked away.

My new wipers beat at the rain and my headlights were only slightly brighter than two fireflies in a sack. The water was flowing over the road, and the wind rocked my car like dice in a Yahtzee cup.

Low on gas and high on energy, by noon I damn near floated into New Long Lincoln. The streets were ankle-deep in water and even old Jefferson Davis's statue looked like it would have liked an umbrella, because it was only a shape coated in dark rain.

There were cars parked at the curb all along Mrs. Chandler's street, so I had to park down away from the house and run along the sidewalk and up onto the porch. I brought my ax handles this time. The door was locked. I used my key to get in. Soaked as I was, the air in there was uncomfortably cool.

I called out to Mrs. Chandler. I felt the floorboards shake

gently, and a moment later she appeared in the kitchen door-way. She looked weaker and even more frail than when I had seen her last.

"You shouldn't have come back."

"Believe me, I know it."

"Wait a moment."

She went away and came back with a towel. I dried off. She said, "Come in the kitchen and have a bite to eat."

I gave her the towel and went in there. She said, "Look in the refrigerator. Fix it yourself. I don't have an appetite or the strength to do much."

"Sure."

Mrs. Chandler draped the towel over the back of a chair and sat in another. I found some sandwich meat that I couldn't identify but that looked fresh, got a slice of cheese, the bread, and mayonnaise, and made a simple sandwich. There was brewed coffee that was a little old and tasted as if it were angry. I ate and sipped slowly. Bad as the coffee was, I enjoyed it.

"I'm not feeling so well, Danny."

"I'm so sorry."

"Me too. Listen here. I hate you came back, and I'm glad you came back at the same time. I been sitting here all morning thinking about what I haven't done."

"You tried with the book."

"That was like peeing in the ocean and saying every little bit helps."

"I have an idea or two," I said, and I told her about the files at the club and what I expected was in them.

"That could be the ticket," she said. "Listen, I have to go lie down. I felt fine enough yesterday, but today...maybe it's the rain. Today I feel like shit in a wheelchair."

"That would be Kate Conroy."

That made her laugh a little. "Guess it would. And you know what saddens me? That bitch will probably outlive me."

* * *

It was late afternoon, and sundown might as well have already happened, though normally during the summer months, it would go down late.

I decided to pack all my stuff. No matter how things turned out, even if I got hold of the files at the club, after tonight I was done being in New Long Lincoln.

I thought about the locks on the file cabinets. We had to get past that. I could jimmy a lock if I had enough time and the right tools, but I thought perhaps a crowbar or the sharp end of a tire tool, though less graceful, could do the work faster.

I put the empty suitcase on the bed, and the lights went out. Okay. That made sense. I had seen them dying all along the road on my trip, but something clicked in the back of my mind, and it was simply that I hadn't seen a flash of lightning or heard a crack of thunder.

Okay. Don't have to. Lights can go out without you hearing a damn thing. It was still rainy and dark outside and maybe something blew down somewhere along the street. Power lines. A transformer.

I heard something that didn't sound quite right. It was a clicking that sounded like the front door being carefully opened, but the front door was locked, and only Mrs. Chandler and I had keys.

Was she up and about?

Maybe.

Was she thinking about a walk in the rain during a near pitch-black afternoon?

I peered between the curtains. There were a few lights across the street in front of the bank. I put my face close to the glass and looked in both directions. There was a stagger of lights, fuzzy through the heavy rain. Okay. No transformers blown.

Someone had thrown the switch in the house fuse box.

I eased to the door and put my ear to it. I thought I heard the front door close and there was air pressure at my door as the one in the hallway was pulled to.

I locked my bedroom door, listened some more.

Was someone on the stairs? I thought I could hear footsteps.

Could it be Mrs. Chandler?

I had heard her come up the stairs many times, and this didn't sound right. It sounded heavy. I moved across the room in the dark and grabbed a chair and put it under the doorknob.

I heard that bad stair near the top squeal, then there was a pause.

Enough time for me to imagine all manner of things went by, then another squeak as weight was shifted off the step.

Okay. Not my imagination, and not Mrs. Chandler, unless she had gained fifty pounds and walked like an elephant.

I picked up one of the ax handles from the corner of the room. The hair on the back of my neck stood up, thick and firm as the teeth in a comb. I rested the ax handle on my shoulder and envisioned swinging for the fence.

I pulled the curtains wide to get more light on the subject from outside. I could hear the doorknob gently turning. The lock held.

All right, Danny. Keep your cool. Stay steady. No one is in the room yet. The door is locked. There's a chair—

The chair scraped backward slightly and the door bumped hard against the lock. I slid over and quietly pushed the chair back into place. The doorknob was definitely turning, and then it went still. I felt clammy and weak in the knees. I started to yell out some kind of threat, like "I have a gun," but restrained myself. Best for them to think the door was locked and I had gone.

No. They were bound to have seen my car out there. So, no good. But wait—I hadn't parked out front. That was something.

They probably had a gun. There could be more than one. They came through that door, especially if they had guns, I didn't want them seeing me right away—

And then at the bottom of the door, I saw a bit of light appear and crawl along the floor outside.

Mrs. Chandler could have a flashlight. She would need one. But if so, why was she at the top of the stairs and why hadn't she knocked or said a word?

Nope. Still wasn't her, no matter how hard I tried to make it be.

More prowling around outside the door. Another turn of the knob, less subtle this time. The chair rocked back a bit. I put my leg against it.

Trembling, I stood with my ax handle at the ready. Then I heard a kind of bark, more than a scream, at the bottom of the stairs. It certainly wasn't a happy sound, and then there was movement outside my door, but it was moving away. I heard the stairs squeak again, and now there was nothing quiet about what was going on out there. My intruder was going down the stairs with all the stealth of a rhinoceros trying out a few dance steps.

I waited. Listened.

My door vibrated when the door downstairs was opened. There was another cry and I recognized that voice.

Mrs. Chandler.

It took all the courage I could muster, along with a lot of foolhardiness, which in the end might be the same thing, for me to move the chair and set it aside.

With the ax handle held over my shoulder, I used the other hand to snap open the lock.

I pushed the door open and no one shot me.

I slipped onto the landing and looked down the stairs. The front door was wide open and rain was blowing up onto the porch and into the hallway, almost to where the stairs began.

Lightning did a little jig through the downstairs window.

I took a deep breath and crept down the stairs. My foot hit that squeaky spot. I froze.

Nothing.

I went down and looked in the living room. No one there either. I went through to the closet in the hall. I opened the closet and took down the box with the pistol.

In the kitchen, I put the box on the table, laid the ax handle beside it. I loaded the pistol, all six shells. My hands shook while I did it. I had to really concentrate to get those shells in the chambers.

I left the ax handle and, carrying the pistol, went to the closet again. I placed the pistol on a shelf, got the single-shot shotgun out, the one Mrs. Chandler had used to frighten Jefferson Davis and Coolie Parker with.

I managed all of this in the dark, but the dark downstairs wasn't as bleak as upstairs, as lights from across the street were stronger and more direct. They poured in through the living-room window. Their glow spread to the closet door and there was light coming through the kitchen window as well. It wasn't a light to do watch repair by, but it was okay.

I scrounged around in the closet and found a flashlight, but it didn't have batteries. I looked for shotgun shells and came across an open box. I felt around in the box with the tips of my fingers. Three shells.

I broke open the shotgun and slipped one into it, put the other two in my pants pocket. I might actually hit something with a shotgun, but shooting someone wasn't high on my list of priorities.

Or hadn't been, but as I stood there in that little hallway in front of the closet, I mentally moved blowing someone's head off to a higher position on my priority list.

I was scared, but I was mad too.

I went into the living room and to the door across from the couch. The door was cracked open. I moved it with my foot, crouched with the shotgun at the ready. I was looking into an empty room.

To be sure Mrs. Chandler wasn't hiding under the bed or in the closet, I gave the room a once-over. This was made easier as she had a flashlight sitting on her end table, along with all manner of bottles of pills. I took the flashlight.

Mrs. Chandler, despite all her bravery, might wish now she had never showed me a thing so she could have died in her own home or in some hospital somewhere pumped full of morphine instead of being placed in a chair with a garrote around her neck, the city council watching as a happy Jack Jr., smiling like a ghoul, slowly tightened it.

(48)

knew Ronnie was coming by later, but I didn't have time for that. I had to call her.

I went to the front door. The wood around the frame was cracked. I pushed the door to. It hung awkwardly, but it was some barrier against the howling wind and the blinding rain.

I called Ronnie at the cop shop, trying to sound friendly and not scared. I had to be careful who I talked to and how I talked. A nice lady, maybe the young lady I had met the first day I'd gone into the cop shop, said she wasn't in, that she was working something, but they'd give her the message when she was back inside her car with her radio.

When I hung up, I only took a minute to consider. I couldn't wait because Mrs. Chandler couldn't wait. They might not have bothered with taking her to the country club; she might already have given them information about the files I planned to steal. She might have told them where Bert's Moonshine Castle was or she might've said I had the files, and I did have the important ones.

I couldn't blame her either way.

* * *

With the ax handles in the back seat, the pistol shoved down under my shirt at my spine, the shotgun on the passenger seat beside me next to the flashlight, I drove through bullets of rain over to Buck's garage.

There was a light on in the office window, to the side of the building.

I parked, got out, and tried the door. It was locked.

By the time I waded through the downpour to the office window, I was drenched and damn near blind from the rain.

I tapped on the window.

No answer. I tapped again.

Nothing.

All right. Who was going to be at work in this weather anyway?

It was me and my weapons and a sinking certainty in my belly that tomorrow they would pull out that insurance policy that would be filed somewhere, and in a few days, I'd turn up bloated and fly-swarmed, and they'd be cashing checks. Kate and Jack Sr. touching champagne glasses together, Judea sleeping nearby with his oxygen mask over his face. Jack Jr. chuckling over his garrote.

When I got back to the car, there was a shape next to it. Someone, I couldn't tell who, until Buck said, "Who are you? Don't get funny. I got a gun."

"It's me, Buck."

Buck flicked on a flashlight and I couldn't see anything but a ball of wet light.

"Damn, Danny. What are you doing here?"

"Looking for you."

"Let's sit in your car," he said.

When he climbed in, he saw the shotgun and moved it to the back seat with the ax handles.

"Either you have a plan in mind or you are terribly paranoid," he said, sliding wetly onto the seat, resting what I knew to be Jefferson Davis's revolver on his knee.

"Why are you out in the rain?" I said.

"You tapping on the window. I didn't know who that was. And after what I heard from you and Jeff, I was being cautious. Snuck out the back way and came around."

"Listen, Buck. I have no right to ask you, but I need your help, and if you can't, you can't, but I couldn't think of anything else. And I'm scared."

"Help for what?"

I told him about Mrs. Chandler. Told how I had to get some of those files as well.

(49)

As I drove, leaning forward to see better, the rain crashing, the wind whistling, there was a sensation of being underwater in a small submarine with a view shield and windshield wipers. The headlights were almost useless, as night had finally set in on top of the clouded, rain-slick darkness.

Was I sorry I asked Buck to come?

Yep. He would be putting a lot on the line.

Was I glad I had asked?

Yep.

His response to my less-than-inviting invitation had been simple. "I'm armed, wet, and ready."

He didn't seem worried, nervous, or scared. Me, I had a lump in my stomach the size of a grapefruit and I could smell the sour stench of my own fear.

"Jefferson Davis?" I said. "How did that work out?"

"You could say he and his car left town."

"Literally or metaphorically?"

"Let me put it like this. He won't be coming back. I'm certain of that. Never mention it again."

The lump in my stomach seemed to be expanding and hardening.

I thought suddenly of that sinkhole of oil and mud that he and Chief Dudley had talked about, the one that had swallowed the jeep. I had no choice but to let that thought go.

I said, "My guess is they are going to punish Mrs. Chandler, put her in the chair. I don't know how much time we have, but we can't pull up to the front door. Those old Prohibition tunnels, that's the way we have to go."

"Flashlight Boy's tunnel. Didn't you say he was on the big and mean side?"

"Big and dangerous, but not mean."

"*Klaatu barada nikto.*"

"You can try that."

"Shit. Look out."

There was a shape in the wet swirl of rain, outlined in the headlights. A figure staggering into the road. The figure appeared to melt into a puddle in front of us.

I slammed the brakes and the car fishtailed and whirled in a circle and went off the road and into a deep ditch with a bone-shaking thump and the sound of metal tearing.

"Goddamn it," Buck said.

We had landed upright, at least. Steam hissed up from under the hood of the car.

I reached for my flashlight, which had tumbled onto the floor-board at my feet, tried my door. I stepped out into knee-deep water. I clawed my way up the side of the ditch. Buck slid across the seat and was close beside me.

When we made the road, I pulled the pistol out from under the back of my shirt. I didn't see any dark forms in the night. Fact was, I didn't see much of anything. I could just make out Mrs. Chandler, a motionless lump in the road.

I still hadn't turned on the flashlight as I feared making myself a target, but finally I chanced it and hustled over to her.

She moved slightly. Buck was covering me in case someone came out of the woods or the curtain of rain. I pushed my pistol back into place. It felt cold against my already drenched skin.

I bent over Mrs. Chandler, put the light on her eyes. Blood was coming out of her mouth and the rain was washing it away. Her eyes fluttered open, then closed. I moved the light away from her face.

"They thought I was dead," she said.

"Let's get her to the car," I said.

"Another hour or two of this," Buck said, "and the water will be over it. Already deep in that ditch."

"It's what we've got for the moment."

I lifted her under her shoulders so that I could scoop her up and still point the light. Buck took her feet. We managed not to drop her as we slid down the side of the ditch carrying her, but we did give her a bit of a dip in the ditchwater.

It took some work, but we moved the ax handles and shotgun onto the floor and placed her on the back seat sitting up, out of the blast of the wind and the rain. The car shook from the power of the storm as me and Buck climbed into the front seat.

Mrs. Chandler leaned against the car door, coughed once, breathed loudly.

I shone the light in her general direction, but not on her face. I said, "What happened?"

"They thought I was dead," she said. "I started coughing up blood. I didn't have my pills. The pain caused me to pass out. Guess they thought they couldn't do anything more to me. They threw me out into the rain like trash and drove off. I woke up, got up, and collapsed in the road. I think they're trying to clean house. They wanted you too. They thought you'd gone from your room, that you'd locked up and left. I told them you had gone back to where you came from."

Since my car hadn't been parked out front, they might easily have believed that. Mrs. Chandler may have saved my life.

"Who's this?" Mrs. Chandler asked.

"Buck Rogers."

"The spaceman?" she said and laughed up blood.

"I'm from the dark side of the moon," Buck said.

I had Buck hand me a small wrapper of tissues from the glove box. I took one and used it to dab her mouth, gave her the rest. She clutched the little package in her fist.

"You've got to end them for good, Danny," she said. "Write that book. Promise me you will."

"Before I do, I want their files. My guess is they're packed with incriminating evidence. They think they're safe up there on their hill, that no one is going to challenge them, look at what they have. I'm going to. First, though, we need to get the car out of the ditch and get you to a doctor."

"I'll stay here."

"You can't stay here," I said.

"No one can help me now. By the time you get the car out of the ditch, even if you could, they might kill someone. They are having a gathering tonight. I heard them talk. Someone will die. It was supposed to be me, but I got the impression they found someone else."

"Who's they?" Buck asked.

"The council. That skinny cop that helped take me."

"Coolie," Buck said.

"Yeah," she said. "Him. And you know who was driving the car? Chief Dudley. It was the two of them that took me, and it was Dudley at the top of the stairs checking your room. He gave up because they believed me, didn't see your car."

"Ah, shit," I said.

"Yeah," she said. "Ah, shit. Funny thing, he really seemed ashamed of himself, like he was glad they didn't find you, like he wished they hadn't found me. But not enough to not go along with it."

"Said you couldn't trust law enforcement," Buck said.

"I know what you got to do," Mrs. Chandler said. "And you need to go do it. As for the water, I'm hoping it will rise and fill the car."

"Don't say that," I said.

"Life seems important until it doesn't seem like life anymore. I'd never make it home even if the car was on the road and running. I'm about out of juice. Listen to that wind howl. I love the rain."

She stretched out on the seat with her head slightly propped up against the door. "Go on," she said.

She closed her eyes. Her breathing was shallow and soon I couldn't hear it anymore.

I took the light off her.

(50)

The water was a couple inches higher than last time we left the car. It was deep enough and strong enough to make the doors harder to open, but with a bit of work, we managed.

I got my impromptu key for the file drawers, a straight tire tool with a beveled edge, out of the trunk of the car.

I left my trusty ax handles. Buck had the shotgun. I gave him the shotgun shells I had. We both had our pistols under our shirts.

"What was wrong with her?" Buck said.

"Cancer."

"Seems like a tough ol' bird," he said.

"Yeah. Come on. Get down the road a piece, I know a shortcut."

I looked through the glass at Mrs. Chandler. Her mouth was open, her hands folded across her chest. Like Elvis, she had left the building.

Me and Buck climbed up onto the road.

* * *

It was hard to know exactly where we were, but I knew we were close to the lake. When we got to the turn off the main highway, I could identify it more out of luck than design.

We practically swam along, and I didn't know we had reached the edge of the lake until there was a hot bolt of lightning that made the sky so bright it was briefly yellow. A strand of it struck the old bridge and made a hissing blue net that trickled across the metal cables from the far end to our end.

In that brief blue fulmination, I could see that much of the lake had already filled with water and was still filling. I could hear the loud gurgling rush of it and see the shadowy shapes of the buildings of Long Lincoln sticking out of it.

When the trace of lightning was gone from the bridge, I rested the flashlight beam on the lake and let it stay there for a moment. To put it mildly, the lake looked troubled. It was still not fully filled, but it was working on it.

I shone the light toward the dam and spillway, but I couldn't really see it clearly. I could hear its roar and make out white explosions of dark water flying out of the spillway gaps and into the lake.

"Damn," Buck said. "Never seen it like this."

"Come on," I said.

I led us along the edge of the lake. The shoreline was growing thinner as the water rose rapidly. The trail that led up the hill and into the trees to the concrete bunker door was mostly concealed by night and rain. I guided us up.

It was a struggle to climb because of the nature of the slope. Gravel came loose under our wet shoes and there were scrubs and small trees we had to work our way around to get up there.

Eventually, we came to the trees and the hill where the door was built into the side.

"Been to this lake a lot," Buck said. "Never knew this was here."

"To find it, you would have to be looking for it," I said. "I think this was just a way for workers to walk in. Other tunnels were designed for trucks and storage. It was like a maze under the old town."

I gave Buck the flashlight and tried to grab the edge of the door with my fingers, but there wasn't much edge to grab. Besides, it was most likely locked. Holding the tire tool with both hands, I stuck the beveled edge into the crack of the door and put all my weight into prying it open.

About the time I felt as if my arms would come off at the shoulders and my balls would blow like strained gaskets, I heard the lock snap and the door moved slightly with a scraping sound. But the door was still too heavy to open.

Buck stuck the flashlight in his back pocket, set the shotgun against one of the trees, grabbed the tire tool with me, and we cranked back on it.

There was a grating noise that put my teeth on edge, then the door opened somewhat and the stink down there came out at us in a wave. When we had it open enough for us to slip inside, Buck used the flash to poke light into the darkness.

Buck said, "Jesus. What a stink."

"Try not to shoot Flashlight Boy. You'll smell him before you see him, even over all this stench."

I shoved the tire tool in my belt, took the flashlight from Buck. He grabbed the shotgun, and we dipped inside, leaving the door open.

The light revealed that the water was higher than before at the bottom of the steps. I thought about how old the tunnels were and how fragile they might have become. I thought too about the great rain that had widened and deepened the river that supplied the lake and how when it hit the spillway, it was hammering it with tremendous force, shooting water through the designed gaps in foaming bursts. That was a lot of water.

The lake and its surroundings were flooding fast due to the ground drying hard and losing its ability to absorb. Being beneath that swelling water in a crumbling tunnel almost unnerved me. It brought back moonlit memories of the dark depths, the taillights of the Buick going down, down, down.

I thought about Mrs. Chandler. Soon the water would be up and in the car. I hated the thought of it, her body floating inside the car the way my father's had. There was nothing I could do. The wet night would claim her and that's all there was to it.

"I think I know the way," I said.

"I'm reminded of Nam," Buck said.

We stepped down the stairs and into the cold water. The air was thick as mud but less tasty. We passed the bricked-in tunnels. Water slipped from cracks in the bricks and trickled down the walls or spilled onto the tunnel floor in spurts that fled into drains at the edges of the walls. We sloshed it about as we went.

Rats moved in the light, running over and under and around one another. Their high-pitched squeaks echoing off the tunnel walls were painful to the ears. They didn't like the water. They didn't like the leaks. Me and the rats had that in common.

(51)

We came to Winston's hidey-hole. None of the dangling flashlights were on. I shone my light around, saw bones, racks, rats, and old clothes, but not him.

I went around and turned on the flashlights hanging from strings, and when I had as many on as I could comfortably manage, that section of Winston's underground world was filled with light. Rats scampered and roaches scuttled into the darkness. But there was no Winston.

"Amazing," Buck said.

"We leave these on, this will be our beacon back."

"Where's Flashlight Boy?"

"He doesn't check in with me, Buck. There are other tunnels, not bricked in, so he could be in any one of them. He may be out in the rain. He's used to weather. He may be stealing flashlights and batteries, trying on new clothes at the graveyard. Come on."

We moved along quickly with the water trickling and the rats running and came to the concrete wall that was actually a door. I pulled the tire iron from my belt, and with Buck holding the flashlight, I stuck it in the crack between door and wall and heaved. It was tough, but not as tough as the outside door. It slid open. The air that sighed onto us was fresh and cold because we were soaked from head to foot.

Not bothering to wipe my shoes, I put the tire tool in my belt and took the light from Buck and guided us up the stairs until we came to the platform where the outside light came through the window and laid a cold creamy square of illumination over us. I could see rain in the light coming from outside, and it came down hard enough to make the window rattle.

I put my ear to the door. Except for the outside rain, it was as silent as Lincoln's tomb. I turned the latch and pushed the door aside. There was the same bit of light like before, shining out from dull bulbs.

I shifted the light to my left hand, pulled my pistol out from under my shirt, and moved along in the dimness of the corridor on tiptoes and wishful thinking. Buck sneaked along behind me.

I came to the ballroom and gently cracked open the door. Dead dark. We went in there, pausing just long enough for Buck to stand under the non-glowing disco ball, cock a hip, and point a finger in the air.

"I was born to boogie," he said.

"I can see that."

His moment of humor passed, and I led us along, careful about it, but moving swiftly as well.

We went up the steps and into the room that overlooked where Creosote Johnny hid patiently in a cabinet, where the garrote chair and the triangular table were kept.

Inching back one of the curtains, I looked down into the room. It was dark. The table and chair and raised stage were merely shapes.

Perhaps after losing their sacrifice, Mrs. Chandler, the council had canceled the night's festivities.

We left that room and I led us to the file room. After we

slipped inside, I closed the door and locked it. Buck leaned the shotgun against the frame of the doorway and I waved the flashlight around.

I picked a file drawer, gave Buck the flashlight again. I stuck my revolver back in my waistband, pulled the tire tool from my belt, and jammed the beveled tip into the edge of that drawer and gave it a sharp pop.

I pulled the file drawer open. There was a fat folder in there. I opened it, thumbed through it.

Buck leaned over my shoulder with the flashlight shining the beam on what I had found.

(52)

We went through file after file, piling them on the long table between the velvet-covered couches. They were all variations of the same thing. Some went far enough back that the big three wouldn't have been old enough to be city council members. Just strange kids who had certain nasty proclivities in common. My guess was a lot of that stuff had been kept in a shoebox until they became rich and powerful.

The oldest files had obviously been cherished. These contained drawings of squirrels, dogs, and cats with ropes around their necks, their eyes marked with Xs, their tongues drawn unnaturally long. What made it so goddamn creepy was how silly it all was and at the same time as earnest as a genital wart.

Also in the drawings were images of Creosote Johnny of the wide smile and sharp teeth, forever squatting, holding his penis like a priceless object.

In later files there were greening Polaroid snaps. In others, more sophisticated photos. The most recent file drawers were larger and contained labeled home movies.

At some point in the later photos, the crude triangular table appeared. There were shots of the three and unidentifiable others sitting at the triangular table. A male child, eleven or twelve, also was shown sitting at the table, and later photos revealed the child had aged and grown to enormous size and was none other than Jack Jr., maturing into a cold, calculating son of a bitch.

In the early photos, the big three ranged from youthful to middle-aged, and the later ones showed they had arrived at the Methuselah district.

The men were dressed in the fashions and hairstyles of the photographic moments: suits with narrow lapels, then broad ones, ties fat and skinny, white belts and mod scarves, cream and lime-green leisure suits, cowboy boots and Italian shoes, short hair, long hair, mustaches and beards and, finally, back to clean-shaven. Kate Conroy appeared with varying hairstyles, wearing poodle skirts, miniskirts, tennis shoes and sensible shoes, go-go boots, high heels, and black flats with all the personality of an afternoon in New Jersey. Frosted lips and ruby lips, mascara thick as a second coating of wall paint, then little to no makeup.

Other photos showed them looking at something, and the something was Creosote Johnny. The figure had been placed in front of a chair. The chair changed, but the person behind the chair twisting a garrote was consistent for a long time in the photos. It was Jack Sr.

In a few photos, when the victim was a child, Kate Conroy was twisting the garrote. Early shots of her when she was quite beautiful were somehow more disconcerting than later photos. A strange contrast of this woman in a miniskirt and jacked-up boots tightening the garrote, the expression on her face akin to sexual gratification.

The occupants of the chair changed, of course. Black. White. Male. Female. Young children, young adults, middle-aged, and old. In a couple of photos, I noted some who had been seated at that triangular table had been demoted to the big chair and the garrote.

The expression on Jack Sr.'s face and, later, Jack Jr.'s as they twisted the garrote was equally as orgasmic as Kate Conroy's. A look of someone having temporarily been invited into a heaven filled with sadists and torturers, given a seat among all the dark angels from the beginning of time.

The faces of the victims were less rapturous. They were obviously drugged, which would, of course, make them easier to handle. Their eyes bulged; their tongues, dark and swollen, stuck out of their mouths like stuffed socks. Their chests were expanded, the toes of their shoes were curled like claws.

In the files, all of their names were listed. These would be those who had been assigned insurance policies they had never paid for and were totally unaware of owning. Sacrifices to Creosote Johnny. The council, a club of ritual killers, had transformed their existence through imagination and greed. They were warped proponents of free enterprise and the American dream. They were the worst manifestation of the American dream.

They were among the self-chosen ones who made the soup, and the rest of us were boiling in it while being told we were merely warm, that there was a God in heaven and all was right with the world, when in truth, we existed only to be ladled into our masters' bowls and consumed.

(53)

We took cushions off the couches and used Buck's pocket-knife to cut the covers off them, and we stuffed those full of the files and videos, made ourselves two bags apiece. We couldn't take all of the files and recordings, but we could take enough for evidence. We carried them carefully to the cellar, which was no easy job. We ended up taking a chance and leaving the shotgun in the file room while we did it to make sure we could manage it all. The flashlight, the tire tool in my belt, our pistols under our shirts, and the bags were controllable. The shotgun was just too much.

We carried them into the tunnel and set them just inside. I decided to close the door, and Buck helped me do it. I then had an idea. I went across to the doors with the big rings and pulled one open and went in and got one of the wheelbarrows.

As I pushed it back through the doorway, Buck holding the door for me, I heard a soft grind. The sound was of the garage door at the far end sliding up. I could hear the purr of a finely tuned motor and see the glow of headlights. Buck left the door open a crack. We peered into the garage. There were headlights, and more behind those.

I could see the rain coming down out there, and it was as if it were being dumped from buckets, and the sound of it echoed inside the garage. The cars, wipers thrashing, glided inside.

It appeared there was some sort of gathering tonight after all.

I eased the door shut. We could hear car doors slamming and voices inside the garage. It sounded festive out there.

"What now?" Buck said. "Do we take the files and run?"

"Might be the smart thing, but I'm wondering if they are still having a, shall we say, assembly?"

"You mean, do they plan to have . . . what would you call it?"

"A sacrifice. Believe me, I know how that sounds. But if that's the case, we need to stop it."

"Depends on how many and who we have to stop."

"You had your chance to bail. Still can."

Buck huffed, then sighed, then grinned at me and said, "Ah, hell, let's go see. Just realized I left my pocketknife in the file room. I want that back."

*　　*　　*

I pushed the wheelbarrow into the tunnel and we put the makeshift bags of files into it. Then we quietly worked our way back to the area above the room with the triangular table in it, cut the flashlight, and sat on the floor next to the tall windows. I eased back a section of the heavy blue curtain that covered one of the windows.

Buck found a spot and did the same. The door opened and an oblong slash of yellow light filled the doorway. The light was marred by the slender shape of a man in the center of it.

The man came into the room and turned on the light. He was the tall cop who I knew now to be Coolie Parker, one of the clowns who'd attacked me twice with his partner, Jefferson Davis.

He was in uniform, bareheaded, a holstered gun resting on his hip. The light he turned on was soft and blue, and it filled the room like a velvet dream.

Coolie's movements under the blue light caused him to appear to be awkwardly swimming in deep water. He made his way onto the dais and to the cabinet behind the tall chair. He took out Creosote Johnny and for a long moment stood contemplating its appearance. Perhaps he was admiring it; perhaps he was wishing on it like a falling star.

He carried the figure to the front of the stage and placed it there as gently as a mother with child. He stepped off the dais, walked to the triangular table, stood at its pointed tip, turned, and examined the dark totem in that sweet, soft light.

It must have satisfied him, because he walked briskly to the open door and its gap of light, went through it with a glance around the room, a lift of his head toward us as we leaned out of the way, then closed the door.

"What do we do if they bring in someone?" I said. "For the business. You know."

"We stop it. That was your idea, remember?"

"Yeah, it was a good thought, but now I'm wondering. Coolie has a gun, maybe the others from the cars do too?"

"We have guns."

"I'm a terrible shot."

"I'm not that terrible," Buck said. "And what the hell else can we do? If we go for help, it'll all be over. And what help? In town, who do we know for sure that's not on their side? Who would help us? Who would believe us, anyway? Hell, I've seen the files, and even I don't believe it."

Buck had a point, of course, and he'd answered my question the way I had already answered it for myself. I hoped that when they finally came through that door and into the blue light, it would be with boxes of pizzas or that cheese tray I had imagined. Maybe there would be a dance party beneath the spinning disco ball, though the main three wouldn't be doing a lot of dancing. Judea Parker didn't even have the strength to nod to the music.

We sat there on the floor in a bit of the blue light that came through the cracks in the curtains. We sat there with no real plan and no real idea of what the hell was up; we waited to see and know. Time skulked by like it was on a respirator. One minute was an hour, two was a century. What were they doing out there?

Then I felt the air change, dust moving about. There was a creak of wood, and I smelled something strong and sweet, realized what was happening too late.

They came into the nearly dark room the way we had come in. Came in with a burst of anger and muscle.

I went for my pistol, but I might as well have been reaching for a star. I was tackled by someone.

Buck jumped up and pushed his back against the wall. He struck out at a tall shape that I figured was Coolie. Coolie went down, supported himself on his hands and knees, shook his head to clear the moss.

Then a big pear-shaped man in a cowboy hat banged Buck's head against the wall by shoving a palm under his chin. A hypodermic needle flashed and poked into Buck's neck.

Buck grunted, let out his breath, and slid down the wall to the floor, not moving. The big man tossed the hypodermic needle aside.

Then all of them were on me. I was so smothered by bodies I couldn't see who was who, but my nose was buried in a dark suit coat, and I knew who it was by the sickly-sweet smell that had entered the room ahead of him. Brut cologne, over-applied and worn by Jack Jr. His scent was so thick, I could have swung a hammock on it.

Someone had hold of my legs. I twisted my head free of Jack Jr.'s coat, and in the faint blue glow slipping through the curtains, I saw it was Coolie.

Then the big man in the cowboy hat pulled something from his shirt pocket. Another hypodermic needle. He popped the cap over the needle, bent down, and tried to poke it into me as I squirmed. I recognized who it was now. It was as Mrs. Chandler had said: Chief Dudley.

"Sorry, son," he said. "You're too goddamn nosy."

One of his cowboy boots stepped on the side of my leg and sent a bolt of fire up it.

The needle jabbed through my short shirtsleeve and into my right arm. I tried to avoid it. I jerked my arm enough that the needle popped loose and the liquid from it squirted onto my flesh like a hot ejaculation.

Then the needle went in again in a different spot. It was like being poked with a railroad spike. As Chief Dudley squeezed the plunger on the hypodermic, my head immediately felt as if it were being blown up with an air pump like a party balloon.

I struggled, and then I didn't. I found a hole in the universe and was working my way inside of it. I was no longer a balloon. I was a cosmic worm in search of nirvana, and nirvana was calm and still and soft and velvet blue.

(54)

All the world was blue and the blue flowed and bubbled and there were sounds in the blue. I think someone hit me once because my head moved but it didn't hurt. At that point, nothing hurt.

I was under the lake, swimming, looking into the depths, seeing the Buick's taillights going down, down, down, popping off and leaving me in the dark. Then above me there was light. I shifted and swam toward the surface. I was so weak I didn't think I could make it.

A dark swift shape came from above, and the shape took hold of me and pulled me up. Then I was jerked back. I looked down. It was Dad, but his face was twisted and his eyes glowed and he was trying to tug me down there with him. But the shape from the surface, from the light, succeeded and pulled me away. I was abruptly on the shore, and the face leaning down to look at me was Ronnie's.

"Danny," she said. "Wake up."

I think maybe she was patting my cheeks. I lay there on the shore of the lake looking up at my mermaid. But she was older, wearing a cop uniform, and I wasn't on the shore of Moon Lake at all. I was in the dark room with thin, blue cuts of light slicing into it. I could hear angry thunder and it made the huge building vibrate. The air was thick and tasted like burned toast.

I expected Ronnie's image to fade away, but it didn't.

I tried to move, but I was too weak to do much. My hands were tied behind my back. Ronnie slipped an arm under my shoulders and lifted me up. My brain slowly un-fuzzed.

"There's a knife in the connecting room, on the table," I said, remembering Buck's pocketknife and that he had forgotten to retrieve it.

Ronnie came back with Buck's pocketknife. I rolled on my side and she cut my hands free. I looked around the room. No Buck.

I felt weak as a birthday wish. I checked for my pistol, but they had taken it, of course. I decided I could get to my knees, and did, with Ronnie's help.

"How did you get here?" I said.

"When you didn't meet me, I thought something was wrong. I remembered your description of the tunnel. The door was open. I had my flashlight and my gun, and I went in. I decided to keep my uniform on. I'm the law."

"See my friend Flashlight Boy?"

"No."

"They've got Buck."

"What?"

I didn't bother to answer. I knee-walked to the curtain and pinched it open slightly, being really careful this time. I had thought I was sneaky before, but Coolie had seen me and that's how they had found us. Had to be. This time I opened the curtain just enough for one eye to see through.

Down in the blue room the light was gentle. Music filled the room and floated up. "Memories," sung by Al Martino.

Always hated that goddamn song, and now I hated it more.

I could see Buck down there in the chair. The rope was stuck through the holes in the back of the chair and went around Buck's neck. Buck's eyes fluttered, but it was obvious he wasn't awake. He'd gotten a lot more of the sleepy shot than I had. No one else was in the room.

The door opened and a blaze of buttery light crushed the blue velvet in the doorway. A procession began.

Coolie pushed Judea's wheelchair into the room. Judea Parker's head leaned to one side. The plastic mask covered his face, and his oxygen tank was strapped to his chair. His mouth hung open. You could have fired a cannon off next to his ear and danced an Irish jig in his lap and he wouldn't have been aware of it.

Coolie pushed Judea to a ramp that had been laid out while I napped. He pushed him up it and onto the dais and placed him beside the chair where Buck sat, then he came down. He had slipped a sports coat on over his uniform. They went together like a lion and a mouse. Coolie moved to stand on the left side of the table, his hands folded in front of him.

Jack Sr. came in leaning on his cane and a crutch. A parade float wearing an expensive suit. Behind him came Jack Jr. He was wearing a black robe with the hood thrown back. He looked big and ominous and at the same time as silly as a cheap party magician.

Moments later Kate Conroy entered the room in her motorized wheelchair. She was dressed in black and her hair was blue as steel in the light.

Estelle Parker was walking behind her. She wore a vanilla gown, and she wore it well. Her skin was peach-tinted porcelain, her hair was ripe wheat, and the gown clung to her legs when she walked. She stopped and stood near the door like a theater usher.

Then Chief Dudley came in. He looked tired and his shoulders were slumped. He trudged more than walked. He wore his uniform and his gun and his cowboy hat. No adjustments for him.

He probably slept in that outfit. He stood near the side of the curtained window.

Okay, they had my pistol, but I remembered the shotgun. I got to my feet, which was like trying to tack a cheap sailboat in a typhoon, but I did it.

"What are you doing?" Ronnie said.

"Shotgun."

I moved free of Ronnie and wobbled my way into the file room. The shotgun was leaning where Buck had left it. They had missed that. It had one shot, but at least with a shotgun, I was more likely to hit my target if I got up close. Problem was, there was more than one target.

I came in with the shotgun. Ronnie had peeled back the edge of a curtain, was peeking down. "Jesus," she said.

I worked my way over and cracked the curtains as well, looked down on what was going on. The music was still playing and now everyone was seated at the table. Jack Sr. and Kate Conroy were positioned on opposite sides, close to the long end of the triangular tip that pointed to the stage. Estelle had joined them. She sat primly on the side of the table closest to the door.

Jack Jr. came up the ramp and onto the stage. Damn, he was big. He had his hood lifted over his head now. His face was a shadow. He paused by Judea Parker, gently removed the oxygen mask from Judea's face.

Judea gulped big, then made several smaller gulps like a fish out of water. While he did this, Jack Jr. turned off the oxygen and then pinched Judea's nose with thumb and forefinger and pressed the palm of his other hand over Judea's mouth.

Jack Jr. yelled out, "For he who has given service!"

"Service" came the voices from below.

I started to move toward the steps that went down to the

hallway, the floor below, but Ronnie grabbed me, said, "Give it a minute."

I thought, Yeah, why not? Judea had reached the end of his usefulness. and my guess was they were all part of this pact, including him. When you were no longer of use, then you added to the success of the others.

Jack removed his hands from Judea's face and put a hand on his chest, feeling for a heartbeat. A moment later he seemed satisfied that Judea was gone. "Memories" had faded, and an older song started, "In the Mood," by Glenn Miller. In spite of myself, I almost tapped my toes to that.

Jack was now behind Buck. He took a moment to better position the rope around Buck's neck.

"The time is now," I said.

Jack called out, "And I crank."

And crank he did, grabbing the stick that was through the loops on the rope. The rope tightened on Buck's neck enough it made him hold his head up. His eyelids fluttered. His mouth opened wide.

"And I crank," Jack said again as we were moving out the door and down the steps toward the ceremony room.

"It's now or never," I said, and I made my way down the steps, trying not to fall over due to the remains of my drug stupor. Ronnie had her service revolver drawn.

(55)

Y ou know how in your thoughts, you plan a thing, and though it may not seem simple, it does have a design, and you feel, yeah, I'll do this or that, and this or that will happen?

I visualized Ronnie and me rushing into the room with our weapons pointed; we would say, "Halt, free Buck," and then ease our way out, and everyone would sit there and watch us leave. But that's the problem with plans. They generally get derailed to some degree or another by unexpected reality.

Of course, it might have helped if Ronnie and I had had a real plan, but we didn't have time for that.

Into and down the hall and through the door we went, and when we entered the room, the song had switched to "Hang Down Your Head, Tom Dooley." Jack Jr. had yelled again, "And I crank," and from the table came "Crank," said by Kate and Jack Sr., and Jack Jr., grinning, wound the garrote again. Buck's tongue was thrusting out of his mouth.

I yelled something, but no one noticed. The music was loud, but I could hear those at the table crying out in chorus, slamming their fists on the table, saying, "Crank it. Crank it."

I speed-walked right past the table, past Chief Dudley. Ronnie was behind me, gun drawn. The music was coming from a black box of some kind on a shelf. I slammed it with the stock of my shotgun. It fell off and the wire came unplugged and the recorder hit the floor. Plastic shattered and a cassette tape slid across the shiny tile.

"Leave him be," I said.

Jack Jr. eyed me as if I were nothing more than a fly and held the garrote tight, but he slowly changed his mindset; a shotgun can be persuasive. He let go of the garrote and it loosened. He started to move toward me. I pointed the shotgun at him. "Take your big ass and sit on the stage by the old dead fart."

Jack Jr. went and sat. In that stupid outfit with the hood, he looked like a sad trick-or-treater who had been robbed of his Halloween candy.

I glanced at Ronnie. She had her pistol on Dudley and then she moved it and pointed it across the table at Coolie, who had gone so far as to rest his hand on the butt of his holstered revolver.

"Please pull it," Ronnie said. "We been to the range together, and you can't hit an elephant in the ass with a load of buckshot at ten paces. Go on. Pull it."

Coolie gave the muscles in his face a workout, but he didn't say anything back. He slowly moved his hand away.

I went over and kicked Creosote Johnny off the stage. It hurt my foot, but I tried not to show it. When Creosote Johnny hit the floor with a thud, I heard Jack Sr. and Kate Conroy let out their breath.

"Think he's going to be mad at you?" I said.

"You little meddling shit," Kate said.

"You old murdering bitch," I said. "You bunch of fucking cartoon villains."

I stepped off the stage, walked over to Coolie with the shotgun pointed at him, said, "Pinch the gun out of your holster and place it on the floor."

He hesitated longer than Jack Jr. had. I cocked back the hammer on the shotgun. The sound was like the latch to hell being thrown open.

"Shit," he said. He pinched the pistol by the butt, slipped it from his holster, and placed it on the floor.

"Step back some."

He stepped back. I went over and stood in front of him. Up close, I could see his face looked banged up from our last encounter. I kicked him smooth in the balls. "That's because I don't like you."

He blew air, bent his knees, and slowly brought them to rest on the floor. He tried to say something, but all his mouth did was open and close.

I picked up the pistol and stuck it in my waistband. I looked at the table. Kate and Jack Sr. reminded me of mummies. It made no sense that they were so powerful. As for Estelle, she looked as if all she had ever wanted was suddenly not worth the match it would take to set it on fire. Her eyes were glazed over and the blue light moved against them like dreams.

I looked at Ronnie. She was crouched, holding her gun on Chief Dudley again.

"I wouldn't have thought it," she said.

Dudley looked like a kid who had just been found jacking off in the holy water by a nun. "Truth is," Chief Dudley said, "neither would I."

"Please do like Coolie and put your gun on the floor."

He did.

"Now step back against the window."

He did that too. "I thought I was someone else," Chief Dudley said.

"I don't care."

"I thought I was really all right, then one day I was them."

Ronnie trembled slightly. She picked up his revolver, dropped that one in her holster, continued to hold hers at the ready.

I crossed in front of the table with the shotgun and stood near the dais. I said to Jack Jr., "Dump dipshit Parker out of the chair there."

Jack Jr. studied me to see if I was serious, decided I was. He stood up and walked behind the wheelchair, took hold of the back of it, and pushed it. He tilted it forward when he was at the edge of the dais. Judea toppled out of it like a rag doll, hit the edge of the stage, then crumpled onto the floor.

"Take the rope off Buck's neck and put him in the wheelchair. And please, act like an asshole and drop him so I can blow a hole through you."

Thunder rolled, doors rattled, the windows shook. I was so engaged in making sure that Jack Jr. did what I asked, I didn't notice that Estelle had stood up and floated away from the table like a vanilla ghost. I only realized it when I heard the fabric of her gown whispering over her thighs.

She looked back at me with her distant eyes, opened the door, and went into the slice of lemon light and on out. She closed the door as if quietly leaving for a bathroom break. I thought, What the hell? But she was gone.

"Nobody else try that," I said.

I took note of Coolie attempting to stand up from the floor. I said, "Coolie, that's not smart. Go sit at the table."

He gingerly rose to his feet, lightly stepped to the table, and sat slowly where Estelle had been seated.

Jack Jr. had not placed Buck in Parker's chair. He had only moved to stand behind Buck in the strangle chair.

"Cut down with that, you get me and Buck," he said.

"I'll get just you," Ronnie said. She was now pointing the pistol at him from across the room. It was a long shot with a handgun, but I had a feeling she could manage it, even with him standing behind Buck.

Jack Jr. decided not to test it. He lifted Buck from the garrote chair as lightly as if he were made of feathers and settled him into Parker's wheelchair.

"Now wheel Mr. Rogers carefully down the ramp and stop in front of Ronnie."

I went around the table to the wider end of it, nearer Ronnie. Jack Jr. stopped the chair about six feet from her.

"Now," I said to Jack, "you go back and sit down where you were, on the edge of the stage."

I could see Jack was starting to get testy, so I tucked the shotgun into my shoulder and eyed down the barrel. Survivalism trumped courage again. He went and sat on the edge of the dais. He rested his feet on Judea Parker like he was a footstool.

It was then that I heard the motor of Kate Conroy's chair. It was humming and she was rolling toward the door.

"Where do you think you're going?" I said.

"Shoot me," she said. "You haven't got the balls. That's why we're us and you're you."

This was true. I didn't feel inclined to blow the head off a geriatric woman in a wheelchair. She reached the door, tugged on the handle. It rattled a little, but the door didn't move.

"Goddamn it," she said.

"I'll be going too," Jack Sr. said. He took hold of his cane and crutch and tried to boost himself to a standing position. "Give me a hand, Coolie," Jack Sr. said. "Get me up on these things."

"Coolie, you I will shoot," I said.

Coolie didn't move.

Jack struggled to rise and balance on his sticks. One of them slipped and he landed on the floor with a smack. That knocked his chair close to Dudley. That made Jack Jr. stand up and start to move toward him.

"Easy," I said. "Put him back in his chair, but nothing else."

"Goddamn door," Kate said. She was still tugging on it. "Someone open this damn thing."

Chief Dudley said, "You know I carry a hideout gun, Ronnie."

Jack eased over and picked up his father and sat him in the chair, gave Senior his crutches.

Ronnie and I had been distracted by Kate's and Jack Sr.'s antics. Dudley had fished a gun from somewhere, a small revolver that looked like a toy. I had no idea where he had been keeping it. He lifted it and pointed it in mine and Ronnie's general direction.

"Now the fucking worm has turned," Jack Sr. said.

"Coolie carries one too," he said and shifted the gun so it was pointing at Coolie, who was reaching into his boot. Chief Dudley shot Coolie through the head. The gunshot sounded like a snap of thunder in that room. Blood jumped across the table and misted in the blue light and sprinkled on the floor. Coolie fell face-first onto the table and one of his hands fluttered at his side for a moment like a dying sparrow, then went still. Blood and strands of brains oozed in a thick puddle from his head, flowed across the table in a stream.

"What the scalded fuck, Dudley?" Jack Sr. said.

Dudley looked at us. He said, "Go. Just go. And Ronnie. I never meant to be this way. It gets in you like tapeworms."

Ronnie got behind the wheelchair with Buck in it, dropped her pistol in his lap, and started pushing him toward the door.

Kate was still rattling the knob. "Open this fucking door."

I backed out behind Ronnie, pointing the shotgun. Just as I was going through the door Ronnie had left open, Chief Dudley looked at me with this little grin on his face, like those jagged kinds you see cut into pumpkins at Halloween. He may have felt like he had redeemed himself.

I thought Senior had transformed into a crippled sloth, but I was wrong, at least in one respect. He pulled a long, thin sword out of his cane and stuck it into Dudley's belly. It went in as smooth as light through a window.

Dudley tried to lift his gun and shoot, but the blade had claimed him. The gun slipped out of his hand and landed on the floor. He slid to the floor so fast, it pulled the sword from Senior's hand and pulled Senior to the floor again.

Dudley's ankles crossed as he sat, and his head and neck rested back against the wall. A blue-lit swell of blood, like a colorful Rorschach pattern, puddled on his belly, then leaked to the floor.

Senior was wallowing on the floor like a turtle on its back. Jack Jr. was already eyeing Dudley's pistol. I didn't like the idea, but when he reached for it, I cut him down with the shotgun.

When I pulled the trigger there was a faint snap, a puffing sound, and a burst of smoke from the barrel. The smoke twisted in the blue light like the arrival of a genie. But there wouldn't be any three wishes.

The shell was a dud.

Jack Jr. smiled.

(56)

I had Coolie's pistol but I didn't think of using it. I was too frightened and confused to think about much.

By this time, Jack Jr. had hold of Chief Dudley's fallen pistol. It looked like a cap gun in his huge hand.

I dropped the shotgun and made a run into the long hallway; the blue light fell in after me, making the photos on the walls appear to move.

Ronnie had already gone through the door at the end of the hall, the one that led to the platform on top of the stairs. The door had closed behind her. I grabbed the latch and turned it as a bullet slapped into the door, just above my shoulder, scattering wood dust. I shoved the door open as another shot picked at the bottom of my ear like an insect bite.

I hopped through the doorway onto the landing, slammed the door behind me, and threw the lock. Ronnie was on the landing with Buck and the chair.

Another volley punctured the door, zipped past us, and rattled down into the cellar.

I got hold of the chair, turned it, started pulling it after me as we went down the stairs, Buck bouncing like a child on a seesaw.

At the bottom of the stairs, I said to Ronnie, "Run for the tunnel. Grab the wheelbarrow inside the gap. It's full of evidence. Go to the end. I'm not there in a few minutes, take the evidence and drive away."

Ronnie slipped her flashlight off her belt, flicked it on, and didn't hesitate. She broke into a run. I wheeled the chair around to start after her. I turned too fast and the chair flipped over and Buck rolled onto the floor.

I set the chair up, got him under the arms, and tried to lift him up. It took some work, but I pulled him over and boosted him into the chair, his head wagging from side to side all the while.

Jack Jr. was banging against the door with all his weight. I heard the lock snap, the doorframe crack. Jack appeared on the landing, standing on top of the broken door he had shouldered down. He looked less like a trick-or-treater now in his robe and more like the angel of death.

I rush-pushed Buck toward the gap in the wall. A shot smacked against the wall and showered me in brick powder. I glanced to see if the wheelbarrow and the makeshift bags were gone, and they were. In a moment, we were bumping down the short row of steps, moving through darkness, the chair's wheels splattering water and frightening rats.

I could hear Jack Jr.'s big feet slapping in the water behind us. Another shot snapped off and reverberated in the tunnel. I could feel it pluck at my hair like a morning breeze, but all that counted was it had missed me.

I made a curve in the tunnel as another shot picked off some brick. Behind me, Jack Jr.'s pursuit was loud, and in the next instant I could smell his cologne, and he was on me.

He gripped me by the shoulders and whirled me away from the wheelchair, slammed me into the tunnel wall. Rats scuttled and I felt stunned. Then he had me again, grabbing me by my shirt. "You ruined everything," he said.

He lifted me as if I were a Styrofoam dummy and sent me sailing along the tunnel floor. I hit Buck's chair and tipped it over, sending Buck into a trail of running water. The chair lay on its side with a wheel spinning.

I got up. If anyone had been there to see me do it, it would have looked like watching the evolution of mankind, the way I put myself together. From all fours to slightly standing to mostly erect to, finally, fully upright.

Jack Jr. was barreling toward me. I reached for Coolie's gun, but it was gone. It had fallen out of my waistband somewhere along the way. I might have found it had I had a flashlight and an hour and a small search party of rats to assist me.

Jack Jr. grabbed me, lifted me, and started to crush me in a bear hug. He had his hands locked behind my back and was squeezing me like a vise. Sweat had collided with his cologne. It was stronger than the stench of the tunnel. I felt an internal organ shift. A fart left me. I began to bend, my head going back. I hammered at him with my fist. I thought I broke his nose, but that might have been wishful thinking.

I tried to claw at his eyes, but I was bent back too far. I felt as if I were going to pass out, and then I heard squeaking and splashing, turned my head, and saw a light coming along one of the side tunnels. The light came quickly and behind the light came that horrid smell I had encountered that night on the lakeshore. Rats squeaked, and in the glow of the light I could see the shape was coated in rats. The flashlight's beam cut across the shadows, made an arc into the side of Jack Jr.'s head.

The glass face of the flashlight shattered, but there were tiny fragments of glass briefly visible in the light from the bulb as the flash came loose from Flashlight Boy's hand, hit the floor, and spun, swinging a thin beam of light around and around.

Jack Jr., as if mildly bothered, dropped me into the cold water that ran through the middle of the tunnel. My hand was touching Buck's hand and it was wet and cold.

I hurt, but I was more afraid than in pain. I regained my feet and grabbed the flashlight. That was one tough flashlight, heavily coated in rubber and made of heavy metal. I poked it in the direction of the battling behemoths.

The light winked off rats leaping from their human taxi as Jack Jr. hammered Flashlight Boy with his fists. It was like a Godzilla and King Kong movie. Something silver winked in the light and shot down, rose up again, shot down again. I realized it was the blade of a pocketknife. The one I had given Flashlight Boy.

Jack dropped faster than a gigolo's drawers and Flashlight Boy leaped onto him. Splashing about in the water, they made sounds like two whales mating. I moved the light from them to look for the pistol. A blasting sound and a burst of red fire flashed in the tunnel. Jack Jr. had found the pistol before me.

Flashlight Boy barked once with pain. He was straddling Jack Jr., still striking him with the pocketknife but doing it slower now. There was another flash and a blast. Flashlight Boy made a weaker sound this time, but the knife rose and went down once more before he slumped over Jack Jr. in a lump.

Jack Jr. struggled his way out from under Flashlight Boy's body. It was a hard go. That man was heavy.

I righted the wheelchair and dragged Buck back into it. He was like a sandbag. Doing this sent fire up my spine where Jack Jr. had compressed it. I turned off the flashlight, dropped it in Buck's lap, and started shoving the wheelchair forward as hard as I could go.

Rats leaped about my wet feet, and chill water sloshed onto my pants legs. Behind me I heard Jack Jr. splashing down the tunnel, coming after me again.

(57)

I passed where Flashlight Boy's flashlights were hanging, bumped my head on one of his unique light fixtures as I went, came to the gap that led into the narrower tunnel, and headed toward the steps that led up to the exit.

Buck sat fully upright for a moment, said, "I think I need some coffee," and then was silent.

As I neared the steps, a light hit my face, causing me to slam to a stop.

"It's me," Ronnie said. "I had to wait, Danny. I couldn't leave you."

"Jack's behind me."

"Get Buck up the steps."

It was like Sisyphus pushing his rock up the hill. I would get Buck almost up and then I'd lose him and he would slide us backward. I had to back-skip to keep from being run over by the wheelchair.

On the third try I broke the curse and pushed him toward where a flash of lightning showed through the breach in the open door to the lake path. Blue needles of rain were briefly visible and then the flash was gone and the rest of it was guesswork.

When I got Buck to the doorway, I paused there, locked the

wheels, and started back down the steps. I could see Ronnie's flashlight shining, and then I heard Jack Jr. splashing in the water. A shot rang out from his direction, then another, and her light went out.

There was one more shot originating near me, and the shape that was Jack Jr. did a soft shoe shuffle to the left and hit the wall. The shape slid into the water.

"Ronnie," I said, looking where her light had been.

Behind me she said, "I'm here."

I turned and we embraced.

"I stuck the light in a crack in the wall," she said. "I fooled the son of a bitch."

"Certainly did."

"I have a penlight too," she said and produced it from what seemed to be Batman's utility belt.

She put the light on Jack Jr. His mouth and eyes were open, but nobody was home. He had a hole in the middle of his forehead and blood was leaking out of it and running down his face. He had wet spots all over his robe where he had been stabbed by Flashlight Boy. His hand, still holding the gun, was by his side in the water.

"I was aiming for his chest," Ronnie said.

"Same result. I think he was running on adrenaline. Flashlight Boy poked some serious holes in him."

"Where is he?"

"Didn't make it. He saved my life, and then you did. Again."

"You just happened to be here."

"Point taken. The evidence?"

"I've already put it in the cruiser. I came back to help."

"Glad you did."

*   *   *

I pushed the chair out of the gap and into the night. The rain on Buck's face stirred him. He looked around; water cascaded off his head and ran down his cheeks.

"I've had a very odd dream," he said.

I pushed Buck where there was no trail, trying to make a path to where Ronnie had parked her cruiser, because down below, the old trail was washed away and the water was rising. There was tangled wet grass, some water, lots of mud. It was like attempting to plow furrows at the bottom of the ocean with a cheap rototiller.

Ronnie helped me push the chair. We fought that damn thing and Buck's big ass all the way to Ronnie's car. I bet it took us over half an hour. When we got to her cruiser, the water had risen almost to the top of the hill. It couldn't have been more than four feet from the car's front tires. The wheelbarrow was parked beside the car and was full of water.

I managed to pull Buck out of the chair and onto the back seat. I left the chair outside. I looked out at the night. I couldn't see the tops of the buildings anymore. I couldn't see the bridge my father had driven through. Just dark water. I remembered what my father had said about dark souls crying and roaming the earth.

The rain made the windshield opaque. Buck had begun to snore. Ronnie started the engine and no sooner had we begun to drive out than there was a sound like a pistol shot and the world lit up bright as a spotlight on a circus act for a long, thrilling instant.

I turned and looked back and saw the trees on the higher ridge above the lake had been struck by that bolt of lightning, and a small fire was trying to rage in the treetops. The intense rain put it out almost immediately and a cloud rose from the trees like a little mushroom burst from a small atomic bomb.

On out of there we went, the windshield wipers going, the headlights fighting to give visibility three feet in front of us. The sides of the road were guesswork. The taillights behind us seemed nothing more than a red foam. Still we went on, Ronnie guided more by instinct than vision of the road.

We nearly went into water-filled ditches a couple of times, and then finally we rolled away from Moon Lake and the great patch of woods that surrounded it. It was a little brighter out there in the clearings, but along the road there were no lights from houses; not even the shapes of houses were visible.

Then, as if someone had turned off a faucet, there was a sudden cessation of the rain, and the clouds slowly rolled back like a terrier ripping the stuffing out of a teddy bear. A fragment of moon. A scattering of stars like damp glitter. The shapes of houses were now visible, but still without lights. The road shimmered as if it were a silver snake.

PART FIVE

THE SOBER LIGHT OF DAY

(58)

When it was done and some time had passed, the whole thing
seemed like a dream, but dreams have cracks in them, and
now and again I fall through them.

In those dreams, I remembered all that had happened, sometimes realistically, but frequently less so. Creosote Johnny would
have legs, Kate Conroy was still tugging on that door, and Jack Sr.
sat silent as the water in the lake rose up through the trees and
tipped over into the bowl of land that contained the golf course
and the great country club with its many rooms.

The water would snap the walls, break through the windows,
and finally, as if in answer to Kate Conroy's pitiful cries, the door
would open easily and the water would rush in thick as mercury.
It would wash over her and everything else, seal the living and
the dead and all the country club inside a pulsating wad of tainted
silver that would float away and rise into the night sky.

Between the wet moon and wet stars, there would be an empty
gap in the vast sky as immense as a solar system. The gap would
have sharp, blackened teeth. The open mouth of Creosote Johnny:
Great eyes like balls of cosmic fire would blaze in the sky above that
mouth, and all the contents of the silver gob would be sucked into

that mouth like phlegm being inhaled. There would then be flashes of lightning inside the mouth and rolls of thunder like Japanese drums, followed by the wild, deafening screaming of souls. And then the mouth would close and there wouldn't be even a murmur. The red eyes would fade and the sky would be black and sleek and clear without moon or stars.

The reality was much the same, but simpler. The bowl of land where the country club stood filled with water and muck and nothing survived. The pseudo-castle proved less stable than the buildings in the original Long Lincoln. It was like cardboard and plywood before the tremendous mass of rolling water. It came apart. Fragments of the roof were found miles away where the lake broke open and filled streams and flooded pastures and drowned cows and a handful of humans. Scatterings of wet photos and soaked videos were found. They added to the better evidence Ronnie had saved. The stuff I had hidden in the house next door to Mrs. Chandler, as well as the materials in the Moonshine Castle. The FBI became involved.

Bodies of the city council members were never found. Kate Conroy's wheelchair was discovered in a tree, but not her. No Jack Sr. either. No Estelle Parker. She may well have made it away before the water washed through the country club, but it's doubtful.

The open tunnel door on the hill and the open door in the country club down in the cellar no longer sealed out the wet. Turbulent waters tucked the tunnels tight. Curiously, both Flashlight Boy's and Jack Jr.'s bodies were located, tangled together in a ball of mud at the foot of the steps that led up and out to the hill.

Chief Dudley's longtime lover, Duncan, packed up in the dead of night and decamped for parts unknown.

I got Christine to come back. The sale of the paper had not been fully executed, and she became publisher and editor again. I wrote the rest of my articles and have used them to sell a book for a nice advance. Everyone feels certain, odd as it all is, true as it all is, that it will be a bestseller. I bought a house already, or bought it with the bank, and I hope I'll be able to pay for it with the profits. The house I bought is the one next door to the Chandler home. No ghost with its head blown apart has appeared from the closets.

All manner of things came out when the city council members were gone. People who knew things, but had not before said things, talked.

We never found the body of Mrs. Chandler or my car that contained her. My guess is it and her are at the bottom of the lake, like those other cars were.

Ronnie and I tried out our relationship for a while, a few months, and it was nice, and then suddenly it wasn't. Jim Crow, like a warlock, still rides the wind in East Texas, especially in a town like New Long Lincoln. Even with its main bad old souls departed, there are remnants. It was okay by me, but it was too much for her. Too many whispers, too many changes even for someone with a mind for change.

I go out to the Candleses from time to time, and sometimes I have dinner with them and Ronnie and her fiancé, Buck Rogers.

We laugh and talk and get along fine, and I die each time his hand touches her, remembering the joy of her flesh, the thrill of her touch.

But it is what it is. Not all skies stay sunny. Not all hopes are fulfilled.

Mr. Candles still trains me in boxing. I use his garage gym sometimes when he's otherwise involved. They are still like the parents I wished I'd had.

An interesting thing was discovered, and Shirley gave me this news. She came to the house I've bought on the edge of town, looking beautiful and smart and prim. In her little sweet voice, she told me that the DNA test I had finally taken had been compared to the DNA in the bones and skin that had been in the back of my father's car. The results were not what I'd expected.

It was my mother.

The starred tooth was a lie. A dentist was finally located, and he confirmed that she had in fact had it replaced in those months she was gone. He could tell. The entire tooth was new. I wouldn't have thought it. Nor would I have thought the jewelry was hers. Seemed she changed everything about herself, like a snake shedding its skin.

That and the DNA killed the idea that she might be out there somewhere. She wasn't. I had my parents cremated. I put my father's ashes in the lake where he wanted to be. My mother's ashes are on a shelf in the bedroom I've turned into a study. They are in a bright blue urn. I'm considering what I will eventually do with them. No answers have arrived.

I guess she'd wanted out of her old life altogether, but there had been one last connection between her and my dad, divorce papers, last words—I can't say. But it had ended with her death. I feel certain now that my father killed her. As had been previously suggested. There was a moment of anger, a quick eruption, and that which had been beautiful and enticing was suddenly stone-still. It might have happened on one of his trips away from the house to get gas or buy groceries with the last of our money. The night we left for the lake, she had most likely been tucked behind the Christmas decorations in the garage.

I must have gone to the bathroom before we left, or gone to get a last bag or a favorite item, and forgotten about doing that. No other way to explain it. Dad had wrapped her in a blanket I didn't recognize, bent her into an embryo position, and boosted her into a suitcase and then into the big Buick's trunk next to the spare tire.

At last I finally knew who he was, and though it was not a

pleasant realization, the facts were out. And my mother was as mysterious as ever.

With my mother in the trunk of the car, Dad had planned to take us all away to Moon Lake. To go down to the bottom of his old world where there had been happier days. Down where he and my beautiful mother had first met and had their hearts sparked by love.

My father no longer comes to me in my dreams.

My name is Daniel Russell. I dream of dark water.

ABOUT THE AUTHOR

Joe R. Lansdale is the author of nearly four dozen novels, including *More Better Deals,* the Edgar Award–winning *The Bottoms, Sunset and Sawdust,* and *Leather Maiden.* He has received eleven Bram Stoker Awards, a Spur Award, the British Fantasy Award, and the Grinzane Cavour Prize. He lives with his family in Nacogdoches, Texas.

MULHOLLAND BOOKS

You won't be able to put down these Mulholland books.

THE QUIET BOY *by Ben H. Winters*

CITY ON THE EDGE *by David Swinson*

MOON LAKE *by Joe R. Lansdale*

THE RETREAT *by Elisabeth de Mariaffi*

ROVERS *by Richard Lange*

GETAWAY *by Zoje Stage*

THE LAST GUESTS *by J. P. Pomare*

Visit mulhollandbooks.com for
your daily suspense fix.